A WIZARD ABROAD

A WIZARD ABROAD

DIANE DUANE

Printed in the United States of America

ADMONITION TO THE READER

Geography in Ireland is an equivocal thing, and perhaps meant to be so. The more solid the borderline, the more dangerous the land's own response to it; the vaguer the boundary, the kindlier. This is best seen in the behavior of the borders between what we consider our own reality, and the other less familiar realities that shoulder up against it. Such boundaries are never very solid in Ireland, and never more dangerous than when one tries to define them, to cross over. Twilight is always safer there than full day, or full dark.

This being the case, I have taken considerable liberties with locations and "established" boundaries, including those between counties and towns. County Wicklow is real enough, but there are a lot of things in the Wicklow in this book that are not presently located in the "real" county—and my version of Bray is not meant to represent the real one . . . at the moment. The description of the townlands around Ballyvolan Farm and the neighborhood of Kilquade is more or less real, though the two are actually some miles apart. And Sugarloaf Mountain looks like parts of its description . . . occasionally.

Most specifically, though, Castle Matrix exists—possibly more concretely than anything else in the book. But it has been moved from its present, "actual" location. Or perhaps one can more rightly say that Matrix has stayed where it is, where it always is, but Ireland has shifted around it. Stranger things have happened. In any case, let the inquisitive reader beware . . . and leave the maps at home.

CONTENTS

I am the Point of a Weapon (that poureth forth combat),
I am the God who fashioneth Fire for a head.
Who is the troop, who is the God who fashioneth edges?

(*Lebor Gabála Érenn,* tr. Macalister)

Three signs of the Return:
the stranger in the door:
the friendless wizard:
the unmitigated Sun.

Three signs of the Monomachy:
a smith without a forge:
a saint without a cell:
a day without a night.

(*Book of Night with Moon,* triads 113, 598)

An tSionainn
SHANNON

The first that Nita found out about what was going to happen was when she came in after a long afternoon's wizardry with Kit. They had been working for three days to attempt to resolve a territorial dispute among several trees. It isn't easy to argue with a tree. It isn't easy to get one to stop strangling another one with its roots. But they were well along toward what appeared to be a negotiated settlement, and Nita was bushed.

She came into the kitchen to find her mother cooking. Her mother cooked a great deal as a hobby, but she also cooked as therapy, and Nita began to worry immediately when she noticed that her mother had embarked on some extremely complicated project that seemed to require three soufflé dishes and the use of every appliance in the kitchen at once. She decided to get out as fast as she could, before she was asked to wash something. "Hi, Mom," she said, and edged hurriedly toward the door into the rest of the house.

"What's the rush?" said her mother. "Don't you want to see what I'm doing?"

"Sure," said Nita, who wanted to do no such thing. "What are you doing?"

"I've been thinking," said her mother.

Nita began to worry more than ever. Her mother was at her most dangerous when she was thinking, and it rarely meant anything but trouble for Nita. "About what?"

"Sit down, honey. Don't look as if you're going to go flying out the door any minute. I need to talk to you."

Uh oh . . . here it comes! Nita sat down and began playing with one of the wooden spoons which, among many other utensils, was littering the kitchen table.

"Honey," her mother said, "this wizardry—"

"It's going pretty well with the trees, Mom," Nita said, desperate

13

to guide her mother onto some subject more positive. Her present tone didn't sound positive at all.

"No, I don't mean that, honey. Talking to trees—that's all right, that doesn't bother me. The kind of things you've been doing lately . . . you and Kit . . ."

Oh no. "Mom, we haven't got in trouble, not really. And we've been doing pretty well, for new wizards. When you're as young as we are—"

"Exactly," her mother said. "When you're as young as you are." She did something noisy with the blender for a moment and then said, "Hon, don't you think it would be a good idea if you just let all this—have a rest? Just for a month or so."

Nita looked at her mother without understanding at all, and worrying. "How do you mean?"

"Well, your dad and I have been talking—and you and Kit have been seeing a whole lot of each other in connection with this wizard business. We're thinking that it might be a good idea if you two sort of . . . didn't see each other for a little while."

"Mom!!"

"No, hear me out. I understand you're good friends, I know there's nothing . . . physical going on between you, so put that out of your mind. We're very glad each of you has such a good friend. That's not a concern. What *is* a concern is that you two are spending a lot of time on this magic stuff, at the expense of everything else. That's all you do. You go out in the morning, you come back wiped out, you barely have energy to speak to us sometimes . . . What about your childhood?"

"What about it?" Nita said, in some slight annoyance. Her experience of most of her childhood so far had been that it varied between painful and boring. Wizardry might be painful occasionally, but it was never boring. "Mom—you don't understand. This isn't something that you can just turn off. You take the Wizard's Oath for *life*."

"I know," Nita's mother said again. "That's what worries me. You're a little young to be making up your mind about what you want to do with the rest of your life."

Nita burst out laughing at that. "Are you kidding? You're the one who's been sitting through all the sessions with the guidance counselor at school! I'm not even fifteen, and already everybody's running off at the mouth about college every five minutes!"

"Now, Nita, that's not the same. That's just going to college. It's not—"

"It *is* the same! They want me to make career decisions, now, about what I'm going to do for twenty years, maybe thirty years, after I get out of college! And I'm not even sure what I want to *do* yet— except be a wizard! But the one thing I *do* want, and *know* that I want to do, you don't want me making decisions about! I don't get it!"

"Oh, honey!" her mother said in some distress, and dropped a spoon, and picked it up, wiping it off. "Why do you have to make this harder than it— Never mind. Look. Dad thinks it would be a good idea if you went to visit your Aunt Annie in Ireland for a month or so, until school starts again."

"Ireland!"

"Well, yes. She's been inviting us over there for a while now. We can't go with you, of course—we've had our vacation for this year, and Dad has to be at work. He can't take any more holiday time. But you could certainly go. School doesn't start until September the ninth. That would give you a good month and a half, now."

There was going to be nothing good about it, as far as Nita was concerned. The best part of the summer, the best weather, the leisure time that she had been looking forward to using working with Kit—"Mom," Nita said, changing tack, "how are you going to afford this?"

"Honey, you leave that to your Dad and me to handle. Right now we're more concerned with doing the right thing for you. And for Kit."

"Oh, you've been talking to his folks, have you?"

"No, hon, actually. We haven't. I think they're going to have to sort things out with Kit in their own way: I wouldn't presume to dictate to them. But we want you to go to Ireland for six weeks or so and take a breather. And see something different: something in the real world."

Oh dear, Nita thought. *They think* this *is the real world. Or all of it that really matters, anyway.* "Mom," she said, "I don't know if you understand what you're doing here. A wizard doesn't stop doing wizardry just because they're not at home. If I go on call in Ireland, I go on call, and there's nothing that's can stop it. I've made my promises. If I have to go on call, wouldn't you rather have me here, where you and Dad can keep an eye on me and know exactly what's going on all the time?"

Nita's mother frowned at that, and then looked at Nita with an expression compounded of equal parts of suspicion and amusement.

"Sneaky," she said. "No; I'm sorry. Your Aunt Annie will keep good close tabs on you—we've had a couple of talks with her about that—"

Nita's eyebrows went up at that—first in annoyance that it was going to be difficult to get away and do anything useful if there was need: then in alarm. "Oh, Mom, you didn't tell her that I'm—"

"No, we didn't tell her that you're a wizard! What are we supposed to do, honey? Say to your aunt, 'Listen, Anne, you have to understand that our daughter might vanish suddenly. No, I don't mean run away, just disappear into thin air. And if she goes to the Moon, tell her to dress warm.'" Nita's mother gave her a wry look and reached for the wooden spoon that Nita had been playing with. "No. We trust you to be discreet. You managed to hide it from *us* long enough, Heaven knows . . . you shouldn't have any trouble keeping things under cover with your aunt." She paused to start folding some beaten egg white into another mixture she had been working on. "No, honey," she said. "Your dad is going to see about the plane tickets tomorrow. I think it's Saturday that you'll be leaving—the fare is cheaper then."

"I could just, you know, *go* there," Nita said desperately. "It would save you the money, at least."

"I think we'll do this the old-fashioned way," Nita's mother said calmly. "Even *you* would have some logistical problems with arriving at the airport and getting off the plane without anyone noticing that you hadn't been there before."

Nita frowned and began to work on that one.

"*No,*" Nita's mother said. "Forget it. We'll send enough pocket money for you to get along with; you'll have plenty of kids to play with—"

Play with, Nita thought, and groaned inwardly.

"Come on, Neets, cheer up a little! It should be interesting, going to a foreign country for the first time."

I've been to foreign galaxies, Nita thought. *But this I'm not so sure about.* But she also had that sense that further argument wasn't going to help her. No matter: there were ways around this problem, if she would just keep her mouth shut.

"Okay," she said. "I'll go.—But I won't like it."

Her mother gazed at her thoughtfully. "I thought you were the one who told me that wizardry was about doing what you had to, whether you liked it or not?"

"It's true," Nita said, and got up to go out.

16

"And Nita," her mother said.

"What, Mom?"

"I want your promise that you will not be popping back here on the sly to visit Kit. That little 'beam-me-up-Scotty' spell that he's so fond of, and that I see you two using when you want to save your train fare for ice cream."

Nita went white, then flushed hot. That was the one thing she had been counting on to make this whole thing tolerable. "*Mom!* But Mom, it's easy, I can just—"

"You can *not* 'just.' We want you to take a break from each other for a while. Now I want you to promise me."

Nita let out a long breath. Her mother had her, and knew she did; for a wizard's promise had to be kept. When you spend your life working with words that describe and explain, and even change, the way the Universe is, you can't play around with those words, and you can't lie . . . at least not without major and unpleasant consequences. "I promise," Nita said, hating it. "But this is going to be miserable."

"We'll see about that," Nita's mother said. "You go ahead now, and do what you have to do."

"Holy crap," Kit said. "This is *dire.*"

They were sitting on the Moon, on a peak of the Carpathian Mountains, about thirty kilometers south of the crater Copernicus. The view of Earth from there this time of month was good; she was waxing toward the full, while on the Moon there was nothing but a Sun very low on the horizon. Long long shadows stretched across the breadth of the Carpathians, so that the illuminated crests of the jagged peaks stood up from great pools of darkness, like rough-hewn pyramids floating on nothing. It was cold there; the wizardly force-field that surrounded them snowed flakes of frozen oxygen gently onto the powdery white rock around them when they moved and changed the field's inner volume. But cold as it was, it was private.

"We were just getting somewhere with the trees," Nita muttered. "I can't believe this."

"Do they really think it's going to make a difference?"

"Oh, I don't know. Who knows what they think, half the time? And the worst of it is, they won't let me come back." Nita picked up a small piece of pumice and chucked it away, watching as it sailed about a hundred yards away in the light gravity and bounced several feet high when it first hit ground again. It continued bouncing down

17

the mountain, and she watched it idly. "We had three other projects waiting to be started. They're all shot now: there won't be any time to do anything about them before I have to go."

Kit stretched and looked unhappy. "We can still talk mind to mind; you can coach me at a distance when I need help. Or I can help you—"

"It's not the same." She had often enough tried explaining to her parents the "high" you got from working closely with another wizard: the feeling that magic made in your mind while working with another, the texture, was utterly unlike that of a wizardry worked alone—more dangerous, more difficult, ultimately more satisfying.

Nita sighed. "There must be some way we can work around this. How are your folks handling things lately?"

At that Kit sighed too. "Variable. My Dad doesn't mind it so much. He says, 'Big deal, my son's a *brujo*.' My mother . . . she has this idea that we are somehow meddling with Dark Forces." Kit made a fake theremin noise, the kind heard in bad old horror movies when the monster is lurking around a corner, about to jump on someone. Nita laughed.

Kit shook his head. "When are they making you leave?"

"Saturday." Nita rested her chin on one hand, picked up another rock and chucked it away. "All of a sudden there's all this junk I have to pack, and all these things we have to do. Go to the bank and get foreign money. Buy new clothes. Wash the old ones." She rolled her eyes and fell silent. Nita hated that kind of rushed busy-ness, and she was up to her neck in it now.

"How's Dairine holding up?"

Nita laughed. "She likes me, but she's hardly heartbroken. Besides, she's busy managing her wizardry these days . . . spends most of her time working with her computer. You wouldn't believe some of the conversations I've heard over its voice-link recently." She fell into an imitation of Dairine's high-pitched voice, made even more squeaky by annoyance. " 'No, I will *not* move your planet . . . what do you want to move it *for*? It's fine right where it is!' "

"Sheesh," Kit said. Dairine, as a very new wizard, was presently at the height of her power; as a very young wizard, she was also more powerful at the moment than both of them put together. The only thing they had on her at the moment was experience.

"Yeah. We don't fight nearly as much as we used to . . . she's gotten real quiet. I'm not sure it's normal."

18

"Oh," Kit said, and laughed out loud. "You mean, like *we're* normal. We're beginning to sound like our folks."

Nita had to laugh at that too. "You may have something there."

But then the amusement went out of her. "My God, Kit," she said, "I'm gonna miss you. I miss you already, and I haven't *left!*"

"Hey, c'mon," he said, and punched her in the shoulder. "You'll get over it. You'll meet some guy over there and—"

"Don't joke," Nita said, irritable. "I don't care about meeting 'some guy over there.' They're all geeks, for all I know. I don't even know if they speak the same language."

"Your aunt does."

"My aunt is American," Nita said.

"Yeah, they speak English over there," Kit said. "It's not all just Irish." He looked at Nita with a concerned expression. "Come on, Neets. If life hands you lemons, make lemonade. You can see a new place, you can probably meet some of their wizards. They'll be in the directory. . . . Give it a chance." He picked up a rock too, turning it over and over in his hands. "Where are you going to be? Dublin? Or somewhere else?"

"That's all there is," Nita said grimly. "Dublin, and the country. All potato fields and cow pastures."

"Saw that in the Manual, did you?"

Nita rolled her eyes. Kit could be incredibly pedantic sometimes. "No."

"I was looking at their chapter in the History of Wizardry section of the Manual a while back," Kit said. "A lot of interesting junk going on over there."

"Kit, I don't care what kind of junk is going on over there! I go on over *here.* This is where I do my work. Where you are. I'm one half of a team. What use am I without the rest?"

"Oh, I don't know. You might be good for something. Scrubbing floors . . . doing the dishes . . ."

"You are a dead man," she said to Kit. "You know that? . . . Look, what are we going to do about the trees? We've got to get this cleared up before we go. I refuse to waste all this work."

"Well, I guess we could get them to agree to another session tomorrow. The part of the negotiation about the roots was doing pretty well. I guess if we can get Aras to loosen up a little about the seedling acorns, Uriv might concede a couple of points regarding the percentage of sunlight."

19

"We could always threaten to uproot them and plant them about three miles apart," Nita said.

Kit sighed and looked at her. "I'm going to miss you too," he said. "I miss you already."

She looked at him, and saw it was true: and the bad mood fell off her, or mostly off, replaced by a feeling of unhappy resignation. "It's only six weeks," she said then.

Kit's face matched her feeling. "We'll do it standing on our heads," he said.

Nita smiled at him unhappily. Since wizards did not lie outright, when one tried to stretch the truth, it showed woefully. "Come on," she said, "we're running out of air. Let's get on with it."

Saturday came.

Kit came with them on the ride to the airport. It was a grim, silent sort of ride, broken only by the kind of strained conversation people make when they desperately need to say something, anything, to keep the silence from getting too thick. At least it seemed silent. She and Kit would pass the occasional comment mind-to-mind. It wasn't all that easy; they didn't do it much . . . they'd gotten in the habit of just talking to each other, since telepathy often got itself tangled up with a lot of other information you didn't need, or want, the other person to have. But now, habits or not, they were going to have to get a lot better at mindtouch if they were going to talk at all frequently.

They reached the airport, met the unescorted-minor representative from the airline and did the formalities with the ticket, checked in Nita's bag—a medium sized one, not too difficult for her to handle herself, though she was privately determined to make it weightless if she had to carry it anywhere alone. And then the annunciator system called her flight, and there was nothing to do but go through security and get on.

She hugged her mom, and her dad. "Have a good time now," her father said.

She sighed and said, "I'll try, daddy. Mommy—" And she was surprised at herself; she didn't usually call her mother "Mommy." They hugged again, hard.

"You be good, now," she said. "Don't—" She trailed off. The "don't" was a huge one, and Nita could hear in it all the things parents always say: *don't get in trouble, don't forget to wash*—but most specifically, *Don't get into anything dangerous, like the last time. Or the time before that. Or the time before that*—

"I'll try, Mom," she said. It was all she could guarantee.

Then she looked at Kit. *"Dai,"* he said.

"Dai stihó," she replied. It was the greeting and farewell of one wizard to another in the wizardly Speech: it meant as much " 'Bye for forever" as " 'Bye for now." For Nita, at the moment, it felt rather more like the first.

At that point she simply couldn't stand it any more. She waved a little, a weak gesture, and turned her back on them all, and slung her backpack over her shoulder, and her warm jacket that her mother had insisted she bring, and, in company with the airline rep, she walked off to go through security, and then down the long cold hall of the jetway, toward the plane.

It was a 747. Her sensitivity was running high—perhaps because of her own nervousness and distress at leaving—but the plane was alive in the way that mechanical things usually seemed to her as a result of working with Kit. That was his specialty—the ability to feel what a rock was saying, reading the secret thoughts of an elevator or an icebox, the odd thing-thoughts that run in the currents of energy which occur naturally or are built into physical objects, manmade or not. She could hear the plane straining against the chocks behind its many wheels, and its engines thinking of eating cold, cold air at 30 below, and pushing it out behind. There was a sense of purpose about it, of restraint, and of eagerness to get out of there, to be gone.

It was a reassuring feeling. She absently returned the smile of the flight attendant at the plane's door, and patted the plane as she got in; let the airline rep help her find her seat, so as to feel that he was doing something useful. Nita sat herself down by the window, fastened her seat belt, and as the rep went away, she got out her manual.

For a moment she just held it in her hand. Just a small beat-up book in a buckram library binding, with the apparent title, SO YOU WANT TO BE A WIZARD?, the supposed author's name, Hearn, and the Dewey Decimal number, 113.26, all written on the spine in white ink. Nita shook her head and smiled at the book, a little conspiratorially, for it was a lot more than that. Was it only two years, no, two and a half now, that she had found it in the local library? Or it had found her; she still wasn't too sure, remembering the way something had seemed to grab her hand as she ran it along the shelf where the book had been sitting. Whether it was alive was a subject on which the

Manual itself threw no light. Certainly it changed, adding new spells and other information as needed, updating news of what other wizards in the world were doing. Using it, she had found Kit in the middle of a wizardry of his own, and helped him with it, so passing through their Ordeal together and starting their partnership. They had gotten into deep trouble together, several times: but together, they had always gotten out again.

Nita sighed and started paging through the Manual, very much missing the "together" part of the arrangement. She had been resisting looking for the information on Ireland that Kit had mentioned until this point, hoping against hope that there would be a stay of execution. Even now she cherished the idea that her mother or father might come pushing down the narrow aisle between the seats, saying, "No, no, we've changed our minds!" But she knew it was futile. When her mother got an idea into her head, she was almost as stubborn as Nita was.

So she sat there, and looked down at the manual. It had fallen open at the Wizard's Oath.

In Life's name, and for Life's sake, I assert that I will employ the Art which is Its gift in Life's service alone, rejecting all other usages. I will guard growth and ease pain. I will fight to preserve what grows and lives well in its own way; nor will I change any creature unless its growth and life, or that of the system of which it is part, are threatened, or threaten another. To these ends, in the practice of my Art, I will ever put aside fear for courage, and death for life, when it is right to do so—looking always toward the Heart of Time, where all our sundered times are one, and all our myriad worlds lie whole, in the One from Whom they proceeded . . .

The whole plane wobbled as the little tug in front of it pushed it away from the gate. Nita peered out the window. Pressing her nose against the cool plastic and looking out, she could just barely make out her mother and father gazing through the window at her; her mother waving a little tentatively, her father gripping the railing in front of the window, not moving. And a little behind them, out of their range of vision, looking out the window too, Kit.

Stay warm, he said in her head.

Kit, it's not like I'm going away. We'll be hearing from each other all the time in our heads. It's not like I'm really going away. . . . Is it?

She was quiet for a moment. The tug pushing the plane began to turn it, so that her view of him was lost.

Yes it is, he said.

Yeah, well. She caught herself sighing again. *Look, you're going to have the trees to deal with again, and you need time to plan what you're going to do. And I need time to calm myself down. Going to call me later?*

Yeah. What time?

This thing won't be down until early tomorrow morning, their time, she said.

Doesn't want to come down at all, from the feel of it, Kit said drily.

Nita chuckled, caught an odd look from a passing stewardess, and made herself busy looking as if she had read something funny in her Manual. *Yeah. Call me about this time tomorrow.*

You got it. Have a good flight!

For what it's worth, Nita said.

The plane began to trundle purposefully out toward the runway. They didn't have to wait long; air traffic control gave them clearance right away—Nita, eavesdropping along the plane's nerves, heard the pilot acknowledging it. Half a minute later the plane screamed delight and leaped into the air. Nita had to smile a little in spite of everything, wondering how much the pilots thought they had to do with the process of flight. The plane had its own ideas.

New York slid away behind them, replaced by the open sea.

Seven hours later, they landed in Shannon.

Nita had thought she would be completely unable to sleep, but when they turned out most of the lights in the plane after the meal service, she leaned her head against the window to see if she could relax enough to watch the movie a little.

The next thing she knew, the sun was coming in the window, and there was land below them. Nita looked down into the early sun—six o'clock of that morning, it was—and saw the ragged black coastline and the curling water, white where it smashed into the rocks, the Atlantic throwing itself in fury against this first eastern barrier to its will. And then green—everywhere green, divided by little lines of hedge; a hundred shades of green, emerald, viridian, khaki, the pale green that has no right to be anywhere outside of spring—hedgerows winding between, white dots of sheep, tiny cars crawling along little toy roads: but always the green. The plane turned and she saw the beginning sprawl of houses, and Shannon town—a little city, barely the size of her own.

The plane was turning to line up with the airport's active runway, and the Sun caught her full in the eyes. Nita shivered, a feeling that had nothing to do with the warmth of the sudden light. That was warm enough, but the feeling was cold. Something about to happen, something about the lances of light, the fire—Nita shook her head: the feeling was gone. *I haven't slept all night,* she thought. *I'm susceptible to weird ideas.* But when wizards have weird ideas, they do well to pay attention to them. She forced herself to relive the feeling, to think again of the cold, and the fire, the sun like a spear—

Nothing came of it. She shrugged, and watched the plane finish its turn and drop toward the runway.

It took them about fifteen minutes to get down, and for the jetway to be trundled up. With her backpack over her back, and yet another (she thought) unnecessary airline representative in tow, Nita went through passport control.

She went up to the first empty desk she found and laid her passport on it, and smiled at the man, a big kindly guy with a large nose and little cheerful eyes. He looked down at her and said, "Here's a wee dote of a thing to be traveling all alone. And how are you this morning?"

"I didn't sleep on the plane," Nita said.

"Sure I can't do that myself," the man said, riffling through her passport. "Keep hearing things all the time. Coming to see relatives, are you? —Here's a nice clean passport then. Where do you want the stamp, pet? First page? or save that for something more interesting?"

Nita thought of the first time she had cleared "passport" formalities at the great Crossroads worldgating facility, six galaxies over, and illogically warmed to the man. "Let that be the first one, please," she said. The man stamped the passport with relish, and handed the passport back. "You're very welcome in Ireland, pet. *Chayd mil'fallcha.*"

She had seen that at least spelled over the doorway past the jetway hall: *cead mile failte*—"a hundred thousand welcomes." "Thank you," she said, and walked on toward baggage claim.

It would be a while yet before the connecting flight to Dublin. On the far side of the baggage hall, and the customs people, Nita found herself in the big Shannon duty-free shop. The airline rep loitered by the entrance and chatted with one of the staff while keeping an eye on Nita, and she for her part wandered around the place with her mouth open for a good while, never having quite seen anything like it before. It was the size of a small department store, filled with crystal and linen and china and smoked salmon, and books. She went straight for the books, not liking smoked salmon much. She found a couple of volumes of Irish stories and mythology, and bought them with some of the odd pastel-colored Irish money. She remembered with some pain her mother looking at the bills and saying, "Who are all these people?"

"Writers," her father had said. "There's Yeats on the twenty, and Duns Scotus on the five: a historian. And Jonathan Swift on the ten. Look at the map of Dublin on the back of that one, I bet you can still find your way around with it—"

Nita put the memory away, hurting slightly. She hadn't thought she would miss her folks so much; after all, it was only seven hours since she'd seen them. . . .

She went along to the gate for the flight that would take her to Dublin.

Another flight, another plane equally eager to be gone. It was about an hour's flight, over the thousand shades of green—and all the bright rivers winding amongst the hills, blazing like fire when the sun caught them. Her ears had started popping from the plane's descent almost as soon as it reached altitude, and Nita looked down and found herself and the plane sinking gently toward a great green range of mountains, and three mountains notable even among the others. Nita's mother had told her about these three, and had shown her pictures. One of them wasn't a mountain, but a promontory: Bray Head, sticking out into the sea like a fist laid on a table with the knuckles sticking up. Then, a mile further inland, and westward, Little Sugarloaf, a hill half again as high as Bray Head. And then westward another mile, and higher than both the others, Great Sugarloaf, *Slieve O Cualann* as the Irish had it: *the* mountain of Wicklow, its name said. It was certainly one of the most noticeable—a grey stony cone, pointed, its slopes green with heather—no tree grew there. The plane turned off leftward, making its way up to Dublin Airport. Another ten minutes and they were down.

Nita was met by yet another airline rep, got her bag back, got a cart, looked around curiously at the automatic change machine that took your money and gave you Irish money back, and briefly regret-

25

ted that she didn't have an excuse to use it. She sighed and pushed her cart out through the customs folk, out through the sliding doors and past the bored uniformed man at the desk who kept people from coming in the wrong way.

"Nita!"

And there was her aunt Annie. Nita grinned. After spending your life with people you know, and then having to spend a whole day with people you didn't know, the sight of her was a pleasure. Nita's aunt hurried over to her and gave her a big hug, signed the clipboard the rep held out for her, and waved the lady off.

Aunt Annie was a big silver-haired lady, big about the shoulders, a little broad in the beam; a friendly face with pale grey-blue eyes. The hair was tied back in a short ponytail behind. "How was your flight? Did you do okay?"

"I did fine, Aunt Annie. But I'm real tired . . . I wouldn't mind going home."

"Sure, honey. You come right out here, the car's right outside." She pushed the cart out into the little parking lot.

The morning was holding fresh and fine. Little white clouds were flying past in a blue sky; Nita put her arms around herself and hugged herself in surprise at the cold. "Mom told me it might be chilly, and I didn't believe her. It's July!"

"This *is* one of the cooler days we've been having lately. Don't worry, though; the weatherpeople say it's going to get warm again tomorrow. Up in the 70's."

" 'Warm,' " Nita said, wondering. It had been in the 90's on the Island when she left.

"We haven't had much rain, either," said her aunt. "It's been a dry summer, and they're talking about it turning into a drought if it doesn't rain this week or next." She laughed a little as she came up to a white Toyota and opened its trunk.

They drove around to the parking lot's ticket booth, paid the toll, and got out. Nita spent a few interested moments adjusting to the fact that her aunt was driving on the left side of the road. "So tell me," Aunt Annie said, "how are your folks?"

Nita started telling her, with only half her mind on the business; the rest of her was busy looking at the scenery as they came out onto the freeway—or the "dual carriageway," as all the signs called it— heading south toward Dublin, and past it to Wicklow. AN LAR, said one sign: and under that it said DUBLIN: 8. "What's 'An Lar'?" Nita said.

"That's Irish for 'to the city center,' " said her Aunt. "We're about 15 miles south of Dublin . . . it'll take us about an hour to get through it and home, the way the traffic is. Do you want to stop in town for lunch? Are you hungry?"

"Nnnnnno," Nita said, "I think I'd rather just go fall down and have a sleep. I didn't get any on the plane."

Her aunt nodded. "No problem with that . . . you get rid of your jet lag. The country won't be going anywhere while you get caught up on your sleep."

And so they drove through the city. Nita was surprised to see how much it looked like suburban New York, except that—except— Nita found that she kept saying "except" about every thirty seconds. Things looked the same, and then she would see something completely weird that she didn't understand at all. The street signs, half in Irish and half in English, were a constant fascination. It was a very peculiar-looking language, with a lot of extra letters, and small letters in front of capital letters at the beginnings of words, something she had never seen before. And the pronunciations— She tried pronouncing a few of them, the last one being *Baile atha Cliath,* and her aunt howled with laughter and coached her. "No, no! If you try to pronounce Irish the way it looks, you'll go crazy. That one's pronounced 'bally ah-cleeah.' 'Dublin city.' "

Nita nodded and went on with a brief version of how things were at home, while looking at more of the signs they passed. There was something vaguely familiar about the language, for all the weirdness of its spelling.

They drove through the center of Dublin, down O'Connell Street. This was a thoroughfare about the width of a Manhattan avenue, three lanes on each side, with a broad pavement in between. People jaywalked across it with such total recklessness that Nita had to shake her head at the sheer brazenness of them. Down the big handsome avenue they went, and through the city, out past shops and stores and parts of town that looked exactly like New York to Nita's eyes, though much cleaner; and then started to pass through areas where small modern housing developments mixed with old brownstones that had beautiful clear or stained-glass fanlights above their front doors, and elaborate molded plaster ceilings that could be glimpsed here and there through open curtains. Then the brownstones too gave way, starting to be replaced by housing developments again, older ones now. The "dual carriageway," which had become just one lane on each side for a while, now reasserted itself.

27

And then fields started to appear, and big vacant lots that to Nita's astonishment and delight had shaggy horses casually grazing on them, right by the side of the road. "Whose are they?" Nita said.

"They're tinker ponies," her aunt said. "The traveling people leave them where they can get some grass, if the grass where their caravans are is grazed down already. Look there." She pointed off to one side.

Nita looked, expecting to see some kind of a barrel-shaped, brightly-colored wagon. Instead there was just a trailer parked off to one side of the road, with no car hitched to it. There were clothes laid over the nearby hedge in the sun: laundry, Nita realized. As they passed, she got just a glimpse of a small fire burning near the trailer, and several small children sitting or crouching around it, feeding it sticks. Then they had swept by.

"Are they gypsies?" Nita said.

Her aunt shrugged. "Some of them say they are. Others are just people who don't like to live in houses, in one place . . . they'd rather move around and be free. We have a fair number of them down by us."

Nita filed this with about twenty other things she was going to have to ask more about at her leisure. They passed more small housing developments—"estates," her aunt called them—where houses sited by themselves seemed to be the exception rather than the rule. Rather, two houses were usually built squished together so that they shared one wall, and each one was a mirror image of the other.

And then even the housing estates started to give out. There was a last gasp of them as they passed through a town called Shankill, where the road had narrowed down to a single lane each way again. Shortly after that it curved off to the right, away from what looked like even a larger town. "That's Bray," Aunt Annie said. "We do some of our shopping there. But this is officially County Wicklow, now: you're out of Dublin when you get near the Dargle."

Nita hadn't noticed the river: it was hidden behind rows of little houses. "That's Little Bray," her aunt said. "And now, here's Kilcroney."

The road widened out abruptly into hill and forest, and two lanes on each side again. "Everything has names," Nita said.

"Every *acre* of this place has names," her aunt said. "Every town has 'townlands' around it, and every one of them has a different name. Almost every field, and every valley and hill." She smiled. "I kind of like it."

"I think I might too," Nita said. A wizard could best do spells when everything in them was completely named: and it was always easier to use existing names than to coin new ones—which you had to do if no one had previously named a thing or place, or if it didn't know its own name already. And the name you coined had to be right, otherwise the wizardry would backfire.

"There," her aunt said, maneuvering around a couple of curves in the road. "There's our mountain."

Nita peered past her aunt, out toward the right. There was Sugarloaf. It looked much different than it had from the air—sharper, more imposing, more dangerous. Heather did its best to grow up its sides, but the bare granite of the mountain's peak defeated it about two thirds of the way up. Scree and boulders lay clear to see all about the mountain's bald head.

The road ran past a service station where geese and a goat grazed behind a fence, watching the traffic; then through a shallow ravine that ran between two thickly forested hills. Sunlight would fall down the middle of it at noon, Nita guessed, but at the moment the whole deep vale was in shadow. "Glen of the Downs," Aunt Annie said. "We're almost home. That's a nice place to hike to, down there, where the picnic benches are."

After driving a couple more miles down the dual carriageway, Aunt Annie turned down a little lane off the dual carriageway. To Nita's eyes this road looked barely wide enough for one car, let alone two, but to her shock several other cars passed them, and Aunt Annie never even slowed down, though she crunched so far over on the left side of the road that the hedges scraped the doors. The road began to trend downward, so that the gently sloping valley beneath it was visible, and beyond that, the sea, with the sun on it, blinding.

"See that town down there on the left? That's Greystones," said Aunt Annie: "we do the best part of our shopping there. But here—" She turned off down another lane, this one literally just wide enough to let one car through. In half a minute they came out in the graveled "parking lot" in front of a little house. Around it, on all sides, fenced fields and farm buildings stretched. It was forty acres, Nita knew: her aunt's life savings had gone into the farm, her great love.

"Welcome to Ballyvolan," her aunt said. "Come on in and we'll get you something to eat."

They did more than that. They gave her a place to stay which was uniquely her own, and Nita was very pleased.

They put her up, not in the house, but in a caravan out in the back: a trailer, as she would have called it. She was getting the feeling that everything here had different names that she was going to have to get used to. But she was used to that; everything had different names in wizardry, too. . . . *It's going to take months to get everything straight,* she thought. And then thought immediately, *I hope not! I don't want to be 'months' here. Six weeks is plenty!* But all the same, the sheer difference of things was beginning to get to her. She had been to other planets and spoken to alien creatures in their own languages, but nothing had yet struck her as quite as strange as being here in this odd place where everything she knew was called something strange; and where people she knew to be speaking English as their first language were nonetheless speaking it in accents so thick she couldn't make out more than one word in three. None of the accents were what she had always thought of as the typical Irish "brogue," either. Evidently there *was* no such thing; the word "brogue" turned out to come from an old, slightly scornful Irish word that meant "tongue-tied," and had originally been used to describe people who couldn't speak Irish. At any rate, the accents came in all variations of thick, thin, light, impenetrable, lilting, dark; and people would run all their words together and talk very fast. Or very softly, so that Nita shortly began feeling as if she was shouting every time she opened her mouth.

They gave her the caravan, and left her alone. "You'll want to crash and burn, I should think," Aunt Annie said. "You come in when you're ready and we'll feed you." So Nita had unpacked her bag, and sat down on the little bed built into the side of the trailer. It was a good size for her. Its windows afforded a clear view of the path from the house, so that if she was doing a wizardry, she had a few seconds to shut it down before anyone got close enough to see what was going on. There were cupboards and drawers, a shelf above the head of the bed, a little closet to hang things in, a table with a comfortable bench-seat to work at, and lights set in the walls here and there, and an electric heater to keep everything warm if it got cool at night.

She leaned back on the bed with her manual in her hands, meaning to read through some of its Irish material before she dropped off. She never had a chance.

Nita woke up to find it dark outside. Or not truly dark, but a very dark twilight. She glanced at her watch and saw that it was almost eleven at night. They had let her sleep, and she was ravenous. *Boy, I must have needed that,* she thought, and swung her feet to the floor, stretching and scrubbing at her eyes.

That was when she heard the sound: horses' hooves, right outside the door. That wasn't a surprise, except that they would be out there so late. Annie's farm was partly a boarding stable, where people kept their horses because they didn't have stables of their own, or where they left them to be exercised and trained for shows. There were a couple of low voices, men's voices Nita thought, discussing something quietly. That was no surprise either: there were quite a few people working on Aunt Annie's farm—she had been introduced to a lot of them when she first arrived, and had forgotten most of their names. One of the people outside chuckled, sighed, said something inaudible.

Nita snapped the bedside light on so that she wouldn't bash into things, and got up and opened the caravan door to look out and say hello.

Except that no one was there.

"Huh," she said.

She went out through the little concrete yard to the front of the house, where the front door was open, as Aunt Annie had told her it almost always was except when everyone had gone to bed. Her aunt was in the big quarry-tiled kitchen, making a cup of tea.

"So there you are!" she said. "Did you sleep well? Do you want a cuppa?"

"What? Oh, right. Yes, please," Nita said, and sat down in one of the chairs drawn up around the big blond wood table. One of the cats, a black-and-white creature, jumped into her lap: she had forgotten its name too in the general blur of arrival. "Hi there," she said to it, stroking it.

"Milk? Sugar?"

"Just sugar, please," Nita said. "Aunt Annie, who were those people out there with the horses?"

Her aunt looked at her. "People with the horses? All the staff have gone home. At least I thought they did."

"No, I heard them. The hooves were right outside my door, but when I looked, they'd gone away. Didn't take them long," she added.

Aunt Annie looked at her again as she came over and put Nita's teacup down. Her expression was rather different this time. "Oh," she said. "You mean the ghosts."

Nita stared.

"Welcome to Ireland," said her aunt.

31

Cill Cumhaid
Kilquade

Nita sat back and blinked a little. Her aunt stirred her tea and said, "Do ghosts bother you?"

"Not particularly," Nita said, wondering just how to deal with this line of inquiry. Wizards knew that very few ghosts had anything to do with people's souls hanging around somewhere. Most apparitions, especially ones that repeated, tended to be caused by a kind of "tape recording" that violent emotion could make on matter under certain circumstances, impressing its energy into the molecular structure of physical things. Over long periods of time the "recording" would fade away, but in the meantime it would replay every now and then, for good reasons or no reason, and upset the people who happened to see it. And if they happened to believe that such a thing was caused by human souls, the effects would get steadily worse, fed by the emotions of the living.

Nita knew all this, certainly. But how much of it could she safely tell her aunt? And how to get it across without sounding like she knew more than a fourteen-year-old should?

"Good," her aunt was saying. She drank her tea and looked at Nita across the table with those cool blue-grey eyes. "Did you hear the church bells, earlier?"

"Uh, no. I must have been asleep."

"We have a little church down the road," Aunt Annie said. "About three hundred years ago, after the English killed their King—Charles the First, it was—his 'replacement,' a man named Oliver Cromwell, came through here." Her aunt took another long drink of tea. "He and his army went up and down this country throwing out the Irish landowners and installing English ones in their places. He sacked cities and burned houses, and got himself quite a name for unnecessary cruelty." Aunt Annie looked out the kitchen window, into the near-dark, watching the apple trees in the back yard move slightly in the wind. "I think what you heard was, well, a reminder of some of his people, who were camped here on guard late at night. You can hear the horses, and you can hear the soldiers talking, though you usually can't make out what they're saying."

"As if they were in the next room," Nita said.

"That's right. The memory just reasserts itself every now and then; other people have heard it happening. It's usually pretty low-key." She looked at Nita keenly.

Nita shrugged in agreement. "They didn't bother me. They didn't seem particularly, well, 'ghostly.' No going 'ooooooo' or trying to scare anyone."

"That's right," her aunt said, sounding relieved. "Are you hungry?"

"I could eat a cow," Nita said, suspecting that in this household it would be wiser not to offer to eat horses.

"I've got some hamburger," her aunt said, getting up, "and some chicken . . ."

Nita got up to help, and poked around the kitchen a little. All the appliances were about half the size she was used to. She wondered whether this was her aunt's preference, or whether most of the stoves and refrigerators sold here were like that, for on the drive in she had kept getting a feeling that everything was smaller than usual, had been scaled down somewhat. The rooms in her aunt's house were smaller than she was used to, as well, reinforcing the impression. "So have you got other ghosts," Nita said, "or are those all?"

"Nope, that's it." Her aunt chuckled and pulled out a frying pan. "You want more, though, you won't have far to go. This country is thick with them. Old memories. Everything here has a long memory . . . longer than it should have, maybe." She sighed and went rooting in a drawer for a few moments. "A lot of history in Ireland," Aunt Annie said, "a lot of bad experiences and bad feelings. It's a pain in the butt sometimes." She came up with a spatula. "Do you want onions?"

"Sure," Nita said. Her aunt came up with a knife and handed it to Nita, then found an onion in a bin by the door and put it on the counter. "Hope you don't mind crying a little," she said.

"No problem."

They puttered about the kitchen together, talking about this and that: family gossip, mostly. Aunt Annie was Nita's father's eldest sister, married once about twenty-five years ago, and divorced about five years later. Her ex-husband was typically referred to in Nita's family as "that waste of time," but no one at home had ever been too

33

forthcoming about just why he was a waste, and Nita had decided it was none of her business. Aunt Annie had three kids, two sons and a daughter, all grown up now and moved out: two of them now lived in Ireland, one in the States. Nita had met her two male cousins some years back, when she was very young, and only dimly remembered Todd and Alec as big, dark-haired, booming shapes that gave her endless piggyback rides.

At any rate, her aunt had moved with her kids to Ireland after the divorce, and had busied herself with becoming a successful farmer and stable-manager. Now she had other people to manage her stables for her: she saw to the finances of the farm, kept an eye on the function of the riding school that also was based on her land, and otherwise lived the life of a moderately well-to-do countrywoman.

They fried up hamburgers and onions. There were no buns: her aunt took down a loaf of bread and cut thickish slices from it for both of them. "Didn't you have supper?" Nita said. "It's way past time."

"We don't have set mealtimes," Aunt Annie said. "My staff come in and get a snack when they can, and I tend to eat when I'm hungry. I was busy with the accounts for most of this evening—didn't notice I was hungry until just now. Unlike some," she said, looking ruefully down at the floor around the stove, which was suddenly littered with cats of various colors, "who are hungry whether they've just eaten or not."

Nita laughed and bent down to scratch the cats: the black and white one, again—'Bronski'—as well as a marmalade-colored cat with golden eyes, and a tiny delicate white-bibbed tabby, and another black-and-white cat of great dignity, who sat watching the others, and Nita and her aunt, unblinking. "Bear," Aunt Annie said, "and Chessie, and Big Paws. All of you, out of here: you had your dinners! Now where's the mustard got to?"

She turned away to find it. Under her breath, Nita said hurriedly in the wizards' Speech, *"You all get out of here and I'll see if I can liberate something for you later . . ."*

They sat looking thoughtful—since almost everything that thinks can recognize and understand the Speech—then one by one got up and strolled off. Her aunt found the mustard, and noticed the exodus. "Huh," she said. "Guess they don't like the smell of the onions."

"It's pretty strong," Nita said, smiled slightly, and started spreading mustard on bread.

When everything was ready, they sat down and ate. "I hope you don't mind being a little on your own tomorrow," Aunt Annie said. "You hit us at kind of a busy time. There's going to be a hunt here in a few days, and we have to start getting ready for it."

"You mean like a fox hunt?" Nita said.

"That's right. Some of the local farmers have been complaining about their chicken flocks being raided. Anyway, some of our horses are involved, so we have to have the vet in to certify them fit, and then the farrier is coming in tomorrow afternoon to do some re-shoeing. It's going to be pretty hectic. If you want to be around here, that's fine: or if you think you'll be bored, you might want to go down to Greystones—it's a pretty easy bike ride from here. Or take the bus over to Bray and look around."

"Okay," Nita said. "I'll see how I feel . . . I'm still pretty tired."

"Traveling eastbound takes it out of you," Aunt Annie said. "It won't be so bad going back."

You said it, Nita thought. *And the sooner the better.* But she smiled anyway, and said, "I hope not."

They finished up, and cleared the table. "If you want to watch TV late, forget about the ground-based stations," her aunt said. "All but one of them shut down around midnight, and the one that's left mostly just shows old movies. There's a fair amount of stuff on the satellite channels, though."

"Uh, thanks. I thought I might read for a while. After that I may just go to sleep again . . . I'm still kind of tired."

"That's fine. You make yourself completely at home." Her aunt looked at Nita with an expression as thoughtful, in its way, as the cats'. "It must have been a bit of a wrench, just being shipped off like that."

What did they tell you, I wonder? Nita thought. "It was," she said after a moment. "But I'll cope."

Her aunt smiled. "Typical of our side of the family," she said. "There's a long history of that. Well, if you get hungry or something later, just come on in and take what you need. Use the back door, though: I'm going to lock the front now, and turn in. I'll leave a light on for you in here. You know where everything is, the bathroom and so forth?"

"Yeah, Aunt Annie. Thanks."

Her aunt headed off. Nita looked around the kitchen to see if there was anything else that needed cleaning up—her mother had drummed into her that she should make sure she returned hospitality by helping out in the kitchen: her aunt hated doing dishes above almost anything else, her mother had said. But there was nothing left to do.

Except something that needed a wizard to do it, and Nita set about that straight away.

She headed out the back door, out through a little archway into the concrete yard again. The only light was the one she had left on in the trailer, and it was dim. She paused outside the door and looked up. Even now, past midnight, the sky wasn't completely black. Nevertheless, it was blanketed with stars, much brighter than she was used to seeing them through the light pollution of the New York suburbs. And there was no sound here but the faintest breath of wind. Even the dual carriageway a mile away made no noise at all. It was as if everyone in this part of the country had gone to bed and turned out the lights all at once. There was only one light visible, about a mile away across the fields: someone's house light. For someone who had always lived in places where the street had streetlights on all night, this utter darkness was a shock.

But the stars, she thought. The Milky Way was clearly visible, even bright. At home it was almost impossible to see it at all. *At least there's been one thing worth seeing here.*

She shivered hard then, and ducked back into the trailer to get her jacket, and her manual.

Once she had them she headed out across the concrete yard again, making for the log fence that separated the land immediately around Aunt Annie's house from the fields beyond it. The closest field was planted with "oilseed rape," or "canola" as they would have called it in the States—tall green plants with flowers at the top so extremely yellow that they had made Nita's eyes hurt to look at them in the sunshine that morning. The field beyond that was clean pasture, grassland being left fallow for this year. That was what Nita wanted, for there was a thick strip of woodland at the far side of it.

She made her way through the oilseed rape, enjoying the fragrance of it, and on to the next fence. This was barbed wire: she climbed one of the fenceposts carefully, so as not to tear anything. Cautiously, for the ground over here wasn't as even as it had been in the rape field, Nita made her way into the center of the field, and opened her manual.

She said the two words that would make the pages generate enough light to read by, though not enough to mess up her night vision. Normally she wouldn't have needed the manual for this spell,

36

which was more a matter of simple conversation than anything else; but she didn't know the name she needed to call, and had to look it up. The manual's index was straightforward as usual. *"Canidae,"* she said under her breath. "Here we go."

The spell was a calling, but the kind that was a request, not a demand. She hoped there would be someone to respond. She recited the standard setup, the request for the Universe to hear. Then, *"Ai mathrára,"* she said in the Speech, "if any hear, let them speak to me; for there's need."

And then she put the book down and sat there in the quiet, and waited.

It seemed to take a long time before she heard the soft sound of something rustling in the grass, about a hundred yards away. Normally she would never have heard it, except that her ears were sharpened by sitting in this total silence. The noise stopped.

"Mathrára," she said then, very quietly, "if that's you, then I'm here."

Another rustling, another silence.

"You speak it with an accent," said a voice in a series of short, soft barks, "but well enough. Let me see you."

Nita saw the long, low, sharp-nose shape come toward her. The dog-fox had a tail bigger and bushier and longer than she would have thought possible. Only the faintest firefly gleam from the manual's pages silvered his fur, giving him enough of an outline to see, and glinted in his eyes.

"So," the fox said.

"What accent?" Nita said, curious. As far as she knew, her accent in the Speech was quite good.

"We wouldn't say *'mathrára'* here. *'Madreen rua,'* that would be it." And Nita chuckled, for that meant "the little red dog" in the Speech.

"Local customs rule," Nita said, smiling. "As usual. I have a warning for you, madreen rua. There's a hunt coming through here in a few days."

The fox yipped softly in surprise. "They are early, then."

"That's as may be," Nita said. "But if I were you, I'd spread the word to keep your people well out of this area, and probably for about five miles around on all sides. Maybe more. And you might lay off the chickens a little."

The fox laughed silently, a panting sound. "They've poisoned almost all the rats: what's a body to eat? But for the moment . . . as you say. I am warned, wizard. Your errand's done." It looked at her with a thoughtful look.

"So then," the fox said. "Go well, wizard." And it whisked around and went bounding off through the pasture-grass without another word.

Nita shut her manual and sat there in the quiet for a while more, getting her breath back. Talking to animals differed in intensity the smarter the animal got, and the more or less used it was to human beings. Pets like cats and dogs tended to have more fully humanized personalities, and could easily be made to understand you; but they also tended to be short-spoken—possibly, Nita thought, because being domesticated and more or less confined to a daily routine, they had less to talk about. Wilder animals had more to say, but it was often more difficult to understand them, the message being colored with hostility or fear, or plain old bewilderment. The fox lived on the fringes of human life, knew human ways, but was wary, and so there was a cool tinge, a remoteness, about the way it came across.

At any rate, she had fulfilled her own responsibilities for the evening. A wizard had a duty to prevent unnecessary pain, and fox-hunting did not strike Nita as particularly necessary, no matter what farmers might say about the need to exterminate "vermin." If a fox was stealing someone's chickens, let them shoot it cleanly, rather than chasing it in terror across half the countryside and getting dogs to rip it to shreds.

Meanwhile, there were other concerns.

Kit? she said in her head.

Yeah!

She paused a moment. *What's that noise?*

I'm chewing, Kit said.

Oh no, you're eating dinner!

It's not such a fascinating experience that I can't take a few minutes out to talk to you, he said. Nita got a distinct impression of slightly lumpy mashed potatoes, and restrained herself from swallowing. *What's happening?* Kit said.

This, she said, and gave him a series of pictures of the day as quickly as she could, ending with the fox. *Great, huh?*

Bored with me already, Kit said. *I knew it.*

Kit—!! She would have punched him hard, had he been in range. As it was, he flinched a little from what he felt her fist and arm wanting to do. *Look,* she said, *I'm wiped. I'll talk to you more in the morning.*

He started to nod and stopped himself. She had to laugh a little. *Have a good night,* Kit said.

Will do.

She let the contact ebb away, then got up and started carefully walking back the way she had come. Behind her, from the woodland, a fox was barking; perhaps a mile away, another answered it.

Nita smiled to herself and headed for the trailer.

As she had thought, she wasn't able to stay up very late that night. She tried to watch some television, but even the sixty-odd satellite channels were fairly dull, either showing old movies that she wasn't interested in, or foreign-language material that was a strain for even a wizard to follow. Finally she turned the TV off and went back to the trailer again to read, though not before opening a small can of cat food on the sly, and parceling it out to the cats. They accepted this with great pleasure, purring and rubbing and making their approval known: but none of them spoke to her.

She went back to bed and slept some more. The dreams were not entirely pleasant. In one of them, she thought she felt the earth move, but it was probably just the wind shaking the trailer. When she woke up everything was quite still. It was early morning, how early she couldn't tell any more without her watch: the different sunrise time here had her thoroughly confused. She found her watch and saw to her surprise that, even though the sun was well up the sky, it was only seven AM.

She got up and dressed in yesterday's clothes, slipped into the house, had a quick shower, dressed again in clean clothes this time, and went to see what there was for breakfast. There were already several people in the kitchen, two of whom Nita had been introduced to before. One was Joe, the stable master, a tall lean young man with a grin so wide that Nita thought his face was in danger of cracking. Another was Derval, the head trainer, a tall curly-haired woman, eternally smoking a hand-rolled cigarette. She had a drawly accent that made her sound almost American.

"There y'are then," Derval said. "You want some tea?"

Nita was beginning to think that every conversation in Ireland began this way. "Yes please," she said, and rooted around in the big ceramic bread crock for the loaf. "Where's Aunt Annie?"

"Down at the riding school, waiting for the farrier. She said to tell you to come on down if you want to."

"Okay," Nita said, and cut herself a slice of bread and put it in the toaster. The butter was already out on the counter, along with a basket of eggs from the farm's hens, various packages of bacon and a gruesome-looking sausage called "black pudding," more toast, some of it with bites out of it, boxes of cereal, and spilled sugar. Breakfast was a hurried business in this house, from the look of things.

Nita sat down with her tea and toast and pulled over the local weekly paper, *The Wicklow People*. Its front-page story was about someone's car catching on fire in the main street of Wicklow town, and Nita sat there paging through it in total wonder that anyplace in the world should be so quiet and uneventful that a story like that would make the front page. Derval looked over her shoulder and pointed with one finger at an advertisement in the classifieds that said BOGS FOR SALE. Nita burst out laughing.

"If you're going to be around the stable block," Derval said to her, going to get another piece of bread out of the toaster, "just one thing. Watch out for the horse in number five. He bites."

"Uh, yeah," Nita said. She had been wondering when she was going to have to mention this. "I'm a little scared of horses . . . I hadn't been planning to get too close to them."

"Scared of horses!" Joe said. "We'll fix that."

"Uh, maybe tomorrow," Nita said. She had been put up on a horse once, several years ago on vacation, and had immediately fallen off it. This had colored her opinions about horses ever since.

Joe and Derval finished their breakfasts and headed out, leaving Nita surrounded by cats eager to shake her down for another handout. "No way, you guys!" she said. "Once was a special occasion. You want more, you'd better talk to your boss."

They looked at her in thinly disguised disgust and stalked off. Nita finished her tea and toast, washed her cup and plate, and then wandered out into the concrete yard again. There was a pathway past the back of her trailer into the farm area proper, and the road that wound past the front of the house curved around to meet it. Here there was another large concreted area with two or three large brown, metal-sided, barnlike buildings arranged in a loose triangle around it. The field on the right-hand side as she faced it was full of horse-jumping paraphernalia, jumps and stiles; all around the edge of it ran a big track covered with wood shavings and chips for the horses to run on. Further down and on her right was the stabling barn, and beyond it what Derval had referred to as "the riding school," a big covered building that had nothing in it except a floor thickly covered with the same chips as on the track outside. This was where the riders practiced when the weather was bad.

Nita took a little while to look around in there, found nothing of interest, and made her way back to the stables. There were about fifteen box stalls with various horses looking out over the doors, or eating their breakfasts, or standing there with vaguely bored expressions. She looked particularly at the horse in number five, who was a big handsome black horse. But he had a bad look in his eye, and when (since there was no human around to hear) she greeted him in the Speech, he eyed her coldly, laid his ears back and snorted, "Bugger off, little girl, or I'll have your arm off."

Nita shrugged and moved on. Other horses were more forthcoming. When she spoke to them in the Speech, they answered, asking her for a sugar cube, or asking if she would please take them out. A few just tossed their heads, blinked lazily, and went back to their eating.

At the end of the stable barn was an extremely large pile of hay, kept under cover there so that the rain couldn't get at it, and the horses could be given it easily. Nita was standing for a moment looking at it, when something small and black, a rock she thought, fell down from the top of it. It tumbled down the hay, and even though Nita sidestepped, the falling black thing fell crookedly, and landed on top of one of her sneakers.

She looked down in shock. It was a kitten, its body no bigger than one of her hands. It more or less staggered to its feet, looked up at her, and meowed, saying, "Sorry!"

"Don't mention it," Nita said.

The kitten, which was already in the act of scampering away after a windblown straw, stopped so suddenly that it fell over forwards. Nita restrained herself mightily from laughing. It righted itself, washed furiously for a second, then looked at her. "Another one," it said. "The wind *does* blow, doesn't it."

"Another what?"

"Another wizard. Are you deaf?"

"Uh, no," Nita said. "Sorry, I'm new here. Who are you, then?"

"I am Tualha Slaith, a princess of the People," she said, rattling it all off in a hurry, "a bard and a scholar. And who are you?"

"I'm Nita Callahan."

"Nita?" said the kitten. "What kind of name is that?"

Nita had to stop for a moment. She was amazed to be getting this much conversation out of a domestic cat, let alone a kitten that

41

barely looked old enough to be weaned yet. "I think it was Spanish, originally," she said after a second or so. "Juanita is the long form."

"Aha, a Spaniard!" the kitten said, her eyes wide. " 'There's wine from the royal Pope / Upon the ocean green: / And Spanish ale shall give you hope, / My dark Rosaleen!' "

"You lost me," said Nita. "Anyway, I'm not a big ale fan . . ."

The kitten looked at Nita as if she was a very dim bulb indeed. "It's going to get crowded in here shortly," the kitten said. "Let's go out." She scooted out the barn door, and Nita followed her, feeling rather bemused: out the back, into the areaway between the riding school and the stable block. The path led up towards the field where the jumping equipment was. There was no one there at the moment.

The kitten stopped several times in her run to crouch down, her butt waggling, and pounce on a bug, or leaf, or stalk of grass, or blown bit of hay; and she always missed. Nita was having trouble controlling her reaction to this, but if there was one thing a wizard had practice in being, it was polite: so she managed. A little dusty whirlwind passed them by as they went between the riding school and the stable block, and Tualha paused to let it go by. "Good day," she said.

"You usually talk to wind?" Nita said, amused.

Tualha eyed her. "That's how the People go by," she said: "the People of the Air. You *are* new here." She scuttled on.

They came to the fence. Tualha made a mighty leap halfway up onto the fencepost, hauled herself up claw over claw, and sat at the top, where she washed briefly.

Nita sat down on the fence next to her. "Aren't you a little young to be a bard?" she said.

The kitten looked Nita up and down. "Aren't you a little young to be a wizard?"

"Well, no, I'm fourteen. . . ."

"And that's what percentage of your lifespan?"

"Uh—" Nita had to stop and figure it out.

"You can't even tell me right away? Poor sort of *ban-draoia* you'd make over here. Maths are important."

Nita flushed briefly. Whatever a *ban-draoia* might be, math had never been one of her favorite things. "And you of Spanish blood," Tualha said, "and you don't know that song, about how the Spanish came to Ireland first? What do you know?"

"Not much sometimes," Nita said, suspecting that here, at least, that was probably going to be true. "I know about the Spanish Armada, a little." Very little, she added to herself. Social studies had never been a favorite with her either, but she was beginning to suspect that that was going to have to change.

"That was only the fifteenth invasion," Tualha said. "The real causes of things go back much further. The wind moves, and things move in it. Now, in the beginning—"

"Do we have to go back *that* far?" Nita said drily.

The kitten glared at her. "Don't interrupt. How do you expect to become wise?"

"How did you do it?"

Tualha shrugged. "I've been in the hills. But also, I had to be a bard: I was found in a bag. It's traditional."

Nita remembered her aunt saying something the previous night about one of the farm cats having been found in a sack by the roadside, abandoned and starving. The starving part, at least, had been dealt with: Tualha was fat as a little ball. "Anyway," Tualha said, glaring at Nita again, "it's all in the Book of Conquests, and the Book of Leinster, and the Yellow Book of Lecan."

"I doubt I could just go get those out of the library where I come from," Nita said, "so perhaps you'll enlighten me." She grinned.

"It's all in the wizards' Mastery anyway," Tualha said, "if you'd bothered to look. But grow wise by me. —In the beginning there was no one in this island; it was bleak and bare, nor was it an island at all. The Flood rose and covered it, and fell away again. Then two hundred and sixty-four years later came twenty-four men and twenty-four women: those were Partholon and his people. At that time in Ireland was only one treeless and grassless plain, three lakes and nine rivers; so they built some more."

" 'Built—' " Nita said. "When was this?"

"Four hundred thousand years ago. Didn't I mention? Now do stop interrupting. They built mountains and carved valleys, and they fought the Fomor. The monster people," Tualha said in obvious annoyance at Nita's blank look; "the ones who were here before. The Fomori made a plague, the sickness that makes those who catch it hate and fight without thought; and the plague killed Partholon's people. So the Island that was not an island was empty. Then after another three thousand years, the people of Nemed came. They settled there and dug rivers and planted forests; and they met the Fomor and caught their plague—fought with them, and lost, and in the great strife of the battle the land was broken away from the greater land, and drowned in ice, and then water. When the ice melted and the water drew back, another people came after: the Fir Bolg. They brought new beasts and birds into the land, and there was song in the air and life in the waters."

"When did the cats get here?" Nita said.

"Later. Shush! —The Fomor came to the Fir Bolg too, though, with gifts and fair words, and married with them, and darkened their minds; and they caught the battle-sickness from the Fomor, and most died of it as all the others had: and the ones that were left had the bad blood of the Fomori in them, and became half-monstrous too. —Are you getting all this?" Tualha said.

"I think so." Nita resolved to have a look at her manual later, though, if as Tualha said all this information was in there. It might have been in a form that made sense to a cat at this point, but Nita was a little uncertain about it all, particularly about some of the dates.

"Well. After this the One grew angry that Its fair land was being ruined, and sent another people to live here. That was the *Tuatha de Danaan*, the Children and People of the Goddess Danu. They tried to parley with the Fir Bolg, but the Fir Bolg were sick with the battle-sickness of their Fomor blood, and would make no parley. So there was a great fight at the Plain of the Towers, Moytura. The battle came out a draw, and both sides drew apart and waited for a sign. And the sign came, sent by the One: the young hero-god Lugh the Allcrafted. He told the *Tuatha* to bring the four treasures of the people of Dana, the cup and stone and sword and spear they had brought with them when they first came there from the Four Oldest Cities. Seven years he reforged those treasures with the power that was in him. Then the Children of Danu went forth to battle once more at Moytura. Lugh went forward with the Spear called Luin, and with it destroyed Balor of the Deadly Eye, and the Fomori."

Tualha stopped, panting a little. Nita made a list in her head. "That's, let's see," she said, "six invasions. If you count the *Tuatha.*"

"It's *all* invasions," said Tualha, "from the land's point of view."

Nita thought about that for a moment. "You may have something there. So then who threw the *Tuatha* out?"

Tualha laughed at her. "Sure, you're joking me," she said. "They're still here."

"Say what?" Nita said.

A leaf went by Tualha on the breeze. She jumped at it, missed spectacularly, and came down on the ground so hard that Nita could hear the breath go out of her in a squeak. Nita couldn't help it any more: she burst out laughing. "I'm sorry, I really am," she said, "but I think you need some practice."

Tualha looked at her scathingly. "When you're a cat-bard," she said, "you get to choose. You get to be fast, or you get to be smart. And no offense, but I prefer smart. Not sure what you prefer, *Shonaiula ni Cealodhain*," she muttered, and scuttered off.

Nita chuckled a little, then got up and made her way back the way Tualha had gone, through the areaway between the riding school and the stable. As she went she noticed a sort of burning smell, and put her head quickly into the stable-block to make sure that something flammable hadn't fallen into the hay. She couldn't see anything but one of the grooms leading a chestnut horse out.

Out in the concreted yard, she found the source of the burning. There was a small pickup truck out there, and a square steel box about two feet on a side had been unloaded from it. *It's a forge*, Nita thought, as the little woman standing by it pulled at a cord handing out of one side, and pulled at it again, and again, like someone trying to start a lawn mower.

The comparison was apt, since a moment later a compressor stuttered and then roared to life. *That pushes air into it*, Nita thought, *and then—* The woman standing by it went around to one side of the portable forge and applied a blowtorch to an aperture there. *How about that*, Nita thought. *Portable horseshoeing—*

Nita went down to have a look as the chestnut horse was led up to the horse to be reshoed. The woman standing by the forge had to be about sixty. She was of medium height, with short close-cropped white hair and little wire-rimmed glasses, wearing jeans and boots and a T-shirt. Her face was very lined and very cheerful, and her accent was lighter than a lot of them Nita had heard so far: in fact, she sounded like an American who had been here for a long time. "Ah, you again," she said to the chestnut as the groom led it up and fastened its reins to a loop on the back of the pickup truck's tailgate. "We'll do better than we did last time. Ah," the farrier said then, looking up immediately as Nita wandered over. "You'll be Miz Callahan's niece."

"That's right," Nita said, and put her hand out to shake. She was getting used to the ritual by now, and was becoming relieved that no one was in a position to offer her any tea.

The farrier held up her hands in apology: they were covered with honest grime. "Sorry," she said. "I'm Biddy O Dalaigh. How are you settling in?"

45

"Pretty well, thanks."

"Have you seen this done before?"

"Only on TV," Nita said. "And never out of the back of a truck."

Biddy laughed. "Makes it easier to get a day's work done," she said, rooting around in a box in the truck and coming out with a horseshoe. She looked critically from it to the horse's feet, then bent down to push it into the aperture of the furnace-box. "Used to be that all the farms had their own farriers. No one can afford it now, though. So I go to my work, instead of people bringing it to me."

Nita leaned against the truck to watch. "You must travel a lot."

Biddy nodded and walked around to the front of the horse, stroking it and whistling to it softly between her teeth. "All over the county," she said. "A lot of horse shows and such." With her back to the horse's nose, she picked up its right forefoot and curled it around and under, grasping it between her knees. With a tool like a nail-puller, she went around the horse's hoof loosening the nails and prying them up one by one: then changed her leverage and knocked the shoe completely up and off. With another tool, a smaller one with a sharp point, Biddy began trimming down the rough edges of the hoof. "Tell Derval," Biddy said to Aisling, the blond groom who had been handling the chestnut, "that he won't be needing the orthopedic any more; the hoof's cleared up."

Nita was surprised. "Orthopedic horseshoes?" she said.

"Oh yes," Biddy said. "Horses have problems with their feet the same as people do. Tango here has been wearing a booster until this hoof grew back in straight—he hurt the foot a few months ago, and that can make the hoof go crooked. It's just an overdeveloped toenail, after all." She patted Tango as she got up. "We're all better now, though, aren't we, my lad? And you'll have a nice run tomorrow." She reached into the truck and came up with a pair of tongs.

"He's in the hunt?" Nita said.

Biddy nodded. "He belongs to Jim McAllister up on the Hill." She rooted around in the forge, stirring and rearranging the coals in it. Nita peered into the opening of it.

"Lava rocks?" she said.

"Oh aye, like in the barbecues. They work as well as charcoal unless you're doing dropforging or some such."

She turned her attention back to the hoof, scraping its edges a bit more. Then Biddy picked up the tongs again. "Here we go, now," she said, and took hold of the hoof again. With her free hand she plucked the horseshoe out of the furnace and slapped it hard against the hoof, exactly where she wanted it. There was a billow of smoke, and a stink like burned hair or nails.

Nita waved the smoke away. "Foul, isn't it," Biddy said, untroubled. After removing the shoe from the hoof and dunking it in a bucket of cold water, she dropped the tongs, took a hammer out of another belt loop, reached into a pocket for nails, and began tapping them in with great skill, each nail halfway in with one tap, all the way in with the next.

Nita watched Biddy do Tango's other three shoes. Then another horse was led out, and Nita turned away: this kind of thing was interesting enough, once. *Maybe I'll go down to Greystones,* she thought. Aunt Annie had told her that the bike was out in the shed behind the riding school, if she wanted to use it and no one else had it. *Or maybe I won't.* It was strange, having nowhere familiar to go, and no one familiar to go with. Being at loose ends was not a sensation she was very used to: but she didn't feel quite bold enough at the moment to just go charging off into a strange town.

I wouldn't mind if Kit were here, though. . . .

Nita wandered back the way she had come, back to the field where the jumping equipment lay around. She climbed over the fence and walked out into the field to look at it all; the odd barber-striped poles, the jumps and steps and stiles, some painted with brand names, or names of local shops.

The wind began to rise. From this field, which stood at the top of a gentle rise, you could see the ocean. Nita stood there and gazed at it for a while. The brightness it had worn this morning, under full sunlight, was gone. Now, with the sun behind a cloud, it was just a flat silvery expanse, dull and pewter-colored. Nita smelled smoke again, and idly half-turned to look over her shoulder, toward the farrier's furnace.

And was shocked not to see it there at all . . . or anything else. The farm was gone.

The contour of the land was still there—the way it trended gently downhill past the farm buildings, and then up again toward the dual carriageway and the hills on its far side. But there were no buildings, no houses that she could see. The road was gone. Or not gone: reduced to a rutted dirt track. And the smoke—

She looked around her in great confusion. There was a pillar of black smoke rising up off to one side, blown westward by the rising wind off the sea. Very faintly in this silence she could hear cries, shouts. Something white over there was burning. It was the little white church down the road, St. Patrick's of Kilquade, with its one bell. She stood there in astonishment, hearing the cries on the wind, and then a terrible metallic note, made faint by the distance: the one bell blowing in the wind, then shattering with heat and the fall of the tower that housed it. A silence followed the noise . . . then faint laughter, and the sound of glass exploding outward in the force of the fire.

And a voice spoke, down by her feet. "Yes, they have been restless of late, those ghosts," said Tualha, looking where Nita looked, at the smoke. "I thought I might find you here. It's as I said, *Shonaiula ni Cealodhain*. The wind blows, and things get blown along in it. Bards and wizards alike. Why would you be here, otherwise? But better to be the wind than the straw, when the Carrion-Crow is on the wing. It always takes *draoiceacht* to set such situations to rights."

Nita gulped and tried to get hold of herself. This was a wizardry, but not one of a kind she had ever experienced. Worldgating, travel between planes, she knew. But those required extensive and specific spelling. Nothing of the sort had happened here. She had simply turned around . . . and been here. "Where are we?" she said softly. "How did we get here?"

"You went *cliathánach*," Tualha said. " 'Sideways,' as I did. True, it's not usually so easy. But that's an indication that things are in the wind indeed."

"Sideways," Nita breathed. "Into the past—"

"Or the future," Tualha said, "or the never-was. All those are here. You know that."

"Of course I know it," Nita said. It was part of a wizard's most basic knowledge that the physical world coexisted with hundreds of thousands of others, both like it and very unlike. No amount of merely physical travel would get you into any of them. With the right wizardry, though, you had to move no more than a step. "It shouldn't be anything *like* this easy, though," she said.

Tualha looked up at her with wide, bland eyes. "It is easier here," she said. "It always has been. But you're right that it shouldn't be *this* easy. There's danger in it, both for the 'daylight' world and the others."

Nita looked at the smoke, shaking her head. "What was it you said? . . . the wind blows, and things get blown along with it?"

Tualha said nothing. Nita stood there and thought how casually she had said to her mother, *If I go on call in Ireland, I go on call, and that's it*. It was not her mother's idea that she come here, after all.

Some one of the Powers that Be had sent her here to do a job. She knew that when she got back to the farmhouse—*if* she got back to the farmhouse—and opened her manual, she would find she was on active status again. And here she was, without her partner, without her usual Senior Wizards' support—for their authority didn't run here: Europe had its own Senior structures. Alone, and with a problem that she didn't understand— She was going to have to get caught up on her reading.

Tualha crouched and leaped at a bit of ash that the wind sailed past her. She missed it. Nita sighed. "How do we get back?" she said.

"You haven't done this before?" Tualha said. "Where were you looking when it happened?"

"At the ocean."

"Look back, then."

Nita turned her back on the smoke and the cries and the brittle music of breaking glass, and looked out to the flat grey sea, willing things to be as they had been before.

"There you are, then," Tualha said. Nita turned again. There was the farm, the riding school, the farmhouse: and the field, full of its prosaic jumping equipment, all decals and slightly peeling paint. "But indeed," Tualha said, "it's as I told you. Something must change. Get about it, before it gets about us."

Brí Cualann
Bray

The next morning, Nita did what she usually did when she was confused—the thing that had made her a wizard in the first place. She went to the library.

She caught the bus in, a green double-decker that stopped at the end of her aunt's road, and climbed up to its second floor of the bus. There was no one at all there, so she went straight forward to take the seat right in front, its window looking directly forward and twelve feet down onto the ground. It was interesting to ride along little country lanes and look right down onto the sheep and the hedges and the potholes from such a height.

But she didn't let it distract her for very long. The section in the Wizard's Manual on Ireland was quite long. This was not a surprise to her, since at the moment the section on the United States was quite short . . . most likely since she wasn't there. The manual tended to have as much information as you needed on any particular subject, and simply waited for you to look for it.

She immediately found that she had been correct to be a little suspicious of Tualha's numbers. The things she discussed as happening four hundred thousand years before had apparently actually happened four hundred million years before. This didn't surprise Nita either; she remembered her Aunt Annie saying yesterday that as far as she knew, the only times cats were really concerned about were their mealtimes.

In any case, the Manual told her of the formation of Ireland, some four hundred million years earlier; of the pushing up of the great chain of mountains that it shared with Newfoundland, and with the Pyrenees. A hundred and fifty million years later, Greenland began to move away from the ancient European continent, creating a huge gap in what was to become the northern Atlantic. The great island that had been both England and Ireland was flooded, as the waters of other seas flowed into the gap, and then split; and the ice came down and tore at it, leaving the terrible glacial valleys of the western Irish coast that Nita had seen when she flew in.

That was just the science of it, of course. Science may accurately reveal the details about concrete occurrences, the "whats" and "hows" of life: but a wizard knows to look further than science for the "whys." And wizards knew that the world was *made*: not created in some disinterested abstract sense, like an assembly line of natural forces stamping out parts, but made, stone by stone, as an artist makes, or a craftsman, or a cook: with interest, and care. The One— the only name wizards have for that Power which was senior to the Powers that Be, and everything else—like a good manager had delegated many of its functions to the first-made creatures, the Powers, which some people in the past had called gods, and others had called angels. The Powers made different parts of the world, and became associated with them simply because they loved them, as people who make tend to love what they've made.

But something had gone wrong in Ireland's making. Someone had been—it was tempting to say "interfering." The manual said nothing specific about this: it tended to let one draw one's own conclusions on the more complex ethical issues. But several times, the Makers had begun to make the island; and several times, something had gone wrong. Cataclysms, a glacial movement that happened too quickly, a continental plate ramming another faster than had been intended. A misjudgement? A miscalculation? Nita thought not. She thought she saw here the interference of her old enemy, the Lone Power, the one which (for good or evil) invented death, and later went through the world seeing what It could destroy or warp.

It seemed that the bright Powers, the Makers and Builders, had not seen, or suspected, the flaws inserted in their building by the Lone Power's working. So Ireland had come undone several times, and had had to be patched. Indeed, the top part of it had only been welded on about two hundred and fifty million years after the original complex began to be formed—after other land that should have been Ireland was drowned beneath the sea.

So then. Two or three attempts to make, frustrated two or three times by the Lone Power . . . and then, as Tualha said, the One had become impatient. Or maybe impatience was an inaccurate emotion to attribute to the Power that conceived the whole universe at its beginning, and through to its end. The One's great intent, along with that of the wizards and the Powers that Be, who do Its will, is to preserve energy—to keep things running for as long as they can be

51

made to run, with what's available . . . and not to waste unnecessarily. Building here was being actively hindered. So a new group of Makers came into the world to shape Ireland: greater powers, more senior, more central, than those who had worked here before. They would set it right.

They tried. Nita saw, between the telling of the manual and what Tualha told her, that just as the One had scaled up its response, so had the Lone Power. The Fomori had been growing more powerful each time they had been challenged. Each time they were put down, they came back more powerful yet. And then came the first battle of Moytura.

The version that Tualha gave her turned out to be much romanticized and classicized. Moytura itself was a great strife of forces over many centuries, as mountains were raised and thrown down, river valleys carved and choked; and the ice rose and fell. You could still see the evidence in places in Ireland—rock more warped and twisted than could be explained by any mere geological uprising or subsidence; places where fires had fallen and melted the stone in ways that geologists could make nothing of. Nita could make something of it. The weapons used to wage war in heaven had been brought to bear on Ireland. The battle went on for a good while.

And then— Nita turned a page over, scanning down it. She was beginning to get the drift of this. Here was the arrival of Lugh of the Long Reach. She thought she knew this particular power. She had met it once or twice. A young warrior, fierce, kindly, a little humorous, liable to travel in disguise: a power known by many names in many places and times. Michael, Athene, Thor—it was the One's Champion, one of the greatest of all creatures: definitely a Power to be reckoned with. As Lugh, that Power had come and poured Its virtue into the great Treasures that the *Tuatha de Danaan* had brought from the Four Cities.

Then he and the *Tuatha* had gone out with those weapons against Balor of the Evil Eye. *Who was he?* Nita thought. *The Lone Power Itself? Or some unfortunate creature that It corrupted and inhabited?* That, too, was a favorite tactic. Either way, Balor had held the humans of the island, and his twisted creatures the Fomori, and the other, lesser powers, in great terror for thousands of years. But then came the second battle, as Tualha had said, and all that changed. War came from Heaven to Earth with a vengeance. The Champion, in the form of Lugh, struck Balor down.

Nita turned another page over and saw why Tualha had laughed at

52

her so. Certainly it was laughable, the idea that anyone could just throw out ten of the senior Powers that Be. But something had happened. After putting down Balor, they had gotten busy finishing Ireland. They raised the mountains and smoothed them down, made the plains and the forests and lakes. And they fell more completely in love with the beautiful, marred place than any of their more junior predecessors had.

This was commoner in the Old World, Nita read, than in the new. In places like North America, where the native human peoples had stories not of specific gods, but instead about heroes and the One, it indicated that the Makers of that place had gone away, well-satisfied with their work. In some places in the world, though, the satisfaction took longer—places like Greece and Rome. Their Makers loved them too much to leave for a long while, though finally they did let go. But there were still a few places in the world where the Powers had never let go. This was one of them.

I bet this is why Ireland has so much trouble, one way and another, Nita thought. *The Powers won't move out and let the new tenants be there by themselves. Us*— For like most other wizards, Nita knew quite well that the good Powers might indeed be good, but that didn't make them safe. Even the best of the Powers that Be could be blunted by too much commerce with humans and physical reality.

Nita read that the *Tuatha de Danaan*, as the Irish had come to call the Builder-powers, had never left. And when the human people, the "Milesians," came at last, the Powers struck a bargain with them, agreeing to relinquish the lands and vanish into the hills. At least, that was how it looked to the humans. They knew that some hills in Ireland, at the four great feasts of the year, became more than hills. The nonphysical then became solider, realer; and the physical, if it was wise, would stay out of the way of what was older, stronger, harder, by far.

They had gone "sideways," had the *Tuatha*. They could not bear to leave Ireland, and so they had gone just one over—or two, or five. It was still Ireland, but it was also a little bit closer to the depths of Reality, where, as Nita knew, lay Timeheart. She had been there several times, for brief periods. It looked different ways, depending on where and when you were. She had seen it look like a city, like the ocean, like the depths of space. What it always *was*, regardless of your viewpoint, was that place where the physical universe was as it would have been, had the Lone Power not taken exception and created something that the other Powers had not intended: entropy

. . . death. The Powers simply moved into that universe nearest to Timeheart which to them looked most like Ireland.

But much coming and going had forged a link, broadening the road from a little track into a highway that it was easy to stumble onto. All of Ireland had become a place where one could suddenly go sideways. This to-ing and fro-ing of the greater and lesser Powers between Ireland that was, and their version of Ireland—*Tir na nOg*, as they called it, the Land of the Ever-Young—was very dangerous. But it wasn't a thing you could just stop: at least, Nita couldn't. And as for her—

Well, she had gone sideways, and it hadn't hurt her . . . but then she was a wizard. If something like that started happening to regular people, though, people in the street who were standing waiting for a bus, and suddenly found themselves in the middle of a Viking invasion—or something worse—Nita shuddered.

The problem with being sent somewhere by the Powers that Be to do a job is that, frequently, they leave it to you to find out what the job is. Nita flipped through the book to the directory pages and saw that, yes indeed, she was on active status, and her aunt's address was listed. There was an address for a senior wizard as well, with an asterisk and a note saying, "Consult in case of emergency."

Well then, Nita thought, *if they've put me on my own on this one, I guess that's what it is. Must be something that having Kit around wouldn't help.* The thought made her ache. Were the Powers trying to break up their partnership? Or on the other hand, was this just the kind of solo work that even a partnered wizard had to do every now and then? Well, either way, she was not going to refuse the commission. She shut the book as the bus bounced into Bray.

It was not a very big town, its main street about half the length of the main street at home; and as usual, everything continued to look small and cramped and a little worn-out by Nita's standards. She berated herself inwardly. *Just because you're used to everything looking slick and neat and new, doesn't mean that it has to be that way here.* Aunt Annie had mentioned to her that Ireland had been in economic trouble for a while, and there just wasn't the money to spend on things that Nita took for granted.

She got off in the middle of town, across from the big Catholic church, and had a look around. There was a sign there that said *Leabhlair poblachta*, public library. She grinned. Finding libraries had never been one of her problems.

The library was two buildings—one older, which had been a

schoolhouse once, a big square granite-built building, very solid and dependable-looking, all on one story; and the newer annex, built in the same stone but a slightly more modern style. She spent a happy two or three hours there, browsing. Nita had had no idea there was so much written in the Irish language—so many poems, so many poets; humor, cartoon books, all kinds of neat things. And structurally the language looked, and occasionally sounded, very like the Speech. But she tried not to be distracted from what she was there for.

She picked out several large books on Irish mythology, and began going through them in hopes of correlating what Tualha had told her with what she had seen in the manual. Mostly she found confirmation for Tualha's version—the terrible eye of Balor that burnt everything it saw: many strange tales of the old "gods and goddesses," the greater and lesser Powers that Be. As usual, the Powers had their jobs divided up. Among many others, there were Govan the smith and beer-brewer, Diancecht the great physician of the gods, and Brigid of the Fires, hearth-goddess and beast-goddess, artificer and miracle-worker; bard-gods and carpenter-gods, builders, charioteers, cooks and warriors.

There were also tales of the "little people." Nita had to smile at that. Worldgating did odd things to the density and refractive index of air. Something close, seen through air whose structure was disturbed by wizardry, might seem far away, or small. But this was an effect of diffraction, not magic. The "little people" were little only to human perceptions, and only occasionally.

And then there were the stories of the saints. Bridget, for example. When the saints came to Ireland, so many miracles attended them that Nita seriously wondered whether the stories she was reading were not in fact new versions of the tales about the Powers, transferred to the saints to make them "respectable" to the new religion. Bridget's stories in particular were interesting, though there was confusion over whether the person they were happening to was the old Goddess in disguise, or the new, mortal saint. Her miracles seemed to be of a friendly, homey sort, more useful than spectacular: she fixed broken things and fed people, and she said that her great wish was that everyone should be in Heaven with God and the angels, and should have a nice meal and a drink.

There was a lot more material, and Nita did her best to digest it. And then digestion came up to be considered seriously, since she hadn't had any breakfast. It was partly out of cowardice; she had wakened up afraid to hang around the farm for long, lest she should look at some common thing and abruptly find herself back in time, or sideways in it. *I'm really no safer here, though,* she thought as she stepped out of the library, looking up and down the little road which ran parallel to Bray's main street. This calm-looking landscape with its brownstone houses ranged across the way, and the truck unloading groceries for the supermarket around the corner, and the people all double-parked on the yellow lines, all this could shift in a moment. A second, and she might find herself outside the stone age encampment that was here once long ago: or the little row of wattled huts that the Romans came visiting once, and never left—their bones and coins had been found down by Bray Head: or the great eighteenth-century spa where people from Britain came on their vacations, promenading up and down the fine seafront, a second Brighton. No, there was nowhere she could go to get away from things.

She went up to the main street and looked around for somewhere to get something to eat. There were some tea shops, but at the moment she felt like she had had enough tea for a lifetime. Instead, near the bridge over the Dargle, there was a place with a sign that said AMERICAN STYLE FRIED CHICKEN. *Hmm,* Nita thought, her mouth watering as she made for it, *we'll see about that.*

She went in. As she ordered, she saw a few heads turn among the kids who were sitting there: probably at her accent. She smiled. They were going to have to get used to the look of her for the little while she was going to be here.

She got herself a Coke and settled down to wait for her chicken to be ready, gazing idly over at the kids sitting at the other table. They were stealing glances back at her, boys and girls together: a little casual, a little shy, a little hostile. In that way, they looked almost exactly like almost everyone she knew at home. They *did* dress differently. Black seemed to be a big favorite here, and a kind of heavy boot that she had never seen before. Everyone seemed very into tight torn jeans, or just tight jeans, or very tight short skirts, all black again; and black leather seemed popular. She felt a little out of place in her down vest and her faded blue jeans, but she grinned back at the other kids and paid attention to her Coke again.

A couple of minutes later, two of them came over to her. She looked up amiably enough. One of them was a boy, very tall, with very shaggy dark hair, a long nose, with dark eyes set very close together, and a big wide mouth that could have been very funny or very cruel depending on the mood of its owner. The girl could have been his twin, except that she was shorter, and her hair was marvelously teased and ratted out into a great black mane. At least parts of it were black; some were stunningly purple, or pink. She was wearing a khaki T-shirt with a wonderfully torn and beaten-up leather jacket over it: black again, black jeans and those big heavy boots which Nita was becoming rather envious of.

"You a Yank?" said the boy. It wasn't entirely a question. There was something potentially a little nasty on the edge of it.

"Somebody has to be," Nita said. "Wanna sit down?"

They looked at her and shuffled for a moment. "You staying in town?"

"No, I'm out in Kilquade."

"Relatives?"

"Yeah. Annie Callahan. She's my aunt."

"Woooaaa!" said the boy in a tone of voice that was only slightly mocking and only slightly impressed. "Rich relatives, huh?"

"I don't know if rich is the right word," Nita said.

"You here looking for your roots?" the girl said.

Nita looked at her hair, looked at the girl's. "Still attached to them, as far as I can tell. Though finding them around here doesn't seem to be a big problem."

There was a burst of laughter over this. "Come on and sit with us," they said. "I'm Ronan. This is Majella."

"Okay."

Nita went with them. She was rapidly introduced to the others, who seemed to alternate between being extremely interested in her, and faintly scornful. The scorn seemed to be because she was an American, because they thought she had a lot of money, because they thought she thought they were poor, and various other reasons. The admiration seemed to be because she was American, because they thought she had a lot of money, and because she could see the big movies six months earlier than everyone else. "Uh," Nita said finally, "my folks don't let me go see that many movies. I have to keep my schoolwork up all the time, or they don't let me go out."

There was a general groan of agreement over this. "There's no escape," said Ronan.

More detailed introductions ensued. Most of the kids lived in Bray. One of them lived as far out as Greystones, but said she took the bus in "for the crack." Nita blinked until she discovered that crack was not a drug here, but a word for really good conversation or fun. Nita was immediately instructed about all the nightclubs and all

57

the discos she should go to. "How many discos do you have here?" she said, in some surprise. It then turned out that "disco" was not a word for a specific kind of building, or a specific kind of music, as it was in the States, but a dance that various pubs or hotels held once or twice a week. Several of them were no-alcohol kids' discos, highly thought of by this group, who went off into enthusiastic discussion of what they would wear and who they would go with.

"You got somebody to go with?" said Ronan.

"Uh, no," Nita said, thinking regretfully of Kit. He loved to dance. "My buddy's back in the States."

"Oooh, she's got a *buddyyyyyy!!*" Nita grinned a little: she was now beyond the blushing point. Her sister had been teasing her about Kit for so long that this was a very minor salvo by comparison.

"Aren't you a little young for that?" one of the girls said, clearly teasing, to judge by the young guy massaging her shoulders at the moment.

Nita arched her eyebrows. "Let's just say that in my part of the world we make up our minds about this kind of thing early."

"Whooooaaaaa!!" said the group, and started punching one another and making lewd remarks, only about half of which Nita understood.

"So if your buddy's there, what are you doing here?" said Ronan.

"I know!" said Majella. "Her folks sent her away to separate them because they were—ahem!" And she shook her hand in a gesture intended to be slightly rude and slightly indicative of what they were doing.

Nita thought about this for a moment, and thought that the simplest way to manage things was to let them think exactly this. "Well, yeah," she said. "Anyway, I'm stuck here for six weeks."

"Stuck here! Only stuck here! In the best part of the Earth! Well, excuse *us!*" they said, and began ragging her shamelessly, explaining what a privilege it was that she should be among them, and telling her all the wonderful places there were to see, and things to do. She grinned at this at last, and said, "I bet none of you do those things."

"Oh, well, those are *tourist* things," Ronan said.

"Thanks loads," said Nita.

They chatted about this and that for a long while. Nita found herself oddly interested by Ronan, despite his looks: maybe *because* of his looks. She didn't know anyone at home who managed to look so dark and grim, no matter how punk they dressed: and there was an odd cheerful edge to his grimness that kept flashing out, a certain

58

delight in having opinions, and having them loudly, in hopes that someone would be shocked. They ranged through music ("Mostly junk except for the Cranberries") and art ("All bollocks"—Nita kept her mouth shut and made a note to find out what bollocks were), and quite a bit about politics, especially Irish politics, much of which left Nita completely in the dark. Ronan's opinions of anyone who wanted to colonize Ireland, from the English on back, were scathing. So were his views on people who thought they were Irish and weren't really, or who weren't Irish and thought they should have something to do with running the country, or thought that the Irish needed any kind of help with anything at all. The others tended to nod agreement with him, or if they disagreed, to keep fairly quiet about this: Nita noticed this particularly, and suspected that they had felt the edge of his temper once or twice. She grinned to herself, thinking that he would have a slightly hotter time of it if he tried it on *her*. She rather hoped Ronan would.

It was amazing how long a couple of pieces of chicken and a few Cokes could be made to last; fortunately, the people running the shop didn't seem to care how long they stayed. Eventually, though, everybody had to leave: buses to catch, people to meet. One by one they said goodbye to Nita, and headed off, Ronan last of them. "Don't get lost looking for leprechauns, now, Miss Yank," he shouted to her over his shoulder as he made his way off down Bray's main street.

She snickered and turned away, looking at the 45 bus pulling up across the street, and thought, *Naah . . . I'll walk home.* It was only eight miles, and through extremely pretty countryside.

Except for the first part, the climb up one side of Bray Head, it was a long, easy walk down, taking her about an hour to get down to Greystones. She strolled down into the town. It was a more villagey-looking street than Bray's, smaller: a couple of banks, a couple of food stores, two small restaurants, a newsagent where you could get magazines and cards and candy. Various other small shops . . . a dry cleaners'. And that was it. After that, the town was surrounded by big old houses, and estates of smaller ones. And then the fields began again—in fact, they began almost as soon as you had left the town. Nita strolled by the tiny golf course, looked down to Greystones' south beach beyond it; walked past a cow with a blank expression, chewing its cud. *"Dai,"* she said to it. It blinked at her and kept chewing.

The road climbed again, winding up through Killincarrig. *Every-*

thing does have names here, Nita thought. *It's amazing. Really must get a map out. There may be one in the manual. . . .*

There was. She consulted it as she went up the road. At the top of the road, another crossed it at a T-intersection: she turned left. That way led toward Kilquade and Kilcoole and Newcastle with its little church.

This road climbed and dipped over a little bridge that crossed a dry river; up between high hedges. Birds dipped and sang high in the air. The sun was quite hot: there was no wind.

There came a point where there was a right turn, and a signpost pointing down between two more high hedges, toward Kilquade. Nita took it, making her way down the narrow road. The houses here were built well away from one another, even though they were small; some were larger, though.

The road dipped and broadened, curving around in front of Saint Patrick's. Nita stopped and looked at it for a moment. It was quite normal. A little white-painted church, with the tower off to one side of the building, and the bell with a circular pulley to make it go. There was a big field on one side, and visible behind it a hedge, and beyond that, some of Aunt Annie's land, another field planted with oilseed rape and those bright yellow flowers. The hum of bees came from it, loud. Nita stood still and listened, smelled the air. No broken stained glass, no fire, no blackening.

She turned and looked off to her right. Well behind her, she could see Little Sugarloaf, which she had passed on her walk. And just beyond it, Great Sugarloaf, a very perfect cone, standing up straight, a sort of russet and green color this time of year; for in this heat, the bracken was beginning to go brown already. *I wonder,* she thought. *Sideways. . . .*

She had done it without wizardry yesterday. She stood there for a moment, and just looked. Not at Sugarloaf as it was, but as it could be; not this brown, but green.

Nothing.

Nothing . . .

. . . But it was green.

Her eyes widened a little. She looked at the nearby hedge. There were no flowers. She looked over her shoulder in panic at the church. The church looked just the same, but it was earlier in the year, much earlier. *I wonder,* she thought. *How far can you take it? Do you have to be looking for anything in particular?* Most wizardries required that you name the specifics that you wanted . . . *All right. What does it look like? she thought. What does it look like for them?*

She looked at Sugarloaf again. *What does it look like? Show me. Come on, show me. . . .*

There was no ripple, no sense of change, no special effects. One minute it was Sugarloaf, green as if with new spring. The next minute—it was a city.

There *were* no such cities. No one had ever built such towers, such spires. Glass, it might have been, or crystal: a glass mountain, a crystal city, all sheen and fire. It needed no sunlight to make it shine. It shed its light all around, and the other hills nearby all had shadows cast away from it. Nita was not entirely sure she didn't see something moving in some of those shadows. For the moment, all she could see was the light, the fire; Sugarloaf all one great mass of tower upon tower, arches, architraves, buttresses, leaping up; an architecture men could not have imagined, since it violated so many of their laws. It was touched a little with the human idiom, true; but then those who had built it and lived in it—were living in it—had been dealing with the human idiom for a while, and had become enamored of it. "They're still here," Tualha had said, and laughed.

Nita blinked, and let it go: and it was gone. Brown bracken again, plain granite mountain, with its head scraped bare. She let a long breath out and went walking again, back up to the last hill that would lead her up to her aunt's driveway. "That simple," she said to herself. "That easy . . ." For wizards, at least. At the moment. *But it shouldn't be that easy. . . .*

Something had better be done.

If only I could find out what . . . !

She headed back to the farm.

The next morning was the foxhunt. She missed the earliest part of the operation, having been reading late again that night, and chatting with Kit. He hadn't been able to throw much light on anything, except that he missed her. "Kit," she said, "I don't know how much more of this I can take."

"You can take it," he said. "I can take it too. I saw your folks the other day."

"How are they?"

"They're fine . . . they're going to call you tonight. They said they were going to give you a couple of days to get yourself acclimated before they bothered you."

"Fine by me," Nita said. "I've had enough to keep me busy."

She had felt Kit nod, thirty-five hundred miles away. "So I see," he said. "I'd watch doing that too much, Neets."

"Hm?"

"I mean, it makes me twitch a little bit. You didn't do any specific wizardry, but with that result—makes you wonder what's going on over there."

"Yeah, well, it can't be that bad, Kit. Look, you come back as easily as you go—"

"I sure *hope* you do," he said.

The conversation had trailed off after that. It was odd how it was becoming almost uncomfortable to talk to Kit, because their conversation couldn't run in the same channels it usually did, the easy, predictable ones. For the first time, she was having things to tell him that he hadn't actually participated in. "How's Dairine?" she said.

"She's been busy with something . . . I don't know what. Something about somebody's planet."

"Oh Lord, not again," Nita said. "Sometimes I think she should be unlisted. She's never going to have any peace, at least not while she's in breakthrough . . . and maybe not later." They chatted a while more, and then trailed off.

Nita was thinking about this in the morning as she got her breakfast. The kitchen was in havoc. A lot of the riders who were picking up their horses from the stable had come in for "a quick cup of tea." Nita was learning that there was no such thing in Ireland as a quick cup of tea. What you got was several cups of tea, taking no less than half an hour, during which whatever interesting local news there was was passed on. "A quick cup of tea" might happen at any hour of the day or night, include any number of people, male or female, and always turned into a raging gossip session with hilarious laughter and recriminations.

Finally the kitchen began to clear out. The people who were in the hunt were splendidly dressed, all red coats and black caps and beige riding britches and black shiny boots. They were discussing the course they would ride—a mean one, from Calary Upper behind Sugarloaf, down through various farmers' lands, straight down to Newcastle. The thing that was bemusing them was that, suddenly, there were no foxes anywhere. Nita smiled to herself as she heard the discussion in the kitchen that morning. Everyone was excessively bemused about the situation. Some people blamed hunt protesters; others blamed the weather, crop dusting, sunspots, global warming, or overzealous shooting by local farmers. Nita grinned outright, and had another cup of tea. She was beginning to really like tea.

"Well, that's all we'll see of *them*," said her Aunt Annie, pouring herself a cup as well and then flopping down in one of the kitchen chairs in thinly disguised relief.

"I thought they were coming through here," Nita said.

"Oh, they will, but that's not until this afternoon."

"No foxes, huh?" Nita said, in great satisfaction.

"Not a one." Her aunt looked over at her and said, "Personally, I can't say that I'm exactly broken-hearted."

"Me either," said Nita.

"Doesn't matter. They'll hunt to a drag—it's just an old fox skin, that leaves a scent for the dogs: they drag it along the ground. They'll have a good time."

Nita nodded and went back to her reading, half-thinking of going down to Bray again that afternoon, to see if Ronan or Majella were around. Then she talked herself out of it. It was too nice a day, the sun was hot . . . there was no reason to go into a smelly town and strangle yourself on the bus fumes and traffic. She would put a towel down outside, and lie out in the sun, and pretend it was the beach. She missed the beaches back home: the water here was much too cold to swim in.

So that was what she did. And so it was, about two-fifteen, that she heard the cry of the hounds. She got up and pulled a T-shirt on over her bathing suit, put the Manual in the trailer, and went to lean on the fence by the back field and see what she could see. She almost missed the first horseman to go by, about a half mile away across the field; thundering through the pasture, one horseman with a long rope dragging behind him, and something dragging at the end of the rope.

There was a long pause. And then the note of the hounds came belling up over the fields, followed by the hounds themselves, woofing, lolloping, yipping. Then, over the rise behind them, came a splendid pouring of horses of all kinds: chestnut, brown, dapple, black, galloping over the hill; and a horn going *tarantara!* And the riders, hallooing and riding as best they could after the hounds.

It took them about a minute and a half to go by. There were about fifty people, all in their red jackets and their beige breeches and not-so-black boots. Then they were gone. The sounds of the hounds and the horses' hooves faded away over the next hill, south of the potato field, and were gone. Nita listened to the last cries fade out, then went back to lie in the sun.

The horses started coming back to the farm, some of them trucked in by trailer from Newcastle, about three hours later. There was much talk of rides and falls and jumps and water barriers, and a lot of other stuff that Nita didn't particularly understand. But everyone seemed to have had a good time. Nita was very glad that it had been able to happen without any foxes being ripped up.

Dinnertime that evening was replaced by a marathon "little cup of tea," as the grooms from the stables got together with the stablemanager and the trainers. It was at least eleven-thirty or twelve before the last of them left, having been given wine and whiskey and everything else that Aunt Annie had.

Nita came in from the trailer, having had enough of the horsey talk about eight, and helped her aunt do the dishes, or at least rinse them and put them in the dishwasher. "There's that done with for this year," said her aunt. She rolled her eyes at the ceiling. "The way they eat!"

"Yeah. You need anything else, Aunt Annie?"

"No, I think we're okay for the night. You ready to turn in?"

"I'm going to have a little walk first."

"Okay. Just watch out for those holes in the pasture. It's pretty torn up out there, what with the neighbor's cows."

"Right."

She got her jacket and went out into the evening. It was twelve-thirty by now, but it still wasn't fully dark; in fact it was beginning, in the northeast, to think about slowly brightening again. Nita cast an eye up at the sky. There was a canopy of thin cloud, enough to obscure all but the very brightest stars, and the occasional planet. Jupiter was high, and the Moon.

She wandered out into the pasture, into the total dark and the quiet, and just stood there and listened. It was the first time she had really felt relaxed since she had come here. She was beginning to feel a little more in control of things: she had done enough reading to at least be able to go and see a senior and tell him or her what she thought her problem was, and to be able to discuss it in terms that made some kind of sense to someone who lived here and was familiar with this kind of situation. In the great quiet she heard birds crying, somewhere a long way away. It might have been a rookery. She had heard that creaky, cawing sound a couple of times now, when the rooks were settled down for the night and some late noise disturbed them.

She stood there under the stars, waiting for the silence to resume. It didn't resume. It got louder.

More rooks. Or no—what was that?

The hair stood straight up all over her as she heard the howl. There are no wolves in Ireland! she told herself. The wolfhounds had been bred specifically to deal with them, and there hadn't been wolves in Ireland since the late 1700's sometime.

But that howl came shuddering out of the night, and several others behind it; followed by yips and barks. And the sound of hooves. Not many sets of them, but just one, a long way off. One rider, one horse, galloping. *What in the worlds—?*

She strained to see in the moonlight. It was hard. Through this thin cloud, the Moon was only at first quarter, and it was hard to see anything but a vague bloom of light over the cropland, black where it struck trees and hedgerows, the dimmest silver where it struck anything else. The hoofbeats got louder; and the howls got louder too.

Hurriedly Nita said the first six words of a spell that had proved very handy to her in other times and places. It was a simple force-field spell, which made a sort of shell around the wizard who spoke it. Blows went sideways from it; physical force stopped at it and just slid off. One word would release it if she needed it—and she had a feeling she would.

In the dark, not too far away, she saw something moving. There were spells that would augment a wizard's vision, but she didn't have any of them prepared at the moment, and didn't have time to do any one of them from scratch. She didn't have her manual. She could just begin to see the faint silvering of moonlight on the big thing galloping toward her.

It was not a horse. No horse ever foaled was that tall. It went by a tree she knew the height of, at the edge of the field, and then by a fencepost that she knew was only six feet high. The top of the post came just below the creature's shoulder, as the massive four-footed shape sprinted toward her. Not a horse, not with those antlers, six feet across at least; not with that skull a yard and a half long; and no horse had such a voice, trumpeting, desperate, a sound like the night being torn edge to edge. She had seen its picture. It was an elk, but not like any elk that walked the earth these days; the old Irish elk, extinct since the ice came down.

It went by her like a piece of storm, the breath like a blast of fog out of it as it went. It shook the ground as it ran, and its feet went deep into the soft pasture, spurning up great sods of grass. It flew on past and gave her never a look. Belling, on it went, with a great roar, a trumpeting like an elephant's. And behind it came the wolves.

They were not normal wolves. All the wolfhounds in Ireland could not have done anything about *these.* These were the wolves that had hunted the Irish elk when they still walked this part of the world. They were four feet high at the shoulder, easily; she saw them come past the fencepost too. They were rough-coated, their eyes huge and dark except when the Moon glinted in the head of one or another thrown up to howl as it ran. A faint mist of light clung to them that had nothing to do with the mist on the field, or the moonlight. Their teeth were longer than a regular wolf's; their feet were bigger, their claws were longer. Their tails were shorter, their heads were heavier and more brutish. They were dire-wolves, the wolves of the stone age or earlier, *Canis lupus dirus.* They were hunting the elk.

It suddenly occurred to Nita that there would be someone following behind this pack, as there had been this morning . . . that single set of hoofbeats, growing louder. And she did *not* want to meet that someone.

The wolves tore toward her. There were about twenty of them. More than half of them held the main course that they had been running, on the elk's track: the rest saw or scented her, she had no idea which, and angled toward her. Nita said the sixth word of the spell, felt the shield wink into place around her. Hurriedly she said the first eighteen words of another spell she knew, one she was very reluctant to use; but she had no weapon-spell handy that was less dangerous, and frankly was more willing to see the wolves dead than herself. *If they can be killed at all. Are they even real?* . . .

Nita braced herself as best she could, and waited. The first wolf hit her shield—and didn't bounce; it knocked her down. Nita got a horrible glance of fangs trying desperately to break through to her— failing for the moment—

In shock she fumbled for the last word of the killing spell, couldn't remember it. Those fangs knocked against the shield, right in front of her face, bending it in toward her—

That was when the hooves came down and broke the wolf's head, and kicked its body aside, and smashed its spine into the ground. There was an immediate flurry of other wolves fastening themselves to the great dark shape that was rearing above Nita, smashing at more of them with its hooves. It had bought her the second she needed; she remembered the nineteenth word. She said it.

The sound that followed was not one Nita enjoyed, but the spell worked, even though the shield hadn't. These creatures were flesh and blood enough that when you suddenly took all the cell membranes from between their cells, the result was emphatic. It rained blood briefly. Nita looked at another of the wolves near her, said the nineteenth word. It turned in mid-leap, and showered down in gore. She said the nineteenth word again, and again, and she kept saying it, having no weapon more merciful, until there was nothing near her but a sickly, black, wet patch in the field, gleaming dully in the moonlight . . . and the Irish elk, standing with its head down, panting, looking at her out of great, dumb, understanding eyes.

Nita let the shield spell go, staggered to her feet, and tottered over to the elk. Its flanks and shoulders were torn where the dire-wolves' teeth had met. *Brother,* she said in the Speech, *let me see to those before you go.*

Hurry, said the elk. *The loss of the pack has slowed him. But he's coming.*

He, Nita thought, and broke out in a cold sweat.

Fortunately there was plenty of blood around, blood being what you needed for almost all the healing spells. Nita had some experience with those. She called her manual to her and it came, hurriedly. She started turning pages, not worrying where the blood went that she was smeared with. "Here," she said, and began reading the quickest of the healing spells, a forced adhesion that caused the damaged tissue to at least hold together long enough for the knitting process to start. The spell was little more than wizardly crazy glue, but Nita was satisfied that the elk's body would be able to manage the rest of the business itself; the wounds weren't too serious.

It took about five minutes' recitation before the last of the wounds shut itself. The elk stood there shivering in all its limbs, as if expecting something to come after it out of the night. Nita was shivering too; the healer always partook of the suffering of the healed—that was part of the price paid.

Go now, she said. *Get out of here!*

The elk tossed its head and leapt away, galloping across the field. Nita stood there, panting, and wondering. *'Get out of here.' Where is 'here' any more? That broke through from 'sideways.'*

She stood for a moment, listening. The sound of hoofbeats was fading: both the elk's, and whatever had been chasing it. She was relieved, though still concerned for the elk. The silence reasserted itself, deep and whole. The Moon came out from behind a cloud.

Nita looked up at it and sighed, then turned and started making her way back to the farm. *I'm going to have to do something about these clothes before morning,* she thought. *I suppose the book has some laundry spells.* . . . But she couldn't push the bigger problem out of her mind.

Without any spell done by me, something came through from 'sideways.' A lot of somethings.

We're in deep, deep trouble. . . .

Ath na Sceire
Enniskerry

It was at that point that Nita realized she needed expert help, and fast.

She pulled out her manual, the next morning, and began going through it looking for the names and addresses of the local Senior Wizards. Addresses there were—there were four seniors for Ireland, one of whom was on retirement leave, two of whom were on active assignment and hence not available for consults, and one, the Area Advisory, who was located in a place called Castle Matrix. This impressed Nita, though not as much as it would have a couple of weeks before, when she had thought that probably half the people in Ireland lived in old castles. Now she hoped her business would take her that way . . . but you didn't go bothering the Area Advisory for a problem that you weren't yet sure couldn't be handled at a less central level.

She therefore concentrated on the addresses of wizards in the Bray and Greystones area. There were about forty of these, which surprised her—she had been expecting fewer. Usually wizards on active status are only about one percent of the population, though in some places it can run as high as ten.

She looked the list up and down in mild perplexity. There was a problem in this part of the world; people tended not to use street numbers unless they lived in a housing estate. Sometimes they didn't even have a street, so that you might see an address that said, "Ballyvolan, Kilquade, County Wicklow"—and if you didn't know where Kilquade was, or what Ballyvolan was, or what road it was down, you were in trouble.

She sighed, ticked off a couple of names in Bray that did have street numbers. That done, she went to find her Aunt Annie.

"Going out, are you?" she said.

"Yeah. Aunt Annie, can you tell me where Boghall Road is?"

"The Boghall Road? That's, um, just off the back road between Greystones and Bray. What for?"

"Oh, I met somebody in one of the cafés in Bray yesterday, and I thought I might go over that way and see if I can find them." This was not entirely a fib—the sound and feel of Ronan's lean, edged, angry humor had kept coming back to her for the past day or so. It was just that the two phrases had nothing to do with one another, and if Aunt Annie thought they did, well . . . that was just fine.

Her aunt said, "Here, let me draw you a map."

"Oh, thank you!" Nita said with considerable gratitude. Her aunt sat down and sketched her a thumbnail map, and said, "If you get off the 45 bus here, at the top of Boghall, it's not a long walk to wherever you're going. That sound all right?"

"Fine, Aunt Annie . . . thanks."

"What time will you be back?"

"Not real late."

"All right. Call if you run into any problems. And take an umbrella or something: the weathermen have been predicting thundershowers."

"Will do." And she headed out.

At first she considered not walking—Kit's "beam-me-up-Scotty" spell could occasionally be extremely useful. However, there was always the danger, when "beaming" around unfamiliar territory, that you might turn up somewhere that had people in it.

However, there was a handy bit of woodland not too far away from where the road from Greystones to Bray started trending downhill toward the down, just outside of the big Kilruddery estate. Nita had noticed it coming upwards, the other day—a stand of five cypresses, very big, very old. Generally the only people who walked up that way were the traveling people who lived in their trailers by the side of the road there.

So Nita popped into that grove of trees and looked around her, and paused for a moment. It was a matter of curiosity. Though you might have a sense of how many wizards were working in the area, there was one quick way to find out. It was difficult for a wizard to spend as much as a day without doing some wizardry, the art being its own delight. She opened her manual, as she stood there under the trees in the summer sun, and quickly did the spell that showed one whatever active wizardries were working in an area. Ideally, what happened was that the world blanked out, and you were presented

70

with a sort of schematic—points of light in a field over which the real world was dimly overlaid. She did not get what she was expecting. Nita staggered back against one of the trees, half blinded. It was not just points of light that she was perceiving, but fields of it, whole patches of it—great tracts of residual wizardry that just had not gone away.

It's not supposed to do that! Nita thought. Ideally, the traces of a wizardry were gone by at least forty-eight hours later. *But this—!* It looked either as if the biggest wizardry on Earth had been done here about two days ago, or else—and this concerned Nita more—all the wizardries done here in the past were still here, in residue.

She shut the spell down and stood there shaking. That last thought was not a good one. Doing a wizardry over another one, overlaying an old magic, was extremely dangerous. The two spells could synergize in ways that neither the wizard who wrought the original spell, or the one presently working, could have expected. The results could be horrendous.

No wonder, she thought. *If that's the reason for last night, something like that— Was I working in an overlay area?* She called up the spell in memory for a moment more to look at it. All Kilquade was covered by one big patch of residual wizardry; all Bray was covered by another. There was in fact very little open space in this area that had not had a wizardry done on it at one time or another. She thought with horror of what might have happened had she done a teleportation spell closer to a more heavily overlaid area, like Bray. It was not a pleasant prospect at *all.*

She walked down the Boghall Road. It was a suburban street, with a church and a school at one end, a computer factory at the other end, and a baker's, little shops, and more houses and housing estates scattered along it or branching off from it. Mothers were out walking their babies in buggies; kids were out kicking soccer balls around. It looked like an entirely normal place . . . and so it was, since there were wizards working in it.

Nita made her way down to the address she was looking for, on a street called Novara Court. All the houses here were very much the same. There was not much in the way of trees, as if people didn't want to block the view of Sugarloaf to the west, or Bray Head immediately to the east. And it was a handsome view.

Nita found the house and had an attack of shyness practically on the doorstep. *How can I just go up and knock on the door and ask if there are wizards there?* But that was exactly what she needed to do, and there was no way out of it. Nita went up and rang the bell.

There was a long, long wait. *Oh good,* Nita was just thinking, *no one's home*—when the door was abruptly pulled open.

It was Ronan, from the chicken place.

He looked at her in astonishment.

She looked at him in much the same mood. Once again she was on the end of one of those coincidences of which wizards' lives are made, and which normal people (incorrectly) never take too seriously. A wizard, though, knows that there are no coincidences. And she *had* said to her aunt that she was coming to see him. *I've got to watch what I say around here!* And there was something else. An odd tremor—anticipation, a shiver down her back at the sight of him scowling at her, tall and dark, that she didn't quite know what to make of—

"R. Nolan?" she said. "Junior?"

"Yeah," he said, perplexed. "You're from—"

"I'm on errantry," Nita said, "and I greet you."

He looked at her with his mouth open. He suddenly looked like one of the terminally shocked fish that Nita had seen in the Bray fish market the other morning. *"You?"* he said.

"Me."

"You mean *you're* one of *us?"*

"Um." Nita made a wry face at him, and lowered her voice. "I've been places where the people had tentacles, and more eyes than you have hairs," she said, "and they didn't make *this* much fuss about it. Can we talk? I require an advice."

It was the formal phrasing for a wizard on assignment who needed technical information. Ronan stared at her and said, "Just a minute. I'll get my jacket."

The door shut in her face, and Nita stood there on the doorstep, feeling like an idiot. After a moment Ronan came out again, and they walked. "Let's get out of here," he said. "I don't want to be seen."

Nita had to laugh at that, though she got an odd twinge of pain when he said it. *Not seen with me? Or what?* "What, am I contagious or something?" she said as they made their way down to the Boghall Road.

"No, it's just—" He didn't say what it was just. "Never mind. —You mean *you're* a—"

"Can we stop having this part of the conversation?" Nita said, both irritated and amused. "There's more stuff to talk about. Listen. This going 'sideways' thing—"

"What?"

"Going 'sideways,'" Nita said, getting a little more irritable. "I assume you know about it. Well, it's happened to me twice in the past two days, and I don't mind telling you that I don't like it very much—"

"You went *sideways?"* Ronan said. "We're not *allowed* to go sideways—"

"Listen," Nita said, "maybe *you're* not allowed to go sideways, fine, but *I* did it, and not on purpose, let me tell you. Now I need to talk to someone and find out what's going on here, because last night I was almost eaten by wolves and nearly stepped on by an Irish elk!"

"Shite," said Ronan, almost in awe.

Nita smiled slightly. "My feelings exactly," she said. Carefully she told him how things had been going for her since she arrived.

"You could have been killed!" Ronan said.

"Tell me something I don't know," Nita said. "And I would like to avoid being killed in the future! Is this kind of thing normal?"

"Not really," Ronan said. "At least, not for us. We're not supposed to be doing that kind of thing. This whole area is badly overlaid."

"I saw that," Nita said. "But look . . . this kind of thing isn't safe. If a nonwizard falls into one of these—"

"You got *that* in one," Ronan said, looking grim. "Jeez, Kilquade, *Kilquade* was supposed to be comparatively quiet. Not like Bray—"

"Things have gotten very unquiet up that way," Nita said. "Do you have a senior around here that we can go talk to? This is not good at all."

"Sure. She's up in Enniskerry."

"Then let's get up there. I'm on active, and I don't know what for, and if I can't do wizardry for fear of overlays, I am going to have a nasty problem on my hands. Have you got your manual?"

He looked at her. "Manual?"

"You know. Your wizard's manual, where you get the spells and the ancillary data."

"You get them out of a *book??"*

Nita was confused. "Where else would you get them?"

Ronan looked at her as if she was very dim indeed. "The way we always have—the way the druids and bards did it for two, three thousand years, maybe more. We do it by memory!"

Now Nita's mouth fell open. "You learn the whole Manual *by heart?* The whole body of spells??!"

"Well, the basic stuff. You have to learn the basic incantations that make more detailed information available. But mostly, mostly you learn it by heart—the area restrictions, the address list—if a change happens, you usually just wake up knowing about it one morning—and you make sure you remember it." He shook his head. "Why? You mean you get it written down?"

Nita pulled out her manual and showed it to him. Ronan paged through it with a mixture of fascination and disgust. "I can't believe this. This makes it too easy!"

"Are you kidding? Do you have any idea how thick this thing can get sometimes? I think we have a little more information to deal with than you do over here."

"Don't be so sure," Ronan said, handing the manual back to her in some irritation. "We may be a smaller place than you Yanks have to deal with, but it's a lot more complicated."

They walked down the street, each in a state of mild annoyance with the other. "Look," Nita said, "let's not fight over details. Are there a lot of you working around here? How many of you are there?"

Ronan shook his head. "Not a lot, really. We don't seem able to keep a lot of our wizards after eighteen or so."

"Why? What happens?"

"Emigration," Ronan said. "To England and the States. There's not much work here. You may be a wizard, but you've got to have a job, too. You can't make food or money out of nothing . . . the universe doesn't allow it."

"No," Nita said.

Ronan looked at her with more annoyance. "But there are still a fair number of locals. Can't understand why they should put *you* on active all of a sudden."

"Mmmh," Nita said. "Possibly past experience." She didn't feel like going into much more detail. "Never mind that. Let's go and see your Senior."

"We'll have to take the bus," Ronan said.

So they did. Enniskerry was about four miles away. You had to cross the dual carriageway, and then go up a twisty turny road which the locals called "the thirteen-bend road." It paralleled the course of the Glencree river as it poured down through beautiful woodland. Occasional old houses were scattered along the way, but mostly the road was bounded by hedges on one side and walls on the other, and the river chattering on the far side of the hedge.

They sat in the top of the bus. "I can't believe it," Ronan kept saying. "I mean, a *Yank*—!"

"Some of us have to be wizards," Nita said, rolling her eyes. "You know that. We can't function *entirely* with emigrants from Ireland." She grinned at him wickedly.

"Well, I suppose. But books!"

"You should see my sister," Nita said. "She gets hers out of a computer."

"Jeez," Ronan said in wonder and disgust.

They came to Enniskerry village. It was a pretty place; there was a handsome little red-and-white hotel with peaked roofs, a pub, some small antique stores and a food shop and florist. In the middle of the town's triangular "square" was a wonderful blocky Victorian clock tower with a domed top and a weathervane. "Do we get off here?" Nita said.

"Not unless you want to spend ten minutes climbing the steepest hill you've ever seen."

"Noooo. . . . I'll pass."

The bus paused in the square for a few minutes, then continued up the winding road that led westward. Where the road topped out, near another housing estate and a little store, they got off. Ronan turned and began to walk back down the hill. "It's over here," he said.

They walked down the hill and crossed the road to a pair of wooden gates between two pillars, one of which had the words KIL-GARRON HOUSE painted on it. "Wow," Nita said.

There was a little side gate; Ronan opened it for her, and they stepped through. Inside it was a curving driveway leading to a large two-storey house, square and blocky, maybe a farmhouse once. It had a beautiful view of the Dargle Valley, leading downward toward Bray, and also of the church and water meadow just down the hill.

They went up to the door and knocked. There was a long pause, and then a little old lady came to the door. She was very fresh-faced and smooth-skinned, and only the fact that her hair was quite silver really gave away much about her age. She was a little stocky, with very sharp, intelligent eyes. "Morning, Mrs. Smyth," said Ronan.

"And good morning to you," she said in a faintly Scots accent. "Are you on business or pleasure?"

"Business," Ronan said, nodding at Nita. "She's on errantry."

"I greet you, ma'am," Nita said, as she would have said to an American Senior she was being introduced to. The lady blinked at her.

"Are you on active status?"

"Yes'm. At least the manual says so."

"Then you'd better come in and have a cup of tea, and tell me what it's all about."

Nita rolled her eyes slightly at the prospect of yet another cup of tea, and resigned herself to the inevitable.

They were made comfortable in the sitting room, and the tea was brought out, and Mrs. Smyth poured it out formally for them, and gave them cookies and sandwiches, and cakes, and encouraged them to eat more of them before she would let them tell her anything about what was going on. Then Nita began to explain again, as she had to Ronan. When she mentioned Tualha, and a few of the things she had talked about, Mrs. Smyth's eyes widened. When Nita mentioned going sideways, Mrs. Smyth's jaw almost dropped. "My dear," she said. "I hope you understand that you must not do that again."

"Ma'am, I didn't do it on purpose the first time. Or the third. The only time I did it on purpose was when I looked at Sugarloaf. I won't do it again."

"I wonder . . ." Mrs. Smyth said. "Well. Something is certainly in the wind. We're coming up on Lughnasád; I'd be surprised if it didn't have something to do with that."

Ronan bit his lip. Nita looked from one of them to the other. "I hope you'll forgive me if I don't know what's going on here," she said, "but if I'm going to be on active status . . ."

"No, indeed. Lughnasád is one of the four great holidays—with Beltain, Samhain, and Imbolc. It used to be the harvest festival, a long time ago: people would celebrate the first crops coming in. And it also celebrated the turning of the heat of the summer toward the cooler weather."

"The heat of the summer?" Nita said, mildly skeptical. So far it had only gotten up into the high seventies.

Mrs. Smyth blinked at her. "Oh, you're used to it warmer where you lived? We're not, though. I think the drought is just about official now, isn't it, Ronan?"

"They said they were going to start water rationing," Ronan said.

"So," said Mrs. Smyth. "I suppose that's another indication as

76

well. Anyway, Nita's quite right; if this is allowed to continue, even the non-wizardly will start to notice it . . . and be endangered by it. This is, mmm, an undesirable outcome."

Nita couldn't help but laugh at that. "But what are you going to do about it?"

"Well, I think we're going to have to get together and discuss the matter."

"But if you don't do something—"

"My dear," Mrs. Smyth said, "you come from a very . . . energetic . . . school of wizardry. I appreciate that. But we do things a little more slowly here. No, we need to call the local wizards and the Area supervisors together, and discuss what needs to be done. It'll take a few days at least."

Nita chafed at that. It seemed to her that a few days might be too long. But she was a stranger here, and theoretically these people knew best. "What do you think they'll decide?" Ronan said.

Mrs. Smyth shook her head. "It's hard to say. If we have here a rising of the old sort—a reassertion of the events associated with this holiday—then normally one would also have to reassert the events that stopped whatever thing it was that happened."

"But what was it that happened?" Nita said.

"The second battle of Moytura," Ronan said. "I suppose you won't have heard about it—"

"I've heard about it," Nita said. "A little cat told me. In considerable detail."

"A cat told you?"

"Yeah. She said she was a bard, and—"

Mrs. Smyth looked at Nita in surprise. "You mentioned this before, but we didn't pursue it. How old was this cat?"

"She's a kitten. Not very old . . . maybe ten weeks." Nita told them, as well as she could remember, everything Tualha had told her.

"That is interesting," Mrs. Smyth said. "Normally cat-bards aren't born unless there's about to be some change in the 'ruled' world, the animal world—as well as the human one. —And she mentioned the Carrion-Crow, did she."

Nita nodded. "I get a feeling that's not good?"

Ronan made a face. "The Morrigan is trouble," he said. "She turns up in the old stories, sometimes, as a war goddess. Or sometimes as three of them."

"It's the usual problem," Mrs. Smyth said, "of the language not being adequate to describe the reality. The Morrigan is one of the

77

Powers, a much diminished one . . . though even the lesser Powers were often mistaken for gods, in the ancient times. She has become, or made herself, the expression of change, and violence. A lot of that around here in the old days," she said, and sighed. "And now. But she's also the peace afterwards . . . if people will just let it be. 'Carrion-crow' she might be, but the crows are the aftermath of the battle, nature's attempt to clean it up . . . not the cause of it." Mrs. Smyth turned her teacup around. "It's dangerous to see her . . . but not always bad. She shows herself as a tall dark woman, a fierce one. But she almost always smiles. She *is* Ireland, some ways: one of its personifications. Or its hauntings."

She looked up at Ronan again. "So, the Morrigan . . . and the Hunt. Some very old memories are being resurrected. The foxhunt's running must have reminded the world of an older hunt over the same ground."

"What were those?" Nita said. "They looked like direwolves, but they had some kind of werelight around them."

"They were faery direwolves," Mrs. Smyth said, "from one of the companion worlds."

"Who was that following them?" Nita said.

Mrs. Smyth looked at her. "I see by the Knowledge," she said, "that you've had a certain amount of dealing with the Other. The head of the Fomori—the Lone Power. I should say, a dangerous amount of dealings with It."

"I don't deal with It," Nita said. "Against It, possibly." She began to go hot. "I don't think you need to doubt which side I'm on. Are you saying that you think I'm attracting this trouble?"

Wizards do not tell white lies to make people feel better. Mrs. Smyth said nothing.

"Well, if I'm here for that purpose," Nita said, "I'm here because the Powers that Be sent me. If I'm a trigger, it's Their finger that's on it, not the Lone One's. The Lone One can't move wizards . . . you know that."

"No, I do know that," Mrs. Smyth said. "There have been changes in the Lone One recently, and you had something to do with those."

"Something," Nita said.

Ronan looked at her, and then back at Mrs. Smyth. "Her?"

"She was involved just now in the Song of the Twelve," Mrs. Smyth said. Ronan looked wide-eyed. "She was also involved in— Well, never mind. It's a distinguished start: if you and your partner survive,

78

of course. Wizardly talent is usually tested to destruction. Your sister," Mrs. Smyth said; "where is she now? Did she come with you?"

"No, she's back in New York."

"Pity," Mrs. Smyth said. "At any rate, I advise you to keep your use of wizardry to the minimum needed. Ronan, you'll want to speak to your friends among the locals, especially the young ones. If anyone finds themselves going sideways, tell them not to meddle."

"What kind of reenactment were you thinking of doing?" Nita said.

"Well, my dear," Mrs. Smyth said. "We have a problem. If there's a reenactment of Moytura to be done, we don't have anything to do it with, even though one or two of the Treasures still exist."

"Then how do you mean you don't have anything to do it with?"

"Nita," Mrs. Smyth said, "it took one of the Powers that Be a very long time to invest those four objects with strength enough to function against the Lone Power in the form It took. The legend says that anything that the Lone One in Balor's form beheld with his eye open, burst straightway into fire and fell as ash, and poisoned the ground for leagues around, so that nothing would grow there, and men who walked that ground died."

"Sounds nuclear," Nita said.

"So it might have been," Mrs. Smyth said. "The Lone One has never minded using natural phenomena for Its own ends. But Its power was so terrible that only an army of all the wizards in Ireland—for that's what the druids were—could even think about going up against him; and without the Treasures to protect them, they all would have been destroyed. The Cup, known as the Cauldron of Rebirth, raised up their fallen, and the Sword, Fragarach the Answerer, held off Balor's creatures, and the Stone of Destiny kept the ground of Ireland whole and rooted when Balor would have dragged it off its foundations and overturned the whole island into the deep. All their power together, and all the wizards', was just enough to buy the time for the Spear of Lugh to pierce Balor's fire and quench it at last."

She took a sip of her tea. "Now, three of the four Treasures we still have—at least one of them is in the National Museum in Dublin. But they have no virtue any more. No one *believes* that the gold and silver cup they have there, the Ardagh Chalice, is actually the Well of Transformations, the Bottomless Cauldron. No one really *believes* that the poor old notched bronze blade in the glass case is Fragarach, even though the legends say so. Its virtue has long since ebbed away as a result: the 'soul' in it, if you like, has departed. And the *Lia Fail* is now just a cracked stone half buried in the ground somewhere up North, with an iron picket fence around it, and tourists come and take its picture because it's supposed to be Saint Patrick's gravestone or some such. Not because of what it really is, or was." Her smile was very rueful. "The thousands of years and the loss of true *knowledge* of the nature of the Protectors have taken them and made them just a cup, just a sword, and a rock."

"What about the Spear?"

"Its 'soul' was the strongest of all of the Treasures," Mrs. Smyth said. "It should be the easiest to find . . . but it's nowhere in the world that we can feel. No, what we're going to do—if a reenact-ment—" She sighed. "I can't say. We're going to have to work some-thing out from scratch. In the meantime, if I were you, I would step lightly. And thank you for coming to me. Where are you staying?"

"With my aunt, Anne Callahan, at Ballyvolan."

"Right," said Mrs. Smyth, and made a note. "Now then; another cup of tea?"

Nita groaned.

They went down to the little tea shop in Enniskerry, and had a Coke to kill the time until the 45 bus was ready to leave. "She's not much like the Seniors at home," Nita said, thoughtful, "except she's as tough."

Ronan was sitting slumped back in his chair, his legs crossed, scowling out at her from under those black brows. The hair rose a little on Nita's neck, and she started to blush, and felt extremely stupid. "Just because she's not like your precious Seniors—" he said.

"Ronan, just shut your face. You think you're the hottest thing on wheels, don't you?" And Nita scowled back at him, mostly to cover her own confusion at her anger. "You've got a chip on your shoulder the size of a two-by-four, and you'd better do something about it before it ruins your wizardry. And I'm not one of your little herd of head-nodders, so don't waste your dirty looks on me. You don't like the news, that's just tough."

He stared at Nita, and his expression had changed slightly when she dared to look at it again. He looked a little shocked, still angry: but there was an odd thread of liking there. "No," he said softly, "you're not one of them, are you? Girls have mean mouths, where you come from."

She blushed again, feeling more like an idiot than ever, not understanding her own discomfiture. "Wizards tell the truth, where I come from," she said, annoyed. "I wasn't criticizing your Senior, as you would have discovered if you let me finish. Your manners need work, too."

"And what else needs work?" he said, that same odd soft tone.

She just looked at him, and her insides roiled. That dark regard was disconcerting when it was bent hard on you. Worse still when he was smiling. *He really is pretty hot,* she thought, somewhat to her own horror. She wondered for a moment what some of the girls at school would think of this guy if they had a chance to see him. She knew what they would think, and what they would say. He was the kind of guy who gets notes passed about him all day, the kind that girls look at from the safety of groups, stealing glances, laughing softly together at their shared thoughts about him. *What would you do if you got him alone? . . .*

And she *was* alone with him.

"Hulloooo!!" he said to her, waving a hand in front of her face. "Earth to Nita!"

"Uh, nothing," she said hurriedly. She finished her Coke in one gulp. "Listen, the bus is starting up."

"What's the hurry? I don't hear—" From outside there came a roar of diesel engine. Ronan looked at Nita oddly, then grinned. She flushed again, and inwardly swore at herself. *Oh, he* is *cute. This is awful!*

"Can't keep the man waiting," Ronan said, and got up. "You going to come with?"

"Uh, no, I'll walk it. Fresh air," she said, mortified at the feebleness of the excuse. "Exercise."

"As far as the bus stop, then."

Reluctantly she walked out to see him that far.

"Do you have my number?" Ronan said as he got on. "Call me if you have any problems."

Problems! Do I have problems! Sweet Powers that Be— "I'll do that," Nita said. "You're in the book."

Ronan made an annoyed face. "I can't *believe* this," he said, and the bus doors shut in front of him.

Nita started home to Kilquade. It was a longish walk, about eight miles: but she was really beginning to enjoy the walking. This was one of the prettiest places she had ever been, and the quiet and the sound of the wind and the warm, fair weather were all conspiring to make it very pleasant. She ached slightly, but there were some things worth aching for.

She couldn't get rid of the look of Ronan's face, the whole feel of him, the uneasy, uncomfortable sense of—power: there was no other word for it. Add to that the fact that he was good-looking, and funny, when he wasn't being angry—even then—Nita smiled grimly at herself, annoyed: it was funny to be so hot for someone she so much wanted to give a few good kicks.

Heaven help me, that's what it is. I've got the hots.

The admission made her nervous. Neither parents at home or the sex education classes at school ever told you anything really useful about how to *handle* this kind of thing. Oh, the mechanics of it, body changes and so forth, and how not to catch diseases, and responsibility, and family planning, and all the rest of it. Not important stuff, like: kissing—how did you do it and still breathe? Is not wearing a bra a come-on? Is it worth chasing someone you've got the hots for, or will it just make you look stupid? And if you catch him, what do you do then?

Or what do you do if you get *caught?* . . .

Nita heard something stirring in the hedge off to the right. At first she thought it was a bird—lots of birds nested in these hedges, encouraged by the thorns—but this sounded too loud. Nita paused, and saw a flash of color, a soft russet red.

"Ai elhua," whispered a voice in the Speech, "I have a word for you."

Nita's eyebrows went up. She hunkered down by the hedge. The red dog-fox was deep inside it, curled up comfortably in a little hide against the wall that the hedge grew against.

"Madreen rua!" she said. "Are you all right?"

"O yes. But that *you* may be—" The fox glanced around, a shifty, conspiratorial look. "And that I may repay a debt and all things be even again. There are wizardries afoot."

"No kidding."

"Then you should get help for them. One of the *Ard-Tuatha* is in hide, not half a mile from here."

Nita was confused: there were several different ways to translate the term. "Ard— You mean, one of the Powers that Be? *Here??*"

"In truth. We are bound, we are all bound not to say exactly where, or who. But it is one of the Old Ones. Catch it at its work, and it must help you, yes?"

"That's one way to put it." Nita frowned. The Powers that Be were required to assist wizards when requested to do so. But you had to catch Them first . . . and They usually made that difficult, preferring to do Their work in secret. It made it harder for the Lone Power to sabotage it.

"Well," she said. "I am warned, *madreen rua*. My thanks."

"All's even," the fox said, and in the tiny space where it lay, somehow managed to get up, turn around, and vanish back through a dark hole under the wall.

Nita got up and went on down the road, trying to make sense of what the fox had told her. *It's hard to believe. Why would one of the Powers be living around* here? . . .

She made her way down the little lane to her aunt's driveway, and the farm. In the field to the right she could see Aunt Annie heading off with a rake over her shoulder, probably to do something about the new potatoes she had just planted. They were a rare breed, something called "fir-apple potatoes," and Aunt Annie raked and weeded them herself every day, and wouldn't let anyone near them.

Nita grinned at this and went inside. She was just in the act of making herself another sandwich in the kitchen, when the phone began to ring. Nita ran for it, picked it up, and as she had heard others do, said, "Ballyvolan."

"Is Mrs. Callahan there?"

"No, she's not . . . can I take a message for you?"

"Yes, please. Tell her that Shaun O'Driscoll called, and ask her to call back immediately, it's very urgent."

"All right." Nita scribbled the message down, and said, "I'll see if I can catch her; she just went out. Bye." And she ran out across the graveyard, vaulted the fence, and headed into the field.

Far away, over the hill of the second field, she could see her aunt walking toward the little rise in the middle of it. Yelling at her seemed ridiculous at this point, so Nita just ran on after her as quickly as she could, puffing. She still ached.

She was rather surprised to see her aunt take the rake off her shoulder, and bang the wooden end of it on the ground.

She was even more surprised when the little hill split open, and her aunt walked into it.

Nita stood very still for a moment, and her mouth fell open.

Oh, no! she thought. And she remembered Tom's voice, from not so terribly long ago, saying to her father: "Well, you know, Ed, it's *your* side of the family that the wizardry comes down from. . . ."

My dad's sister. . . .
My aunt's a wizard!
Half torn between terror and laughter, Nita ran after her, toward
the gaping darkness in the side of the hill.

Faoin gCnoc
Under the Hill

The chasm was deeper and wider than it looked. *Is this happening in the real world?* Nita thought, and paused for a moment to try to see with double vision, as she had seen the other day. True enough, mere daylight vision showed her a smooth hill, no crack; nothing. But then no one in the house had seen her aunt . . . and *she* had. Nita *was* seeing sideways where her aunt was, and this was sideways too. Not as sideways as it might have been, of course.

"Aunt Annie," she said, not loud, but urgently, and loud enough to carry. Ahead of her, her aunt stopped in shock, standing there with the rake.

She looked back at Nita and said, "Oh, no."

"Aunt Annie," Nita said, grinning a little in spite of herself, "what *did* they tell you about why they'd sent me here? . . ."

Aunt Annie's mouth opened and shut, and then she said, "When I get my hands on Ed. . . . I'm going to pull his head off and hand it to him."

"They couldn't exactly tell you," Nita said, immediately wanting to defend her father. "It's not his fault."

"Maybe not," Aunt Annie said, "but, Nita . . . ! I had no idea!"

"Actually, I was hoping you wouldn't," Nita said, wry. "I don't usually try to advertise it."

"But how can you *be* here?" Aunt Annie said. Then she shook her head. "Never mind that now. That you're here means you're intended to be. I've got business. Let's go see them."

"Them?"

"Be polite," Aunt Annie said. "And follow my lead."

Nita was entirely willing. She followed her aunt into the hill.

It was not a hill. It was a city. It was like the one that Nita had seen crowning Sugarloaf, but smaller, more intimate. It could not, of course, be inside the hill. It was two, three—ten? fifty?— universes over from the "real world." Broad streets, airy; shade, the sound of running water, stone as fluidly formed as if it had been clay once, or flesh—but paused in mid-movement, possibly to move again some day. There were echoes among the buildings of thatched houses, and old castles, and castles no human being could have imagined, hints of architecture Nita recognized as extraterrestrial from her travels: apparently the builders had had connections elsewhere.

The light was different too; harder, somehow clearer than the light that rested on the fields around Aunt Annie's farm. Things seemed to have sharper edges, more weight, more meaning. Nothing here needed to glow with magical light, or anything so blatant. Things here were too busy being *real* . . . more real even than the "real world." It was a slightly unnerving effect.

"Oh, and one other thing," her aunt said. "Don't eat or drink anything here."

Nita burst out laughing. "There had to be *one* place in Ireland where no one was going to make me drink tea or eat anything," she said.

Her aunt looked at her cockeyed, then laughed. "Well, you keep thinking of it that way."

They walked on among the high houses. "Where are we going?" Nita said.

"To talk to the people who live here," said her Aunt Annie. "I do have certain rights. This is my land—I am the landowner—" She chuckled then. "As if anyone in Ireland can really *own* land. We all just borrow it for a while." She looked sidewise at Nita. "Where were you last night?"

"I was out with some very very large things that should have been wolves, but weren't," Nita said. "Oh, by the way. There was a phone call for you. A Shaun O'Driscoll—"

"I just bet," said Aunt Annie. "The Area Supervisor. Well, we'll see him shortly, but I need to deal with these first."

"These people—"

"You know the name," her aunt said. "We don't usually say it . . . it's considered impolite. Like shouting at someone, 'Hey, human!'."

The Sidhe, Nita thought. *The people of the hills . . . the not-so-little people.* "You see them often?" Nita said.

"Often enough. 'Good fences make good neighbors,' as the poet says. However, every now and then, when you share common ground, you need to have a good long chat over the fence. That's what this is about."

They came to the heart of the city. There were twelve trees in a circle, and three bright chairs under the trees, seemingly resting on the surface of a pool of water. Or rather, the chairs on either side of the central one were true chairs; the central one was a throne. The trees moved in the wind, and the shadows thrown by their branches wove and shifted on the surface of the bright water in patterns that seemed to Nita to be always on the edge of meaning. People stood around and watched from under the shade of those trees; tall people, fair people, with beautiful dogs at heel. Handsome cats sat here and there, watching; unconcerned birds sang rainbows in the trees. Nita tried to look at a few of the people, and found it difficult. It wasn't that they were indistinct. They were almost too solid to bear, and their clothes and weapons, in an antique style, all shone with certainty and existence.

The chairs on either side of the throne were filled; a man sat in one, a woman in the other. The throne was empty. Aunt Annie walked straight toward the three seats, across the water. Nita watched with professional interest. She knew several ways to walk on water, but she felt safe in assuming that the water here was more assertive, and didn't mind being walked on without more active spelling. She headed out after her aunt.

Aunt Annie stopped about ten feet away from the central throne, acknowledged it with a slight nod, and then looked at the person sitting in the right-hand chair. "The greeting of gods and men to you, *Amadaun* of the People of the Hill in Cualann. And to you, lady of this forth."

The lady bowed her head. "To you also, *Aoine ni Cealodhain,* greeting," said the man in the right-hand chair. "And greeting to you, *Shonaiula ni Cealodhain.*"

Nita was slightly out of her depth, but she knew how to be polite. She bowed slightly and said, "I am on errantry, fair people, and the One greets you by me."

"This we had known," said the woman in the chair.

"Then perhaps you will explain to me," said Aunt Annie, "why my niece was chased halfway across my field last night by that one's hunt. I thought we had an agreement that if you saw any power of that kind waking, you would warn me so that I could take appropriate action."

"We had no warning ourselves, *Aoine,*" said the lady.

"I would then appreciate your view of what's happening here. It's most unusual for you to have no warning of so major an intrusion, and that you didn't means we have trouble on our hands."

87

"Trouble rarely comes near us, *Aoine*. But it would be true to say that the past is becoming troublesome. We have had a messenger at our gates . . . one of the Fomori."

"And what did this messenger say?"

"That the old shall become new in our fields, and yours. He offered us . . . what we were offered once before. The end of your kind, once and for all."

Aunt Annie said nothing. The young man, the *"Amadaun,"* looked at Nita and said, "You must understand that the children of the Milesians are not looked upon with favor in some of the Fifth House."

"If you mean that some of the nonhuman species think humans were a dumb idea," Nita said, "yes, I've heard that opinion before."

"There are those powers in this part of the world, and children of the Powers—powers fallen lower than we—who never looked kindly on human folk, and would be glad to see them all dead. At their own hands, or by the hands of other humans—so that old angers are inflamed, and old hatreds seem to live uncannily long."

"Yes," Nita said, "I've noticed that."

"It is the land, of course," said the fair young woman. "The land remembers too well. It saw Partholon come; it saw Nemed; it saw us, and the Fir Bolg, and the hosts of man. One after another of us it threw off, in its way, having been taught to do so by the Lone One, and given a memory that other lands don't have—a sense of injury. Long time we've tried to heal that, but there is no healing it now. The old angers waken again and again."

"There must be something that could be done," Nita said.

"If there is an answer, we do not have it," said the lady of the forth, "and the Fomori are at our gates. Soon enough they'll be at yours."

"They have been at *our* gates, they and their children, for a long while," said Aunt Annie, "under various names. We do what we can, as do you. What are the Fomori threatening you with this time?"

"Nothing concrete as yet. Of course they demanded tribute. They have done that before. We will of course refuse to give it; we have done that before too. And then they will begin to strike, here, and there, at the innocent, the ones who have no defense."

"That too we know about," said Aunt Annie, "for a long time now. Nonetheless, something needs to be done. I think all the wizards will now be called together. Probably there should be another meeting between us once that has happened. Doing seems to have passed into our hands, these days, and out of yours."

"That seems to be true," said the *Amadaun*. "Advise us what you do. We will back you as far as possible. Mean time, rain has not fallen here for too long. We seem to be losing the ability to order our world as we used to. Something outside is becoming very strong . . . and Lughnasád is coming, when old battles are remembered. Even with the power of the Treasures, it was very close. We almost lost, last time. Without the Treasures—" The form on the left shook her head. "There is no saying. We need your help."

"Keep your people in, then, if you would," said Aunt Annie. " 'Sideways' and the not-sideways parts of the world are getting too close together at the moment; we need to part them until this is resolved."

"We will do that. And you—" The *Amadaun* looked at Nita. "What would you say to us?"

Nita looked at the shining forms all around her, and shook her head. "I think you owe me one," she said. "For the other night. If your carelessness let that happen, I think you owe me a favor one of these days."

There were shocked looks at her boldness, and Aunt Annie looked at her sideways. But there was a wry smile from the *Amadaun*. "Our people have long known that a favor given must be returned, and a wrong done must be avenged," he said. "Come here, then, and let me speak a word in your ear."

Nita stepped up to him, wondering. The *Amadaun* leaned over and whispered; and the hair stood up all over Nita. It was a word in the Speech, a name . . . but not the kind of name mortals had. There was too much power in it, and too much time. She glanced sideways in shock, and met his eyes, and found no relief there: the time was in them too.

"Should you need help," the *Amadaun* said, "name that name."

"Thank you," Nita said, trying to get some of her composure back. "I'll do that. Meanwhile, I hope you do well, and that things are quiet for you."

"A mortal wishes what we wish," said the lady of the forth, smiling. "There's a change."

"Thank you," said Aunt Annie.

Nita rejoined her, and together they walked out the way they came. The sunlight looked thin and wan when they came out, when it should have looked golden; everything seemed a little unreal, a little fake, compared with the way it had earlier.

Nita looked at Aunt Annie and was a little surprised to find that she had sweat standing out on her forehead. "Are you okay?" she said. "You look pale."

"I'm all right," said Aunt Annie. "It's just a strain talking to those people. They don't see time the way we do."

"I kind of liked it in there," Nita said.

Her aunt looked at her. "Yes, I thought you might. They prefer the young; the younger wizards have always bent a little more easily to their ways. I make *them* uneasy, too; I'm a little too close to mortality for their liking. . . . But anyway, I still can't believe it. You're a wizard!"

"At times I find it hard to believe myself," Nita said. "Like last night. My wizardry was not working terribly well."

"Yes, it's a problem we have around here," said her aunt. "The overlays. . . . If I'd have known, I could have warned you."

"How could you have known? How was I supposed to tell you?" She broke out laughing. "What *did* they tell you when they sent me out here?"

Her aunt shook her head. "They said you were getting too involved with your friend Kit. —He's your partner, I take it."

"Yeah. They're really nervous about it, Aunt Annie. I try to calm them down. . . ."

"Listen, you're lucky. At least you were able to tell your folks. I was never able to tell your grandma and grandpa."

"Even when they know," Nita said drily, "it doesn't always make for the best of times. But Aunt Annie, look, what are we going to *do?*"

"We can't do anything just yet."

Nita groaned. Her aunt looked at her with a sympathetic expression. "Look, honey, I know. But the tradition of wizardry is different in this part of the world. They've been doing it for thousands of years longer than there even *were* American wizards. And don't forget that at home you're working in a relatively clean environment; the magic of the Amerind wizards was of a much more naturalistic kind. There was practically no overlay, since it worked so completely in conjunction with nature and the environment. Over here we're dealing with the equivalent of wizardly toxic waste. . . . the accumulation of thousands of years of buildup. No, we take our time. We need to get everyone together to talk."

90

"When is this *Lughnasád* thing?"

"It starts tomorrow, really—"

"Tomorrow?!"

"It goes on for two weeks . . . don't panic. The first is the beginning of it: August 15th is the end. It's the end that we have to worry about . . . things will be building up, forces will have to be released. It's going to be like a dam breaking. If we can dig a channel somehow, something for the power, the flow, to run off into . . . Otherwise—"

"Otherwise even the nonwizards are going to notice."

Her aunt laughed. "Nita, nonwizards have been noticing for *years.* Fortunately, Ireland just has a reputation for being a strange place. So when people hear these weird stories, they discount them. . . . It's not always a bad thing: for example, this is one of the only places in Europe where there were almost no witch trials. People were simply so used to bizarre things happening that there didn't seem any point . . . *everyone* knew someone who was a little strange. . . . But meantime, we'll get the wizards together and talk to them. Meantime, try to restrain yourself. I know the urge to do wizardry all the time is very strong, especially at your age. But don't—you know—just *don't.*"

And that was the last that was said about it for a while. Aunt Annie went into the estate office and shut herself in, and started making phone calls. Nita took herself off to her trailer to do some more reading in the manual.

As she turned the corner, she froze in surprise: the trailer shifted slightly as she looked at it. Someone was in there. She paused and tried to see through the window before coming any closer. Inside, someone bent forward into the light: a shadow moved—

She ran to the trailer door and threw it open. On the bed, Kit looked up in surprise, blinked at her. "Hi, Neets. What's the scoop?"

Nita stood there with her mouth working, and nothing coming out. "What are you *doing* here?" she said finally.

Kit opened his mouth, too, and closed it, and then said, "I thought you'd be glad to see me."

"You turkeybrain, I *am* glad to see you! But what are you doing *here?* I thought—"

"Oh." Kit turned red, then started laughing. "Neets, uh, I feel like a dork."

She withheld comment for the moment. "Oh?"

"Well, I mean, you promised your folks that *you* wouldn't come back to see me. But *I* never said anything of the kind. No one asked me. So I said to my mom, 'I have to go out for a while, I'll be back for dinner.' And she said, 'Fine, have a nice time. . . .' "

Nita climbed into the trailer, sat down on the bed and began laughing. "You're kidding."

"Neets," Kit said, "I think they still don't get it about me being a wizard. Not really. But who cares? As long as I come home on time for dinner, no one minds me being here."

"Dynamite! Come see my aunt."

She dragged him inside. Her aunt had taken a little while off from phone calls to feed the cats, and now stood there looking at Kit with a can of cat food in her hand, and a somewhat bemused expression. "Aunt Annie," Nita shouted, "this is Kit!"

"Ah." Her aunt blinked. "Half a second, then, and I'll feed him too."

Nita snickered and sat him down at the table, and started making tea. Out of the tangle of mewing and hollering cats, one detached itself and strolled over to the kitchen table, jumped up on it, and regarded Kit with big eyes. It was Tualha. "And who is this?" she said.

Nita had to laugh a little at Kit's bemused expression. "Kit, Tualha. She's a bard. Tualha, Kit Rodrigues. He's a wizard."

"Dai stihó," said Kit.

"Slán," said the cat, looking him up and down. To Nita she said, "I see the Spanish have finally arrived."

"What?"

"Kit, don't get her started. She'll be reciting poetry at you in a minute."

"I don't mind that."

"So listen," Nita's aunt said then, coming over to the table and sitting down as she dried her hands on a dishcloth. "Kit, you're welcome here, but one question. Do your parents know you're a wizard?"

"Oh, yeah."

She shook her head. "It's getting easier these days than it used to be." She looked at Nita, and then at Kit, and at Nita again. "Listen," she said, "I want the straight word from you on this. You two aren't doing what your mom and dad were concerned you were doing—I mean, what they told me they'd thought you were doing. Are you?"

She had the grace to look embarrassed as she said it. Nita and Kit could do nothing but look at each other and then burst out laughing.

"Why does everyone think that?" Kit said, sounding momentarily aggrieved. "Do we go around panting at each other or something?" Then he lost it and cracked up again.

"No," Nita said to Aunt Annie. "We're not."

"Well," said her aunt, "never mind, then. It's matters here that really concern me, and I've got enough on my plate at the moment. You know anything about it?"

"There was a precís in the manual of what's been going on here," Kit said. He sighed. "We've got problems."

That "we" was one of the nicest things Nita had heard in a long time. She had had enough of working by herself. "Yeah. Well, the Seniors here seem to have at least a handle on what to do. I just hope it works. —Did you read about that?"

"Yeah. It seems they already made some progress. There's a stone, is it? That they had to wake up—"

"It was half awake already," Nita said. "It's the other three that are going to be a problem."

"Yeah. They said one of the other objects was 'dormant,' and the third and fourth were 'unaccounted for.' That doesn't sound terrific."

"Nope."

"Listen," Aunt Annie said, "I'll leave you two to chat. I've got to get back on the phone." She smiled at them and headed out of the room.

"Phone? What for?"

"Other wizards," Nita said.

Kit looked mystified. "To just talk to them? Why don't they—"

"NO DON'T DO THAT!" she said, sitting bolt upright as she felt him starting to casually line up the beam-me-up spell in his head. "You can't do that here!"

"Why not?"

"Feel around you for the overlays! They're all over the place! And you better watch how you go home, too."

He paused a moment, and then looked surprised. "Wow, you're not kidding. How do you get around here?"

"I walk. Or there's a bike to ride."

"Well, let's go do that, then. Sounds like I've got a lot of catching up to do."

Nita slipped into the office, bent over Aunt Annie at her desk, scribbled a note on her pad: GOING OUT BIKE RIDING, OK?

Her aunt nodded and went right on with her conversation about spell structure.

They were out for a long time. Part of it was Kit rubbernecking at the scenery while they talked. But part of it was the weather turning odd. The thunderstorms the weathermen had been predicting materialized, but they dropped hail rather than rain. They had to take shelter from several of these showers, and when they finally got down to the dual carriageway again, they found hailstones as big as marbles lying around on the road, steaming bizarrely in the bright sunshine. The sound of thunder rumbled miles away, sporadic but threatening, all through the ride.

They had been taking turns riding, or sometimes Kit would ride and Nita would sit on the crossbar, or the other way around. At the moment Kit was walking the bike beside her, looking around appreciatively. "This is great," he said. "I guess if you had to be sent someplace, this is as good as any."

"Huh," Nita said. "I don't remember you being real excited about it at first."

He colored somewhat. "Yeah, well."

Nita grinned. "Listen, how's Dairine doing?"

"Okay, as far as I can tell. I think she may be on assignment; she doesn't seem to have been around your place much in the past few days. Busy."

"I bet. Wizards all over the place are real busy around now." Nita shook her head. The oppressive, thunderstorm-about-to-happen feeling had not stopped. She was still prickling, but not so violently as she had been this morning.

"Here it comes," Kit said, looking up at one thundercloud that they had watched drifting halfway between them and the sea as they turned down the Kilquade road. Almost immediately as he said it, Nita saw the bolt of lightning lance down and strike one of the hills behind the farm. Silently she started counting seconds, and had barely gotten to "two" before the crack of thunder washed over them. "A little too close," said Kit. "Let's get inside."

They headed down the driveway in a hurry, and came out into the gravelyard in front of the house. Nita was heading for the front door when Kit looked around him with a sudden surprised expression. "Wait a minute. What's that?" he said.

"That what?" Nita was feeling a little cross. She could feel the rain coming on in the air, and didn't want to stand around outside waiting for it, after all she'd been through today.

"That," Kit said, swinging around as if looking for something. "Can't you feel it? Inanimate. Strong."

Nita shook her head, wondering what he was talking about. Kit was staring down toward the farmyard, between the buildings. "There's something going on down there," he said. "Something alive."

"This place is full of horses and sheep and cows," Nita said. "Kit—"

"No," he said. "Not something that's usually alive. It's inanimate, it's a thing, it's—come on!"

He started down that way. There was another roll of thunder. Nita didn't see the lightningstroke this time. She went after him, muttering to herself. The problem was that Kit frequently sensed things she didn't, just as she sensed things he didn't. They had areas where their talents overlapped, certainly, but Nita's specialty was live things; Kit had always been more for inanimate objects. And if he really felt he was on the trail of something important—

"It's really weird," he said as she caught up with him. "It's nothing—I've never felt one that alive before."

"One what?"

He looked into the farmyard and shook his head, and gestured. "That," he said.

Nita looked. There was nothing in the farmyard but Biddy the farrier's pickup truck, with its forge on the back. "That?"

"It's not the truck itself," Kit said. "That's a little more awake than usual, but nothing really strange. It's the thing in back. That box. What is that?"

"It's a forge, a portable forge," Nita said, mystified. "She's the lady who comes and puts the horses' shoes on."

Right then, Biddy herself came out of the hay barn, in the act of shrugging into a windbreaker. She looked up at the sky, pausing for a moment; then headed toward the truck.

"Uh oh," Kit said, looking up too, with a panicked expression. And a second later, the lightning came down.

That was only the first thing that happened. As Kit said "uh oh," Nita had felt the potential building in the air become suddenly unbearable, not just a prickling but a pain all over her. It was a matter of a second, even with her brains as tired as they were from spelling, to put a shield spell up around herself and Kit. She saw Biddy look up; she saw the lightning lance down at the truck. The breath went right out of Nita in horror, for there was simply no way she could quickly extend her shield so far—

Biddy lifted her hand abruptly—

—and the lightning simply went elsewhere. It didn't strike anything else, it didn't miss; it just stopped. And went away. There was not even a thunderclap.

And Biddy stood there, looking up at the sky, and glanced around, looking to see whether anyone had been watching. Then she smiled very slightly, and got into the truck.

"Now what was that?" Kit whispered.

Nita pulled him behind the nearby smoking shed, out of sight of the truck as it turned, heading for the driveway. He barely noticed; he was watching the truck. "Who is that?" he said. "Is that your aunt?"

"No. I told you, that's the lady who puts the horseshoes on. Biddy."

"She's a wizard!"

"She's not," Nita said. "She can't be." It just didn't feel right. "That wasn't a wizardry. Wizards can hide . . . but the magic still feels like magic, whatever."

Kit shook his head. "Then how do you explain that? She swatted a lightning bolt away like a bug. And her truck, or that forge in her truck anyway, is alive. That *I* can feel."

"I don't know," Nita said. "Things are getting weird around here. . . ."

" 'Getting!' " Kit laughed, then looked thoughtful. "You going to tell your aunt about this?"

"I don't know," Nita said. "I think. . . . I think I want to talk to Biddy first."

"Makes sense," Kit said. "Then what?"

"Check with the Seniors. They seem to be running this show."

"Okay," Kit said. "You're on."

They talked until nearly midnight. The last thing Kit said was, "You been meeting a lot of people around here?" he said. "Kids, I mean?"

"Some. They're OK."

"Are they nice to you?"

Nita thought of Ronan, and immediately flushed hot. How was she supposed to explain this to Kit? *Explain what?* some part of her mind demanded. *Heaven only knows what he thinks about you: if anything,*

96

he probably thinks you're too young for him. "They're fine," she said after a moment. "They're not geeky, the ones I've met."

"Some of the kids back home," Kit said, "were saying that I had 'gotten you in trouble.'"

She burst out laughing. "No wonder you jumped when Aunt Annie poked you. Kit, who cares what they think? Idiots." She punched him. "Go on home, it's your dinnertime."

"Oh, crud, I forgot!" He got up hurriedly and started riffling through his manual.

"Don't forget the overlays!!" Nita said. "You leave them out of your calculations, you'll wind up in the middle of the Atlantic."

"So? We have friends there." He found the page he was looking for.

"Kiiiiiit!" Nita said, annoyed, until he looked at her. "Just be *careful.*"

He nodded, and started reading the transposition spell under his breath. At the very end of it, on the last word, he looked back up at her.

"Don't be late tomorrow," Nita said quietly.

He nodded, and grinned, and the air slammed into the space where he had been.

Nita went to bed.

Baile atha Cliath

Dublin

The next morning, when Nita came into the kitchen, Aunt Annie was sitting at the kitchen table with a portable phone and a cup of tea, going through the yellow pages. She looked up and said, "Want to go into town?"

"Bray?"

"No, Dublin—"

The phone rang again. It had been doing that all morning: Nita had been able to hear it even out in the trailer. Aunt Annie sighed and picked it up. Nita went off to get herself a cup of tea.

After a while Aunt Annie hung up and looked over at Nita. "We'll be meeting at a pub in town tonight," she said, starting to dial another number. "This should be fun for you; you haven't been in a pub yet."

Nita blinked at that. "Am I allowed?"

"Oh, yes, it's not like bars in the States." She started dialing another number. "You can't drink, of course, but you can be in a pub all right, as long as you're over a certain age and it's earlyish. Different pubs have different policies. But you'll have no problems." Aunt Annie chuckled, then, and said to the phone, "Doris? Anne. Johnny says tonight at nine, in the Long Hall. Will you call Shaun and Mairead? —Right. Yes, we are. Right. Bye."

"How are we going in?" Nita said. "Driving?"

"No, we'll take the train," Aunt Annie said. "Doris will give us a ride back; we're more or less on her way. Have your breakfast and we'll go. We can slouch around and do tourist things." Aunt Annie smiled at her. "I think I owe you that much, after the other night. . . ."

Nita grinned back and went to get her jacket.

It turned out that she didn't need it. It was another hot day, up in the eighties now. They drove into Greystones to catch the shuttle train to

98

Bray—the line was only electrified from Bray inward— and stood on the platform, looking out toward Greystones' south beach. Dogs ran and barked, and there were even a few people in the water, which astonished Nita; it was some of the coldest water she had ever tried to swim in and bounced out of with her teeth chattering. Most of the people were out in the sun on the sand, turning very pink.

"Most of the time you can tell right away in the summer when someone is from Ireland," Aunt Annie said, "especially when the sun's been out. It doesn't seem to occur to people here to use sunblock, since they see the sun so rarely . . . They all turn into lobsters, the poor things." She shook her head. "Not this year, though. People are actually getting tans."

Nita looked toward the big orange and black diesel train that was pulling in. "Global warming?" she said.

Aunt Annie just shook her head. "Take one of the right-hand seats," she said. "You'll get a better view of the water as we go in."

Nita did. The train pulled out, and Nita looked out at the north beach as they passed it; more sunbathers, someone riding a horse at the gallop.

"Aunt Annie," she said, "you know something— Why didn't I see your name when I went through the manual and looked in the wizards' directory?"

"Confidentiality," her aunt said. "I wasn't 'out' to you yet. The manual senses such things." She looked at Nita thoughtfully. "I suppose I really should have anticipated it; my kids came out nonwizardly, after all. But anyway, I was looking at the manual this morning. . . . You've been busy."

"You got that in one," Nita said.

Aunt Annie smiled. "Not unusual. Things quiet down, though, after you get to be my age. I remember when I first got my manual, I had about three years when I hardly had a moment to myself. Then things got calm when I went off to college."

"Did you have a partner?"

The train went abruptly darkish, lit only by the feeble ceiling lights, as it passed into the tunnel bored through Bray Head. "I did for a while," she said. "But she and I parted company eventually. It happens," she said, at Nita's shocked look. "You grow apart . . . or one partner finds something more important than the magic . . . or you start disagreeing about how to work."

Nita shook her head, shocked. She couldn't imagine not agreeing with Kit on a plan or course of action within a matter of seconds; and indeed, there had been times when if they hadn't been able to agree that fast, they would have been dead. "Do you still talk?" she said.

"Oh, yes, pretty often. We're friendly enough."

The train burst out into the light again, revealing the beach on the other side of Bray Head, and the iron-railed Promenade with its hotels and arcade, and the new aquarium. "Don't worry," said Aunt Annie. "I think maybe you and your partner have been through enough trouble together that you'll be working together for a long while."

They pulled into Bray station and changed to the sleek little bright-green Dublin Area Rapid Transit train waiting at the next platform over. About half an hour later, the train slid into Tara Street station. Nita and her aunt got out and made their way through the orange-tiled exterior, beneath the skylights and down the escalator, and went out into the streets of Dublin.

It was a fascinating combination of old and new, and Nita was rather bewildered by it all at first. There were tiny cobbled alleys that seemed not to have been repaved in a hundred years, or maybe two, right next to broad streets roaring with traffic and alive with lights and people shopping; old, old churches caught in the middle of shiny new shopping centers; shouting, cheerfully messy street markets in the shadow of big department stores.

"It takes a little while to get used to," her aunt said, as they crossed the street south of O'Connell Bridge and headed down past the stately fronts of Trinity College and the Bank of Ireland, on the way to the pedestrian precinct at Grafton Street. "If you come from one of the big cities in the States, Dublin can seem very small at first, sort of caught in a time warp; slower, more casual about things. Later . . ." She chuckled. "You wonder how you ever put up with a place where people are in such a hurry all the time. And you find that life can go along very well without all the 'conveniences' you were used to once." She smiled. "It's the people here: they make the difference."

They turned left at the corner of Grafton Street, heading for the National Museum. It was next to the Dail, the Irish houses of parliament, and Aunt Annie clearly knew her way around it. As soon as they had paid their admission fees, she led Nita down a flight of stairs, past a sign that said TREASURY. "There are a lot of gorgeous things here," she said, "but this is probably the most famous of them."

They stopped in front of a glass case that was thicker than any of the others scattered around the big room. No one else was nearby. Nita moved close to look at it. The cup inside it sat on a big lucite pedestal; a bright spotlight was trained on it from above. Nita thought this might have been unnecessary . . . since she suspected it might be able to glow by itself.

"The Ardagh Chalice," her aunt said softly. Nita looked at it; not just with the eyes, but with a wizard's senses, and looked as hard as she could. The chalice was about two feet high and a foot wide, mostly gold, with elaborate and beautiful spiral patterns worked on its sides in silver, and ornamented with rubies and topazes. The jewels were lovely enough, but Nita had more of an eye for the engraved and inlaid "knotwork" ornamentation on the sides. They were spell diagrams in a very antique style, and though they looked simple, that was an illusion created by the extreme skill of whoever had designed them. They were subtle, and potentially of huge power; but they were quiescent, emptied of their virtue.

"It's not really very old," Nita said.

"The physical aspects of it, no." Her aunt looked at it. "This chalice was made in the second century."

"Not the Holy Grail, then," Nita said.

Her aunt smiled slightly. "No. And yes. The Treasures might have been made by gods, but they were made of mortal matter . . . and matter passes. The problem is, of course, that the power put in them—the soul of the Treasures, more or less—is as immortal as the powers that made them. The soul passes on when the envelope wears out—'reincarnates,' finds another 'body' that's suitable. This cup was a vessel, for a while. But not any more, I think. Do you feel anything different?"

Nita looked at the cup again, longer this time. Finally she said, "I don't know. It's as if . . . if you knew how to shake this awake, this 'soul,' you might do it. But you'd have to know how."

Her aunt nodded. "We may have to figure out how. Come and see the Sword." They went up a flight of stairs, through another room or two. The room they finally stopped in was full of ancient gold work: torcs and stickpins and necklaces and bracelets of gold, beads and bangles, carved plates of gold linked together. "It used to be mined in Wicklow," her aunt said, "not too far from us. But by the fourth century most of it was gone. Anyway, this is worth more than any of them, if you ask me."

The central case held the sword. It lay there very plain against red velvet; long and lean, shaped like a willow leaf, with no gold or jewel anywhere about it—a plain bronze blade, notched, scraped, some-what withered-looking. Nita bent close to it, feeling with all of her. "Now *this* is old," she said.

"Older than the cup," said Aunt Annie. "Bronze age, at least."

Nita nodded. There was a faint feeling of purpose still in the old bronze, like a memory impressed on matter by a mind now gone: like the ghosts in Aunt Annie's back yard, a tape still replaying and very faintly to be heard. But there was no vigor in it, only recollection: wistful, mournful, feeble. . . . "It might have been the real Sword once," Nita said. "But it's almost forgotten. It's not nearly as much there as the Cup. You're going to have a hard time waking it up."

Her aunt nodded. "That's what I think too."

Nita shook her head. "And there's nothing else in the building that's even this much awake. . . ." She sighed. "So we have the Stone, and *maybe* the Cup, and something that *might* work for the Sword, but probably won't . . . and no Spear."

"That about sums it up, yes. The wizards around the country will be looking for other swords that might work better. But the spirit of the Spear Luin seems to have passed completely. Either no 'body' was strong enough to contain it . . . or it was just too powerful to be contained any more in a universe that had no suitable envelope for it, and it passed out entirely."

Nita rather thought that it had passed. Spears were symbols of the element of Fire, and fire was the most uncontainable of the five elements, next to plasma. Nita began to worry. Three of the Trea-sures would not be enough, to judge from what the *Sidhe* had hinted. But she was fresh out of ideas about what to do.

She looked at her aunt. "Are we done here?"

"I think so. Want to go over to Grafton Street?"

"Sounds good."

They spent the afternoon doing, as her aunt had promised, touristy things; touring the shopping center at Saint Stephen's Green, having tea in the Shelbourne Hotel, listening to the street performers play-ing on pipes and banjos and occasionally spoons. They walked over O'Connell Bridge to look up the Liffey at the Halfpenny Bridge's graceful curve, one of the trademarks of Dublin; and browsed through the shops on the south side of the Halfpenny Bridge, Dub-lin's so-called "Left Bank." They sat by the statue of the goddess of the river Liffey in her stone Jacuzzi, and were grateful for the spray, for it was hotter that afternoon than it had been all summer. Mothers put their little children in the fountain, and they splashed happily, and the patrolling Gardai smiled and looked the other way.

About seven o'clock, Aunt Annie said, "Dinner?" Nita agreed happily, and they went off to have a very New Yorkish pizza in a little restaurant in South Anne Street. Then they went a few blocks westward in the city, to the pub where that night's meeting would take place.

The Long Hall was a handsome place, fronted in beveled glass and stained glass, all arranged so that people standing inside, in front of the windows, couldn't quite be seen from outside. Above, the glass was clear, showing the beautiful carved and painted plaster ceiling, and the gas fixtures still hanging from it. Some of them had been converted for electricity, some hadn't. They walked in, and Nita gazed admiringly at the huge polished hardwood bar, and the antique mirrors, reaching nine feet up from the back of the bar to the ceiling, on the wall behind it. Carved wood and beveled glass and brass railings were everywhere. So were many cheerful people, drinking, but talking more. The place was filled with the subdued roar of a hundred conversations.

"We're in the back room. Hi, Jack," said Aunt Annie to one of the men behind the bar. He was busy filling a glass with the creamy-dark Guinness from one of the arched taps at the bar: he nodded to Aunt Annie, didn't say anything.

"Jack Mourne," Aunt Annie said to Nita, as they made their way through a low carved archway into the "back room." "He owns the place."

"Does he know what's going on?"

"I should think he does: he's one of the Area Advisory-Specialists. What would you like to drink, hon?"

"Can I get a Coke?"

"No problem. Be right back."

Nita found herself a seat at a small round wooden table with ornate iron legs, and waited, fidgeting a little self-consciously. She had never been in a bar by herself, though Aunt Annie seemed to think that this wasn't quite the same. *She might have a point, though,* Nita thought. Here, the drinking looked almost incidental. People were shouting at each other across the back room, chatting, arguing, laughing, pointing, hollering.

"Here you go," Aunt Annie said, sitting down next to Nita with a relieved look. She handed Nita her drink and sipped briefly at her pint. "Perfect," she said. "Jack pulls the best pint in this part of town."

"Aunt Annie," Nita said, "if this is a wizard's meeting—how are you going to keep the regular people out of here?"

"Spell on the back-room archway," Aunt Annie said. "Look closely at the carving when you go to the rear ladies' room. Nonwizards hit it and decide they don't feel like going back there after all—on normal nights, Jack just takes the spell finial off: that little carved flower in the lower right-hand corner. And no one can hear us through all this din anyway; but there are voice-scramblers on anyway. Jack makes anything wizardly come out sounding like an argument about football. Nice scrambler, took him a while to write. But he's one of our best writers. You need a custom spell in this part of the world, it's Jack you come to, or Marie Shaughnessy down in Arklow, or Charles and Alison Redpath up north in Aghalee."

"Then all these people back here are wizards?" Nita said, looking around her in astonishment. She had never been in such a large gathering of her own before.

"Oh yes. All that could come at short notice, of course. Relax a while; we can't do anything until Doris and Johnny get here."

So Nita drank her Coke and listened to the accents around her, and chatted every now and then with the people who came up to her aunt to say hello. If she had been mired in Irish accents before, the situation got much worse now: she heard about twenty more from as many different people, no two of them the same, and some very odd indeed. In addition, there were a lot of people from Northern Ireland down for this meeting, and their accents astounded her; they sounded more like New Yorkers than anything else, though more nasal. They all seemed very open, friendly people, which to Nita seemed a little strange at first: seeing what most Americans saw of Northern Ireland from the news, she half-expected them to be furtive and depressed, as if afraid a bomb might suddenly go off under them. But none of them were. One man in his thirties, a jocund young man in a leather jacket covered with patches, told Nita he had never seen a bomb or been within fifty miles of one, nor had anyone he knew. The peaceful small-town life he described seemed hard to reconcile with all the news shots Nita had seen of taped-off, shattered buildings, and the people with ski masks and rifles.

There was a slight commotion at the door as Mrs. Smyth came in under the archway. "Hey Doris, how they cuttin'?" someone shouted. Doris Smyth looked at the speaker and said something clear and carrying in Irish that provoked a roar of approval from the listeners, and caused the person who had asked the question to be genially pummeled.

Behind Mrs. Smyth, someone else came in; a short man in a long overcoat and plaid scarf. At sight of him, many of the wizards in the room called, "Johnny!" or "Shaun!," and there was a general stir of approval through the back room. Nita bent over to her Aunt Annie and said, "Who's that?"

"Shaun O'Driscoll," said Aunt Annie. "Or Johnny, some people call him. He's the Area Senior for Western Europe."

"Wow," Nita said, never having seen so high-ranked a wizard before. Area Seniors answered only to Regional Seniors, and Regionals to the three Seniors for Earth. When she thought of the Senior in charge of all wizards from Shannon to Moscow and Oslo to Gibraltar, she had imagined someone more imposing—not a little man with thinning hair and (as he took his coat off) a leisure suit. He didn't look very old. He had a fierce-looking mustache, and his eyes were very cool; he looked around the room and returned all the greetings without ever quite smiling. It was the kind of effect, Nita thought, that made you want to try to get him to smile. It would be worth seeing when it happened, for his face was otherwise a nest of laugh-lines.

Doris and Johnny were gotten pints by another of the gathered wizards, and people started settling down, leaning against the walls when they ran out of seats. Johnny didn't sit, but stood in the middle of the room, waiting for them to settle, like a teacher with a big unruly class.

"Thanks for coming," he said. "I know this was short notice, but we've had some serious problems crop up in the past few days, and there was no way to hope to manage them except by requiring an intervention meeting."

There were some heads turned at this, and some murmuring under breath among the assembled wizards. "I know that wasn't the way it was announced," Johnny said, "but we turn out to have less time for this discussion than was originally thought when we organized this meeting via the phone tree last night and this morning. We have had serious transitional leakages all over the island, with some sympathetic transitionals on mainland Europe; and this condition has to be contained as quickly as possible. There have been echoes and ripples as far away as China and Peru."

More stirring at this. "Anyway," Johnny said, "I want to thank those of you who were in the middle of other assignments and found them changed, or who were off active and were suddenly reactivated. The Powers that Be may not thank you until later, but I like to do it early. I also want to welcome those of you who have come unusual distances, including Nita Callahan. Stand up, honey."

Nita flushed fiercely, and hoped it didn't show too much in the pub's dimmish light. She stood up.

"Nita has been reassigned here temporarily courtesy of North American Regional. She has blood affinities with this area, and was recently involved in the New York incursion and the Hudson Canyon intervention in June, and more recently, with the Reconfiguration; Dairine Callahan is her sister."

There was a stir at this which surprised Nita somewhat. She nodded, smiled a little uncertainly at Johnny; he gestured her to sit down. "We're glad to have you," he said. "Bear with us: we do things a little differently here than you're used to, and if you think of anything that seems useful during this discussion, don't hesitate to sing out."

Huh, Nita thought, sitting down. And, *Reassigned courtesy of North American Regional? Who's that? Not Tom and Carl. Someone—or something—further in, or higher up?* But she put the thought aside for the moment.

"Over the past four nights we've had 'sideways' leakages in thirty-three out of thirty-six counties," Johnny said, "and how Monaghan, Wexford and Westmeath were missed is a mystery to us, especially since Westmeath contains the Hill of Tara. In the thirty-three counties, about ninety wizards have experienced timeslides, live remembrances of the so-called 'mythological' period, 'solid' remembrances that returned interactions, viewings of extradimensional objects without doing the wizardries required for such viewings, and even physical intervention by nonphysical entities or creatures not native to this reality, including physical attacks on occasion. One of us met Cuchullain in warp spasm, which is enough to turn anyone's hair: that it happened in the middle of the big shopping center in Tallaght didn't help, either. The Brown Bull of Cooley was seen crossing the dual carriageway north of Shannon; it wandered down onto the Iarnrod Eireann tracks and caused a derailment, though fortunately neither the train drivers nor any of the other people on the train saw it, and by great good luck no one was hurt. Possibly most to the point, there was an earthquake in the fields north of Naas, at the old site of the Battle of Moytura."

More stirring over this, and some anxious looks. Johnny made quiet-down gestures. "It was only about three point one on the Richter scale, and nothing came of it but some broken china. The *Lia Fail* is still managing to hold this island in one place and one piece, no matter what the politicians say. But how long it can hold matters so stable is a good question. Much of its old virtue is gone, as you know. Another such attack will certainly be more effective, on both natural and supernatural levels."

"Johnny," said one of the wizards sitting back by the wall, a handsome little dark-haired woman with a sharp face, "these transitional leakages, are we sure that something else isn't causing them? Something European?"

Johnny shook his head. "I'd prefer to blame Local Europe myself, Morgan, but we're out of luck on this one. All indications point back at us."

"Then what are we going to do?"

Johnny looked grim. "We're going to have to recreate Moytura, I think. Unless someone else can think of something better."

Half the room started muttering to the other half. Johnny waited for it to settle down. "Recreate Moytura with *what?*" said the Northern-based wizard Nita had been talking to, the young guy in the leather jacket.

"Good question," Johnny said. "Two of the Four Treasures are still with us, though diminished, as you know. In their present state, they're too diminished to be of any use. But the 'souls' of those Treasures are still in the world, or the Worlds, somewhere. We are going to have to recall those souls to suitable envelopes, and then take them out into battle against the Lone Power. We know that with them, we have a chance. Without them—" He shrugged.

Relative silence fell for a few moments. "Who does the 'going into battle' bit?" said another voice from somewhere against the back wall.

"Lacking one of the Powers that Be, probably Doris and I to lead," Johnny said. "And all of you we can get together in one place."

"Where are you going to get 'suitable envelopes', then?" said another voice.

"We'll try to use the old ones," Doris said. "They've worked before: with a little coercion, they'll work again . . . or we hope so. The *Lia Fail* is still working; the Ardagh Chalice we think we can reawaken."

107

"Don't you think the Museum will miss it?" said the young wizard in the leather jacket.

Doris smiled slightly. "Not if a wizardry that looks and weighs exactly the same is sitting in the museum case," she said. "If the Taoiseach can borrow the Chalice just to show it off at a politicians' dinner party in Dublin Castle, I think *we* might take the loan of it for a night or so, for something important, and not feel too guilty afterwards. But everything depends on the circumstances, and the power of the ritual used to call the Cup's soul back. Which is what we're going to have to work on. It's not just warriors we're going to need to make this work, but poets. Where are Charles and Alison?"

"Stuck in traffic," said someone from the bar side of the room.

Johnny grinned. "Ah, the 'real world.' But at least Liam and Mairead and Nigel are here. I'll be wanting to talk to you three afterwards. The rest of you: I want you all to talk to your area supervisors about your schedules for the next two weeks. Any one of you may have to drop everything at a moment's notice and lend a hand. Also, given the seriousness of the situation, travel restrictions on teleportation are off for the duration. Just use your judgment, and be very careful about the overlays!"

More chatter erupted. In the middle of it, someone said, "But Johnny, wait a tick! Isn't this going to make things worse?"

Johnny waved for relative quiet. The room settled a little. "How do you mean?" he said.

"If you're going to call back the souls of the Treasures—if you can," said the speaker, a tall dignified-looking wizard with a mighty mustache, "isn't the land going to get even more awake and aware than it already is? I mean, the Treasures are the land, in some ways. At least that's what we were always told: four of the five Elements, in their most personified forms. Air and water and earth and fire are going to wake up more than ever, until the situation is resolved and everything is laid to rest again."

Johnny nodded slowly. The room got quiet as people looked at his expression. "Yes," he said after a while. "It's going to get much worse. Which makes it to our advantage to get the situation resolved, as you say, as quickly as possible. Otherwise first Ireland, then the rest of Europe, and eventually all the other continents, are going to be overrun with the past happening again, and the dead walking, and all kinds of other inconveniences. If we can't stop this, then the barriers between present and past will break down everywhere, and the physical world will be progressively overrun by the nonphysical:

all the myths, and truths that became myth, all the dreams and night-mares, all the more central and more peripheral realities, will super-impose themselves on this one . . . inextricably."

"For how long?" said a small voice out of the hush.

"If that level of imposition ever takes hold fully," Johnny said, "I don't see how the process could *ever* be reversed."

Silence, broken only by the noise of cheerful conversation in the frontmost, nonwizardly part of the pub. "Right," said the man with the mustache again. "But in the meantime, while you seniors are intervening, Ireland's dreams and nightmares are going to keep com-ing true—even more than they have been—and the past will keep happening, and the dead and the undead and the immortal will walk. And 'other inconveniences.' "

"That's exactly right, Scott," Johnny said.

There was another long silence. Then a voice said, "I need an-other pint."

A chorus of other voices went up in agreement. Nita noticed that her Coke was long gone, and she was very thirsty.

"I'll get you another," her Aunt Annie said, and got up. "Anybody else? Katherine? Nuala? Orla? Hi, Jim—" She moved off.

Nita sat there feeling somewhat shaky. "Hey, you look like a sheet," said a voice by her. She looked up: it was Ronan.

She smiled faintly at him as he sat down, and did her best to control herself. He looked, if possible, even cuter than he had previ-ously. Black leather suited him, and so did this subdued lighting. "I feel like one," she said. "How about you?"

"Sounds pretty bad," Ronan said. But he looked and sounded remarkably unconcerned. "Don't worry about auld Shaun there, he just likes to sound like doom and destruction all the time. Comes of being Area Senior; they all sound like the world's ending half the time."

Probably because it is, Nita thought. It was only the sheer number of wizards in the world, and the sacrifices they kept making from week to week, that kept civilization on an even keel; or so it seemed to her. "Look, can I ask you something?"

"Sure."

"I'm just curious. Was your Ordeal bad?"

He looked peculiarly at her. "Almost got me killed, if that's what you mean."

"So will crossing O'Connell Street," Nita said. "Never mind . . . I don't know what I mean. I mean, it seemed to me that my Ordeal

109

was pretty awful. I was just curious whether I was an exception, or whether everyone had that bad a time. My sister did, but she's not exactly a normal case. And I haven't had that many chances to discuss it with other wizards."

Ronan looked thoughtful and took a drink of his orange-and-lemon drink. "I got timeslid," he said.

Nita shrugged slightly. "We bought a timeslide from our local Seniors for ours," she said.

"I didn't buy mine," Ronan said. "I *got* it." He took another drink. "One day I took the Oath—the next I was walking up Vevay Road, you know, at the top of Bray by the Quinnsworth, the supermarket? Well, it stopped being Vevay Road. It was just a dirt track with some thatched huts down near where the school would be, at the bottom of the hill, and it was raining cats and dogs. Thunder and lightning."

Nita shivered: she disliked being caught out in the rain. "What did you do?"

"I went up Bray Head," Ronan said, bursting out in a laugh that sounded as if, in retrospect, he didn't believe his own craziness. "I wanted to see where everything was, you know? It was a mess. You know how the sea gets during a storm. Well, maybe you don't—"

"I live on Long Island," Nita said. "We get high-force gales on the Great South Bay, when the hurricanes come through. The whole sea one big whitecap, spray so thick in the air you can't see—"

"Driving inland," Ronan said. "Between the rain and the spray, there was almost no difference between being in the water and on the land. Well, I saw the boat come in, straight for the rocks. Little thing." He saw Nita's blank look and said, "The Romans."

That made her raise her eyebrows. She had seen the Roman coins that had been found at the base of Bray Head: she had seen a reconstruction of the archaeological site, with their bones. "They were going to try to set up a colony, weren't they?" she said.

Ronan nodded. Nita watched him. She remembered that afternoon in the chicken place in Bray, and the vehemence of Ronan's feelings about colonizers of any kind. But at the moment, Ronan just sat, and flushed a little, and looked away from Nita as he said, "Well, they were going to get killed, weren't they? Them and their little boat and all, in that sea. One of the lifeboats couldn't have stood it, let alone that little smack. So I 'took the sea in.' "

Nita stared at him. What Ronan was describing was temporary but complete control of a pure element: using the wizardly Speech to describe every molecule of an object or area so completely and accurately that for a short period you became it. Control was barely the word for it. It became as much part of you as your body . . . for a while. Then came the backlash: for human beings are not really meant to have more than one physical body at a time. You might find the association impossible to break—and have to spend the rest of your life coexisting with what you had described: which would surely drive you insane. Or the strain of the wizardry itself might kill you. An adult wizard, full of experience, might have done such a wizardry once . . . and no other wizardry, ever again. A young wizard, on Ordeal, or soon after, could have done it and lived . . . maybe. It was a good question whether his head would ever be entirely right again.

But here sat Ronan, still blushing slightly, and said, "It wasn't much of it I had to take, just the sea around Bray Head. They jumped ship and made it ashore. I couldn't save the boat, it went all to pieces when I lost control. I must have passed out up there—the slide came undone after a while, and some tourists doing the cliff walk from the Greystones side found me slipping down the rocks on the seaward side, and they called the Guards. I spent a few days in the hospital." He shrugged. " 'Hypothermia,' " he added, and laughed. "Too true—but they never knew from what."

"Wow," Nita said under her breath, almost lost in admiration of him. She was starting to blush, but she ignored it as she looked at him again. "But you knew," she said. "That there was just the one boat. The Romans never made it here except for those people. Britain was giving them too much trouble. You could have let them go under."

If there was a little challenge in her voice, Ronan didn't rise to it. "Could I?" he said. "I knew it was a timeslide. Would I have been changing history? Did I have any choice?"

"Damn straight you did," Nita said, again under her breath.

Ronan heard it. He looked up from under his brows at her, that familiar scowl. "That's as may be. What could I do? Seeing them waving their arms and trying to get off, and knowing they would drown if they tried it, in that water." He looked away again, as if slightly embarrassed. "Sure nothing came of it anyway. They were marooned there; no one ever came after them. They settled down there, and married the people there, some of them. I'm related to them, for all I know."

Nita smiled slightly. "You didn't *know* that no one would come

111

after them, though. Suppose you *had* changed history? Suppose you had just saved the lives of the people who were going to report back to Rome and bring in the conquerors?"

Ronan drank his drink and looked away.

Nita reached out and patted his arm—a casual enough gesture, she did it with Kit all the time, but as she did it to Ronan, the shock of it, the closeness of actually touching him, ran up the arm like fire and half wilted her. "Never mind," she said, trying to get some control back. The point of each wizard's Ordeal was always a private thing: that Ronan should share this much of it with her was more than he had to do. "You want another of those?" she said. "What did you call it?"

"A St. Clements. 'Oranges and lemons, say the bells of St. Clements—' " He burst out laughing at Nita's uncomprehending look. "Don't know that one, I take it. Not in America's Top 40."

Nita knew when she was being made fun of, and knew when not to take it seriously: her heart warmed that he liked her enough to do it at all. "Eat turf and die, Paddy," she said, and got up, feeling in her pocket for change.

She got Ronan's drink, and when she got back, found her own waiting for her, and rather to her surprise, Johnny sitting in her seat and chatting with Ronan. "Here," Johnny said, and got up; "I was holding it for you. Listen, dear, I have a message for you. Tom and Carl send their best."

"You know them? How are they?!" Nita said, sitting right up. "Are they okay? It was them, then!"

"They're fine. I consult with them fairly often, especially Tom: he's an advisory to the North American Regional for compositional spelling. *What* was 'them'?"

"I mean, it was them who sent me on assignment. They, I mean."

Johnny smiled very slightly, and all his wrinkles deepened. "Ahh . . . no. Not even a Regional Senior, or one of the Planetaries, can actually put a wizard on active assignment. No matter how certain we are that the world's ending." He shot a humorous look at Ronan, and Ronan looked like he was tempted to try to pull his head down inside his black turtleneck. "No, those decisions are made higher up. I might have mentioned North American Regional, but there are more than humans involved in that. Never mind for now. I take it Doris had a talk with you about our local problems."

Nita opened her mouth to answer, and was startled by a sudden shout from up front. "LAST ORDERS NOW, TEN MINUTES GENTLEMEN, LAST ORDERS PLEASE—!"

Johnny laughed at the look her face must have been wearing. "All the pubs have to close at eleven-thirty this time of year," he said. "Anyway, Doris says she told you the ropes."

"If you mean she told me not even to sneeze in the Speech," Nita said, "yes."

Johnny laughed under his breath. "It must seem hard. Believe me, it's for the best . . . and there'll be enough magic around here for anybody, come the end of the month, if things keep going the way they've been going. We'll be in touch with you, of course."

"Johnny," Ronan said suddenly, "this may be out of turn—"

"Knowing you, my lad," Johnny said, "probably."

"Johnny—Look, it's nothing personal," Ronan said, glancing at Nita and blushing furiously again. "But why can't this be handled locally? Why do we need blow-ins?"

Nita went red too, with annoyance. She thought of about six different cutting things to say, and kept her mouth shut on them all.

But Johnny simply looked mildly surprised. "Self-sufficiency, is it?" he said. "Have you fallen for that one? It's an illusion, Ro. Why do we 'need' the help of the *Tuatha de Danaan*? Why do we need the Powers that Be? Or even the Lone Power?—for that One has a function in the universe, too. You know that. The whole lot of us are interconnected, and there's no way we can get away from it, or any one group of us solve even the littlest problem entirely by ourselves. This matter *is* being handled locally. It's being handled on *Earth*. Next thing, you're going to ask me what the Northern Irish wizards are doing here." His eyebrows went up and down. "You've been listening to too many politicians. —Better apologize to her before she turns you into a soggy beermat," Johnny said, patted Nita on the shoulder, and moved on.

"TIME NOW GENTLEMEN, TIME NOW, TAKE THOSE GLASSES AWAY CHARLIE!," Jack was shouting from the front of the pub. Nita did her best to keep her face still. She had gone quite hot and tight inside, and was holding onto herself hard; controlling her emotions had never been her strongest suit, and she had no desire to say something stupid here, where she was a guest and could make her aunt look bad. *Besides, I'm a wizard among wizards. It should take more than some provincial punk with a chip on his shoulder to get me annoyed—!*

113

"Look, Nita," Ronan said. He sounded slightly desperate. "I didn't—"

"You bet you didn't," she said. And shut herself up: and then lost it again. "Look," she said, her voice low but fierce, "do you think this was *my* idea? Do you think I wouldn't rather be back home with my partner taking care of business, than messing around in this dumb little place where you can't even twitch without permission? Do you think I don't have better things to do? 'Blow-ins,' " she said bitterly, and picked up her drink and began to drink the whole thing at once, to shut herself up: at least she couldn't say what she was thinking while she was drinking something.

It was the wrong drink. In the middle of the second swallow she spluttered in shock at the alcoholic black-bread taste of it, and from beside her Aunt Annie said, "You're going to get us thrown out of here, you know that? Here, have a napkin."

Nita gasped and choked and took the napkin gratefully, and began mopping Guinness off herself and the table. Ronan was leaning against the wall and laughing, soundlessly, but so hard that he was turning twice as red as he had been. Furious, Nita felt around in her head for the small simple spell that would dump his own drink in his lap: then remembered where she was, and in rapid succession first shoved the sodden napkin down the neck of his turtleneck, and while Ronan was fumbling for it, knocked his glass sideways with her elbow. "Oops," she said in utter innocence, as it went all over him.

"COME ON NOW GENTS, TIME NOW, TIME, HAVE YOU NO HOMES TO GO TO? YOU TOO LADIES, NO OFFENSE MEANT," Jack shouted from the front of the pub. The conversations were getting louder, if anything. Ronan sat and stared at his lap, and just as he lifted his eyes to Nita's, Johnny went by and patted him on the shoulder, and said, "I *told* you she was going to turn you into a soggy beermat. No one ever listens to me. 'Night, Annie, give me a call in the morning. . . ." And he was away.

"I guess we'd better go," Aunt Annie said, as the lights began flashing on and off to remind people that it was time to drink up and get out. "Doris is waiting. Ronan, do you need a ride home?"

"No thank you, Mrs. Callahan," he said, "I came in with Barry."

"Right, then. Come on, Nita, let's call it a night."

Nita got up, and looked down at Ronan. He was gazing back at her with an expression she couldn't interpret. Not anger, not amusement—what was it? She refused to waste her time trying to figure it out. "Keep your pants dry," she said to him, trying desperately to

keep her face straight, and losing it again. Gratefully she followed
Mrs. Smyth and Aunt Annie out, grinning to herself.

Blow-ins. Huh.

She grinned all the way home . . . and wasn't quite sure why.

Slieve na Chulainn
Great Sugarloaf Mountain

"What's going on?" Kit said the next afternoon. "How are things going with the Treasures?"

They were sitting around the kitchen table, looking at the papers. "Well," Nita's aunt said, "Doris and a couple of the other seniors are going to go in tonight and lift the Ardagh Chalice. They'll leave a perfect copy in its place. They think they have a guess at how to make it wake up. Apparently whatever they did with the Stone worked better than they thought; it seems your friend Tom is quite an asset," she said to Nita. "They were able to wake it up on the first try, using the spell he wrote for them."

Nita nodded. "He says it's because he used to write so many commercials."

Aunt Annie chuckled. "I guess I can see the point. Well, anyway, it's awake. As you will have noticed, the land is getting, uh, restive . . . more than it was, anyway."

"Are they going to bring the stone here? Or somewhere special?" said Kit.

"Oh, no . . . there's no need for that. The Stone *is* the earth of Ireland, some ways; anywhere there is earth of Ireland, the Stone is there in essence. The same way that the Cup *is* the water of Ireland, and all wells and pools; the Sword *is* the air of Ireland, the Spear *is* the fire. The Treasures exist in essence in all the things they represent. But when they're awake, they co-exist many times more powerfully than before. They themselves become weapons of considerable power; and the earth and air and water and fire themselves become weapons that we can turn to our advantage. We sincerely hope." She took a drink of her tea.

"What about the Sword?" Kit said.

"It's hard to say," said Annie. "The Cup is more awake than any of the envelopes they're thinking about using for the Sword; so they're going to try the spell on the Chalice first, and see how the

116

reanimation works on that. If it does, they'll move on and try it on the sword in the Museum."

"And the Spear?" Kit said.

Aunt Annie shook her head. "No news. There are a lot of spears and pikes and whatnot lying around, but none of them seem ever to have been the Spear Luin. Which is a problem, for Luin was *the* weapon that overthrew Balor. The others were basically support for it."

Kit shrugged. "Well, something'll turn up. Something always does."

"I wish I had your confidence," Aunt Annie said, getting up to pour herself another cup.

"Something has to turn up," Kit said. *"We're* here."

Nita punched him lightly. "Something's always turned up before," she said. "This is not like before. . . ."

Kit shrugged again. "Listen, if I can't keep your spirits up, you won't do good work."

"How can my spirits be other than wonderful when I have this to look at?" she said, pushing the paper at him.

The *Wicklow People* had come out that morning, and the usual details of the fortunes and misfortunes of Wicklow people overseas, or the failure of the county council to do something about an urgent local problem, or the accusations of one of the local political parties about the purported bad behavior of one of the others, had been forced off the front pages. Other people besides Nita had been having problems.

SILLY SEASON COMES TO NORTH WICKLOW, said the headline. Underneath it was the beginning of a three-page feature story concerning the bizarre occurrences in the county that week. The trouble had started in the country. A farmer had claimed that a dinosaur—a small one, but still plainly a dinosaur—had been eating his sheep. These claims had been greeted with amusement by his neighbors, some of whom had suggested that he had, in the local way of putting it, "drink taken."

The Gardai declined comment on this business, as they did about the reports of rocks rolling uphill at Ballywaltrim, or the problem incurred by the dairy cattle farmer over by Kilmacanogue, who claimed his Guernsey herd was stolen—driven away across the dual carriageway by a man who said he was Finn MacCumhal, and was entitled to take any cattle that their owner was not strong enough to defend in battle. There were a chorus of noisy protests to Bray Ur-

117

ban District Council and Wicklow County Council about this—some people insisting that the psychiatric hospital at Newcastle needed to look into its security.

Matters were no better anywhere else in Ireland. There were reports from all over of people's lives being suddenly turned topsy-turvy by the appearance of ancient heroes, ancient villains, and ancient monsters, with which Ireland was well supplied. Several people dug up buried treasures after being told where to find them by kindly ghosts; unicorns were seen in Avonmore Forest Park: merfolk were heard singing off Howth. The Gardai had no comment on these matters, either.

They were perusing these accounts when Johnny O'Driscoll arrived. Nita put the newspaper aside and introduced Kit to him. "You're very welcome," Johnny said to him. "Your friend here will have warned you about the overlays, though."

"She mentioned, yes."

"Well, be careful. We have enough problems at the moment."

Nita poured a cup of tea for Johnny; he took it, drank it with a thankful air, and said, "Everyone else I've talked to this morning has had a problem, so I might as well hear yours, too. What happened to you yesterday?"

"Nothing really," she said. "But I did have an interesting conversation with a fox the other day." And she described her meeting with the dog-fox, and the information he had given her.

Johnny looked thoughtful at that. "I have to say," he said, "that I'd suspected for some time that at least one of the Bright Powers was in the area, in human form. I had no solid confirmation. Normally, if one of Them is going to be in the area on business, the Manuals give warning of it: or the Knowledge does, depending on which you use. But there's been no such warning. Then again, this isn't a normal situation. Anyway, I had other indications. Interesting to hear them confirmed."

Nita glanced over at Kit. "Why do They hide?" she said.

"To keep the other side from knowing that they're here. Except that the other side seems to know already, so that reason doesn't work in this case." He shook his head. "I don't know. The Powers are frequently beyond our ability to explain . . . but there's nothing strange about that. They're the next major level of creation up from us, after all. Should a rock expect to be able to explain a human being?"

"We have enough trouble with that ourselves," Kit said.

"Just so. Anyway, whatever Power it is doubtless has good reasons for wanting to stay hidden. I wouldn't want to break Its cover prematurely."

Kit and Nita looked at each other.

"Meanwhile," Johnny said, "Anne, if it's all right with you, Doris will be stopping in this afternoon with what she's picked up. The Enniskerry area is too badly overlaid for her to keep it up there for a few minutes without the area remembering all kinds of things that are better not roused. Down here is a little cleaner; you and I can do something to suppress those memories about the church and Cromwell's people."

"No problem," said Aunt Annie. "We'll put it in the back office."

"Fine. Your staff don't usually go in there?"

"Only my secretary. I can ask her not to."

"Fine. These Treasures are proving a little more dangerous than we thought. Harry, who went up to do the work on the Stone, did it all right . . . but I think he's probably not going to be worth much of anything for the next few days. We have to be very careful that we don't let people spend too long near these things. If you show me where you want to put it, I'll build a warding for that room, and see that it doesn't do anyone any damage."

"But how can these be hurting people?" Nita said. "They're *good!*"

"Oh, absolutely," Johnny said. "There are probably no more powerful forces for good on the planet . . . except for human beings, naturally. But just because they're good, doesn't mean they're *safe.*"

"Listen, Shaun," Aunt Annie said then, "is there any plan yet for where we're going to do the big ceremony, the reenactment?"

"It'll have to start up at Matrix," Johnny said. "It has all the necessary 'equipment.' That's right," he said to Nita, "you haven't seen my place yet, have you? Not really 'my' place, of course. No one owns Castle Matrix but itself . . . and whatever's under it. You'll see." He got up. "Anyway, Matrix is where it'll start. But where it'll end . . ." He shook his head. "I have to go down to Bray. Either of you need a ride?"

"Thanks," Nita said. "We were going to take the bus, but if it's OK . . ."

"Sure, come on."

Johnny dropped them more or less in the center of town, where Herbert Road crosses Main Street. They waved goodbye to him as he drove off, and Kit said, "I didn't have any breakfast . . . I'm an empty shell. Is there anywhere to eat around here?"

"There's a chicken place over here that's not too bad," Nita said. "I've got some money. Let's go in there."

They walked in, went to the counter and ordered. Nita took one quick glance at the back of the restaurant, and her stomach turned over inside her in nervous response. Ronan was sitting back there. He shot Nita one quick glance and then looked down again at the Coke he was busy with.

"You okay?" Kit said, as they turned away with their own drinks and went to sit down at a table. "Your face is all weird."

"Uh," Nita said. "I poured a drink over a guy the other night."

"You were out with a guy?"

Nita blushed. "No, not me. A bunch of us were out."

"What, a bunch of the kids around here?"

"What is this, the Spanish Inquisition? I was out with my aunt. There was a big wizards' meeting in town."

"Oh," Kit said. He started to go red again.

Nita rolled her eyes and said, "Spare me! Never mind that." She took a drink of her Coke—her mouth was suddenly dry—and said, "Half a second." Then she got up and went back to Ronan's table.

He looked up at her with an expression partly unease and partly annoyance; and he still managed to smile on top of it all. "You forgot your Coke," he said.

"No, it's back there."

"I mean, I thought you were going to pour it on me."

She looked at him ruefully. "Listen, Ronan, I'm sorry. Look, come on and sit with us, and meet my partner."

"That's him?" He craned his neck a little.

"Yeah, he's just in from the States. Come on and sit with us."

Somewhat reluctantly, Ronan got up, bringing his Coke, and went and stood by the table. "Kit," she said, "this is Ronan. Ronan, Kit Rodrigues."

They shook hands, Kit willingly enough, Ronan with some reserve, and they looked at each other. *"Dai stihó,"* Kit said.

Ronan raised his eyebrows as he sat down. "You can tell?"

Kit looked surprised. "It sticks out all over you."

"Your partner couldn't."

Nita went hot with embarrassment at that. Kit shrugged. "It's always easier for guy wizards to tell guys, and girls to tell girls. Anyway, Neets has other things to think about. And she's in a weird place:

you get thrown off. I didn't know her aunt was one of us till she was pointed out to me."

There was tension in the air. Nita had thought this would be a good idea, at first; now she was beginning to regret it. "I was just telling Ronan," she said to Kit, "that I was sorry I dumped the drink on him the other night."

Ronan looked bemused. "Watch out for her. She's got a temper."

"I've noticed," Kit said. "Just hope you never see her sister lose hers. Whoo! But Neets is no prize either."

"Will you two stop talking about me as if I'm not here?" Nita said, annoyed. Then they both grinned at her, and she went hot again. *Bad enough being teased from just one direction. . . .*

"Shove over, Kit," she said, sat down next to him, and started working on her Coke again. Then she said to Ronan, "How was *your* day yesterday?"

There was an abrupt sound of breaking glass from outside. All three of their heads jerked up at the same time. "What the heck—!" Kit said.

"Probably an accident," Ronan said, getting up hurriedly. "The corner next to here's a bad one, people are always coming around it too fast—"

The next sound of glass breaking was the shop's own window, and it was not a car that broke it. Something big, dark and blunt slammed into it from one side, and plate glass rained in. The ladies behind the counter cried out in surprise and headed for the back of the shop in a hurry. The shop's three other patrons followed them, leaving Kit and Nita and Ronan standing there.

Something stepped in through the broken glass. If you had taken a human being, and coated it with tar, and rolled it in gravel, and then turned it loose to walk around blindly smashing things, it might look something like this. At least, it would if it were about five feet tall, and about four feet broad, with arms and thighs as thick as a man's waist, and a round ugly face like a boulder.

They looked at it in shock as it came toward them. "It's a drow," Ronan whispered. "Fomori. . . ."

They could see others like it stalking past, out in the street. The sounds of breaking plate glass were spreading down the road; cars screeched to a halt, horns blasted. There was one long screech followed by the sound of more breaking glass, and the crunch of metal too, this time.

"Someone's hit one," Kit said.

"I feel sorry for their car," Ronan said. "Come on."

"How do you stop them?" said Nita.

"Stop them?! You don't stop them. You run away!" Ronan said. He grabbed Nita's arm with one hand, and Kit's with the other, and hustled them out the back door.

They ducked out the back of the chicken place and into Castle Terrace behind it. Nita looked down to the end of the street, toward the remains of the old castle. Several of the drows were there, tearing the place up, or down. They appeared to be made of good Wicklow granite, and to dislike everything they saw. Several of them, a little nearer down the street, were punching holes in the walls of the Bank of Ireland: its alarm bell was ringing disconsolately. Another one, in Herbert Road, was busy turning a car over, while people struggled and screamed and tried to get out of it.

"This is not good," Nita muttered. "We can't just leave these things running all over the place!"

"There's no wizardry that can deal with these," Ronan said, "not with overlays all over the place! You've just got to get away! If they—"

That was when the heavy hand fell on Ronan's shoulder. "No way!" Kit said. He then spoke three words, very short and sharp. The drow screamed, a high thin whine, and reeled back, mostly because it had no head left. Rock dust sifted down past Ronan as Kit pulled him away. "You were saying?" Kit said, breathing hard.

The drow kept screaming. A great crack or fissure ran down it, from its head straight down its centerline. It staggered, and the crack spread. But something else happened as well. The drow got wider. It seemed to have two heads. Then six arms; then eight. It fell to the ground with a terrible crash, and broke in two; and got up . . . twice. It had twinned.

"I was saying *that*," Ronan said. "Run!"

The way westward down Herbert Road was blocked by more drows. The three of them dodged around the formerly single drow and ran into Main Street. People were running and screaming in all directions. Cars were being overturned, windows and walls being bashed in or pulled down. Two drows were in the process of overturning the monument in front of the Royal Hotel. "What the heck is *this* supposed to be a reenactment of?" Nita said, looking around in panic.

"It's not a reenactment. They're Fomori, doing what they always do . . . destroying everything in sight."

122

Nita looked up Main Street toward the old beam-and-plaster building that had been the town's market hall, and was now the tourist center and museum. It was still fairly clear up there. "Come on," she said.

They ran up that way, accompanied by a lot of other people who apparently had the same idea. They didn't get much farther than the little arcade of shops in the middle of the main street before they saw the first squat, grey forms appearing down at the other end of the road. One of them began pulling at the gryphon-topped granite fountain in front of the heritage center.

They stopped. "No good," Nita said. "We don't dare use spells— they'll just backfire. We've got to do something else."

"Such as?" Ronan said, desperate.

She smiled at him, rather crookedly. She was beginning to shake. "Let's try this," she said.

There was a format for these things. She swallowed, and called the name once; she called it twice. The second time, it made her throat hurt—more in warning, she thought, than because of the sound of it. Something was saying to her, *Are you sure? Very sure?* She gulped, and said the name the third time. It shook her, and flung her down.

Nita sat up on the sidewalk, slightly dazed. It took a swallow or two to get her throat working again. Then she shouted in the Speech, *"Pay me back what you owe me—and do it now!"*

It being wizardry involved, she expected immediate results. It being wizardry involved . . . she got them.

Over the screams and the breaking glass, over the crashes of cars and the howling of the sirens of the Gardai, came another sound: bells. Not church bells. It was as if someone had taken the sound of hoofbeats, and tuned them; as if what came galloping did so on hooves of glass, or silver, a clangor of relentless and purposeful harmonies. Other bells were the sounds that bridles might make if each one were built like a musical instrument, made to be carried into battle and shaken to frighten the enemy, a sharp, chilly sound. The galloping and the sound of the bells came closer together, and were joined by a third sound, a high, eerie singing noise, the sound that metal might make if you woke it up and taught it how to kill. The faces of the buildings up near the Heritage Center flushed bright, as if a light came near them.

And then the tide of color poured itself down into Main Street from both sides of the Heritage Center, and the first of the drows fell away from the gryphon fountain, screaming as a crystal sword pierced it. The horses shone, the riders shone; not with any kind of light. They were simply more *there* than the main street was, more *there* than the broken glass, and the crashed cars, and the grey things; more vivid, more real. Everything went pallid or dull that was seen in the same glance with them—the crimson of cloaks and banners that burned like coals, the blues and emerald greens like spring suddenly afire amid the concrete, the gold of torcs and arm-rings glowing as if they were molten, the silver of hair burning like the moon through cloud, the raven of hair burning like the cold between the stars. The riders poured down into Main Street, and the drows fled screaming before them—not that it helped. Two of them took refuge in the smoked-glass-and-aluminum phone booths down at that end of the street; the faery horses smashed them to splinters with their hooves, and the drows afterwards. Down past the Chinese restaurant, down past the real estate agents and the appliance stores, the riders came storming down between the cars, or through them, as if the cars were not real to them: and perhaps they were not. The riders' hands were not empty. Their swords shone and sang where the sunlight fell on them, that high, inhumanly joyous keen of metal that will never know rust. The riders had spears like tongues of fire, and sickles like sharpened moons, and bows of glass which fired arrows that did not miss. The grey things went down like lumps of stone when the weapons struck them, and lay like stone, and didn't move again. The only screams left were those of the drows, now; everything mortal was hiding, or standing very still, hoping against hope it wouldn't be noticed by the terrible beauty raging down through the main street of Bray.

The riders swept down the street to where Nita and Ronan and Kit stood, backs against the wall next to the pub by the arcade; and swept on past them, toward the Dargle, driving a crowd of the drows before them. A Garda sergeant in his blue shirtsleeves stood astounded on the corner and watched them pass, too dumbfounded to do anything at the moment but cross himself; and several of the riders bowed to him as they passed, and smiled as they did it.

One of the riders turned aside from the bright tide, and paused by them, looking down at Nita. He said, "Are you repaid, then?"

Nita looked up at him, the crimson and emerald and golden splendor of his clothing, the impossible handsomeness of his face, and she felt dingy and shopworn by comparison. Her heart ached in her with pity for the wretched ordinariness of life, seen next to this awful, assured beauty. But she said, "Yes, thank you. Thank you very much."

"I would have saved the favor, myself," said the black-haired rider, "for you'll need it more later. But what's done, is done. And now get up and ride, for the Queen desires to speak with you."

Ronan put his eyebrows up at that. "Which queen?"

"Not any mortal one," said the young rider on the horse, looking at him with mild amusement. "The Queen whom it is unwise to refuse . . . as it is unwise to refuse her Fool."

"The *Amadaun!*" Ronan said, his eyes going wide. "Do what he says," he said to Nita. And she caught a flash of unnerved thought from him: *he can kill with a look or a touch, this one, if offended—*

"No problem with that," Nita said, at the moment having no time for Ronan's nervousness. "But one thing first." She looked around her in distress: the cars stopped or crashed in the street, the shattered glass, the stunned townspeople standing around. She beckoned Kit and Ronan off to one side a little, and said, "We can't leave the place this way. Little hiccups in daily reality, people can deal with— but this? They'll never be able to explain it to themselves—"

"Or their insurance companies," Kit muttered.

Nita shook her head. "They'll lose their grip—"

Ronan looked at them curiously. "What are you thinking of doing?"

Kit looked thoughtfully at Nita. "Patch it?"

Nita nodded. Ronan stared at her. " 'Patch it'? Patch *what?* With what?"

Nita bit her lip. "Time," she said. "With a spare piece. It's basic alternate-universe theory, you must know about this. Somewhere parallel to our universe, where this happened, there has to be one where this *didn't* . . . where the drows never popped out, where this damage wasn't done. You patch this timeline with an equivalent piece of that one." She looked around her, considering. "The area and the timespan's small enough not to have to get an authorization, the way you'd have to for a full timeslide. And the reason's good, which is the whole point."

"But the overlays—"

"Ronan," Kit said, holding his voice very steady in a way Nita knew he was fighting not to lose his temper, "we can't sit around debating this all day. A few minutes more, and what's happened will have printed itself too strongly on these people's minds to be patched over. We'll be careful of the overlays. You in, or what?"

125

Ronan looked from him to Nita. She shrugged, nodded.

"All right—"

"Here it is," Kit said, riffling through his manual. "We're inside the time limit, we can do the short form. Ronan?"

"No," Ronan said, looking slightly off to one side like someone having an idea, "I see it. You start."

Kit and Nita started reading together: Ronan joined them. It was a little odd to hear the Speech for the first time in an Irish accent, but Nita didn't let that distract her, concentrating instead on the part of the spell that located and verified the piece of alternate spacetime they needed, "copied" it into the spell buffer prepared for it, and held it ready. Then the second part of the spell, which bilocated the copied spacetime with the one presently proceeding locally.

Kit looked up after a moment, breathing hard. Everything around them suddenly looked a little peculiar, as if every object had two sets of outlines, which were vibrating, jarring against one another. "Come on," he said to Nita and Ronan, "let's get out of here and drop it in place."

"How are we going?" Nita said, glancing up at the *Amadaun*.

There were abruptly three more horses beside him; bridled and saddled, ready to go. "Can you ride?"

"I can be carried," Nita said, utterly unhappy about the idea.

"Up, then."

Kit helped her up. "Where is the Queen?" she said to the *Amadaun*. "Did she come out with you?"

"She did not: she goes not foraying any more," the *Amadaun* said. "Though because of you, that may change."

Nita thought about that one for a minute. Ronan meanwhile swung up in his saddle with perfect ease, gathered up the reins and sat there like a lord. Kit clambered up into his saddle, clutching the pommel of it.

"Don't fear," the *Amadaun* said. "You won't fall."

Nita desperately hoped that was true. "Okay," she said to Kit. "As soon as we're clear, let it drop."

The *Amadaun* turned his mount and led them at a walk up Herbert Road. By the entrance to the church parking lot there Kit paused, looked over his shoulder, said one word. Looking back toward the main street with Ronan, Nita saw the outlines of everything tremble, then suddenly solidify. With that, the glitter of broken glass in the road was gone, and a sudden confused silence fell over the shouting that had started in the street.

126

"Good," Kit said. "It took, nice and solid. Let's go."

And they rode. Nita knew these horses from old stories, but she still was not prepared for how fast they went. One moment she was trying to find a way to sit so that she wouldn't slip sideways: the next, she was galloping. Though it physically felt as if she was trapped in a dream sequence in a movie, the horse moving in slow motion, everything else blurred past her with such speed that she could hardly tell which way they were going. Apparently the Good People's horses didn't care about roads; rough or smooth was all one to them, for they ran "sideways," across water, or fetlock-deep through a hillside in their path. The country around them appeared as it had—how many hundreds of years ago?—before there were roads, or people, or anything else to trouble the serenity of the world. It was an Ireland of apple trees in flower, of long hillsides green with flowery meadows, deep forests, thickets of hazel and rowan. They rode westward out of Bray, and made for Sugarloaf.

In the sideways world it was no mountain, but a city that stood up huge and golden there, the towers lancing up as Nita had seen them from a distance that afternoon, back in Kilquade. The rider alongside them looked at Nita, and at the view ahead, and smiled slightly. "It is the chief of our *dúns* in these parts," he said. "And the fairest. Other mountains are higher, but none was so well shaped, we thought."

"I saw."

"So you did. You have the gift; it comes of the blood, I suppose." The Fool looked at her. "Not a safe gift, though."

"Neither is wizardry," Nita said.

The Fool nodded. "As you will no doubt keep discovering, before the end. No matter. We're here."

They dismounted before the great gates. The horses tossed their heads, somehow losing their saddles and tack at the same time, and wandered off into the surrounding meadows. "Come then," said the Fool. "The Queen holds summer court."

They did not go though the gates. The Fool led them instead a short distance around the high shining walls, to where an open pavilion of white silk was pitched in the meadow. Inside it was a simple chair, and several young women standing around it; in the chair sat another woman, who watched them come.

The Fool led them just inside the pavilion, before the lady in the chair. Afterwards Nita had some trouble remembering her face; what chiefly struck her was the woman's hair, masses of it, a beautiful mellow gold like the wheat ripening in Aunt Annie's third field over. The thick braids of it that hung down reached almost to the ground; the rest was coiled up, braided and wound around her head, the only crown she wore. She was dressed all in a white silk much finer than that of the pavilion, and she held something wrapped in more silk in her lap.

"The greeting of gods and man to you, wizards," she said.

They all bowed. "And to you, madam," Ronan said, "our greeting and the One's."

She bowed her head in return. "I may not keep you long here," she said; "you are on errantry, and we respect that. But word has come to us of what the wizards are doing. We know a little of *draoiceacht* ourselves, and we have something here that may be of use to you."

She turned her attention to the bundle in her lap. "Madam," Kit said, "may I ask a question?"

She looked up, and her eyes glinted a little with merriment. "Could I stop you?"

"Who are you, please?"

She sat back in the chair at that. "Bold one," she said. "But the stranger in the gate has a right to ask. I am one who 'died into the hills.' " Ronan turned his face away. "Feel no shame," she said. "The name is long given to us by humans, and we are used to it. The first of us who lived here after the Making, and could not bear to leave, slipped sideways here, by what art you know; it is part of wizardry. We took ourselves to live outside of the world's time, and exiled ourselves as a result; we cannot go back except for a little while, every now and then. A night of moon to dance in; a morning, or an afternoon, on each of the four great turning-days of the year, when the hills stand open, and there is easy commerce between this world and yours. We are near one of those days now, which is why you can be here at all."

She turned back a bit of the silk of the wrapped thing in her lap, toying with it. "Now and then, the desire for the physical world becomes too much for us, and one or another of us crosses back into it—to live the lives of human beings, in a world where things are definite and deadly, and what one does matters forever. We age swiftly when we do that, and our passions rule us; we do terrible deeds sometimes, forgetting the calm of the slower-running time outside the world. I have been back several times, and returned here after each visit, which makes me unusual . . . for many of us have

128

gone over to try death, and have not come back from it. —Your world would know me by several names. I was called Aoife, and Fand, and Macha, and other names besides: but most important at the moment, I was called Emer, the wife of Cuchullain mac Sualtim, who was Hero of Ulster. And that is how I come by this."

She looked down at the bundle in her lap, and slowly unfolded the wrappings around it. "After Cuchullain died," she said, "I gave it to Conall of the Hundred Battles. It passed from him, eventually; he could not bear the spirit that was in the thing. It was in pain, because there was no hand mighty enough to wield it any more, and no mind that understood its power. Our wise folk thought at last that it ought to be brought out of the world, and 'into the hills,' to spare its pain. And so it was. See—"

She slipped the silk aside, and held up what had been in it. It was a sword. There were no jewels on it; the hilt was plain gold, riveted with silver, and the blade was a long graceful willow-leaf curve of mirror-polished steel, about two and a half feet long, coming to a "waist" about a foot above the hilt, then flaring slightly outward again. There was a wavy pattern in its steel, but more than that, the blade itself seemed to it waver slightly in the vision, as if seen through a heat-haze. Even in this golden light, with the summer of the Otherworld all around them, the Queen looked pale and plain as she held it up; the sword made whatever one looked at with it seem less than real, as the *Sidhe* had done in Bray.

"*Cruaidin Cailidcheann,* he called it; the Hard, Hard-Headed. But it had another name, first. Cuchullain's true father was not Sualtim, but Lugh of the Long Reach; and this is Fragarach, the Answerer, the Sword of Air, which Lugh sent to him. Take it."

Nita put her hand out to it, and felt a cold fire burning, and a pressure of wind forcing her hand away. "It doesn't want me," she said.

"No. It has its own desires, and I can only hold it because I am one of the Undying. One of you," she said to Kit and Ronan.

Ronan put a hand out, and then snatched it back, and scowled. "It doesn't want me either."

"You then," she said to Kit. "Take it, young wizard: and give it to the Senior, with my blessing. He will be the one to wield it, I think. Say also to him," she said, turning to Ronan, "that I ask him again the question I have asked him before; and ask whether he has any new answer for me."

"I will," Ronan said, but his eyes slid sideways to Fragarach.

Kit bowed slightly. "And I'll deliver this." He took the sword, and apparently had no trouble with it.

"Go, then. The *Amadaun* will see you home. And have a care; for the One-Eyed is very strong. He is not as strong as he was once . . . but neither are the Treasures." The Queen's green eyes were troubled. "Nonetheless, they may serve. They must serve."

They nodded.

"Go now."

The horses were brought for them, and they rode back to Nita's aunt's. The dual carriageway wasn't there, but they could recognize the Glen of the Downs as the Good People's horses left it swiftly behind them. The sea glinted before them with colors they had never seen before, under the Otherworld's sun, as they rode down the hill toward Kilquade; then the new colors faded, and there was nothing shining on the sea but mundane sunlight. The road faded into visibility around them at the end of Aunt Annie's driveway.

"Go well," said the *Amadaun* as they dismounted, and their three horses faded away. "We can do no more for you. One treasure from the land itself; one from the hand of the People; one from humankind. The fourth must come from elsewhere: from one of the Powers, or not at all."

"You say you're a Fool," Nita said. "Are you making a joke?"

"Always. But the jokes are always true. Beware," he said. "And the One go with you."

He faded away as well. They turned and headed down the driveway, Kit carrying the sword across his hands and looking extremely nervous.

"You said things around here are *getting* weird?" he said to Nita.

She sighed. "Don't ask me for hints that they might get *less* weird," she said. "My money says things get worse yet."

Cheárta na Chill Pheadair
Kilpedder Forge

There it lay in the middle of the kitchen table, along with old Lotto tickets and a tea-stained copy of the *Wicklow People*, on top of the placemats, next to a plastic cookie tray with nothing but crumbs left in it, and the milk jar and sugar bowl; Fragarach the Answerer, shining under the light that hung down from the ceiling. They sat around it, nursing their tea, and looking at it. It was hard to look at anything else. The cats sat up on the kitchen counter, the way they did when waiting to be fed, and stared at it too, big-eyed.

"And that was it," Kit said to Nita's aunt. "They said we would have to come up with the fourth one ourselves, somehow."

"Did they give you any hints?" Aunt Annie said.

Nita shook her head. "Unless you caught something that I didn't, Ronan. I can't always understand the way people talk around here."

Ronan shook his head. "I heard what you heard, more's the pity. I was hoping they might come up with the Spear, too."

"You and me both," said Aunt Annie. She stretched, and slumped in her chair. Nita noticed how tired she looked, and felt sorry for her.

"Did you do the warding you were going to do?" she said.

Her aunt nodded. "The back office is ready for the Cup," she said. "Johnny went to help Doris with it; apparently it's more alive than they had expected, and it was causing them trouble. They should be here in a while. Anyway, when you're in the back of the house, watch out for the office door. I had to draw the spell pattern partway up the inside of it to miss the rug in there, and if you open the door, it'll break the circuit. Just reach in through the door if you need something."

They nodded. "Aunt Annie," Nita said, "I was going to ask you. Where does Biddy the farrier live?"

She tried to make it sound nonchalant, and had no idea whether she had succeeded. Her aunt looked at her a little curiously. "Just up the road in Kilpedder," she said. "Next to the shop across the dual carriageway. She has her regular forge there. Why?"

Nita tried not to squirm. "I had a couple of questions I wanted to ask her," she said.

"About her forge," Kit said. "It's really neat . . . I hadn't seen a portable one like that before."

"Oh. Well, it's getting close to teatime: you should be able to find her up there in a while—her work rarely keeps her out much later than this."

Nita became aware of a low buzzing, and looked around her. "Is that the oven timer?" she said.

Aunt Annie looked bemused. "No, the oven's not on."

They looked at each other as the buzzing got louder. Some of the spoons on the table began to vibrate gently, moving along the table a little.

"Look at the sword!" Kit said. "It's vibrating."

It was. The low humming sound that Nita had mistaken for the oven timer was coming from it, and it was getting louder. "It sounds a little like feedback," she said.

A faint beep-beep sound came from outside. The sword's hum got louder, and (Nita thought) more threatening. "Ohmigosh," her aunt said, "it's Doris and Johnny, and they've got the Cup!"

"Neat!" Kit said, and got up. "Let's go see!"

"No!" Aunt Annie said, sounding panic-stricken. "We don't have the place prepared to have *two* of the Treasures here at once! Put two of these things together without adequate preparation, and you're going to get something that makes atomic critical mass look like a wet firecracker!" She looked around hurriedly. "Crikey, I can't leave now! Kit, quick, take it and get out of here!"

He picked it up, rather nervously. It jumped and jittered in his hands, and the hum started to scale up into a howl. "Where?!"

"Anywhere! Somewhere far! More than fifty miles. I'll cover you for the overlays, just *go!*"

He looked at Nita. "Copernicus," he said, and said three words, and vanished.

The air went *whoomf* into where he had been: not the usual explosion. Nita smiled slightly, considering that Kit had been as impressed by Johnny's expertise as she had.

Outside, car doors slammed. "Here, let me get that for you, Doris," Johnny's voice said.

They all went to the door. Johnny was pulling the glass sliding

132

door aside. Behind him came Doris Smyth, holding something wrapped in a pastel-striped pillowcase. The something shone through the pillowcase as if it were on fire: a still, cool, changeless fire that nonetheless rippled and wavered on everything it touched, like the sun looked at from underwater. "Back office, Anne?" said Doris's voice, sounding strained but cheerful.

"Right. Don't open the door, just walk through it."

"Certainly. Johnny, you handle that; I have my hands full."

There was no room for them all, down that narrow hall. Nita and Ronan stood there and watched as the three older wizards walked down past the bookshelves and turned the corner, out of view. Except that they weren't entirely out of view at all; they were faintly visible in the reflected light from the Cup, even through the intervening walls. Nita shook her head.

"Don't do things like this at home, do you?" Ronan said.

She grinned at him and headed back into the kitchen. "Neither do you, buster. Not as a rule, anyway."

She went to fill the kettle for the next inevitable round of tea. "Where's Copernicus?" Ronan said.

"On the Moon. Southern hemisphere."

"The Moon?!"

Nita shrugged. "She said more than fifty miles. That should be enough." Then she looked at Ronan's face as she plugged the kettle in. "Haven't you been there?"

"To the Moon? No!"

"Why not? It's neat." He opened his mouth, and Nita suddenly felt annoyed at herself. "The overlays, I guess. I'm sorry. Look, there have to be some places you can teleport from safely. If you can find one, and hop over and see us, we'll run the wizardry through for you, and show you around. It's no big deal."

"I'd like that," he said, and smiled slightly. It was a look Nita hadn't seen on him often; the chip off the shoulder for the moment, and just a touch of wistfulness. "It must be grand," he said, "being where you don't have to be afraid to do all the wizardries you know can be done."

She laughed a little, and leaned against the counter, waiting for the kettle to boil. "It has its downside—you wouldn't believe the trouble you can get into. Remind me to tell you about the shark who almost ate me. . . ."

"Want a look?" Aunt Annie said, coming back into the kitchen, with Johnny and Doris behind her.

133

"Yeah!" Nita said. She headed down the hall, with Ronan behind her.

There was no need to do anything special. Walls meant nothing to the light of the Chalice—or rather the light of what was inside it. The Chalice sat on its pillowcase, with the gold inlay on the outside of the bowl, and in the spirals and curves that ran down its stem and massive foot, all burning as if molten and ready to flow off the chalice at a moment's notice. The burning came from the blue-white light filling the Chalice's foot-and-a-half-wide bowl, a light that was liquid, and still trembling slightly from having been moved. It shone through the metal as if it were glass, and through everything else it touched. Nita looked at her hands, and saw through them as if they were a sketch held up to sunlight; an incomplete and smudgy sketch, possibly in need of revision.

She looked at Ronan, and away again, shaking her head. Words seemed inadequate, and out of place. But at the same time she couldn't help noticing his expression, like that of someone struggling with a memory: and oddly, not trying to remember, but to forget—

Maybe he felt her eyes on him: he turned his gaze away from the Cup, and looked at her with a troubled expression. "Let's get together some time soon," he said. "I need to talk."

Nita suddenly found herself afraid to find out what he wanted to talk about. She nodded, and went away hurriedly, back down to the kitchen.

The three older wizards were sitting around the kitchen table, waiting for the teapot to finish brewing. "There's a message for you from the Queen," she said. Johnny looked at her questioningly, and Nita repeated the message.

He smiled very slightly, and it was a sad look. "She's asking," Johnny said, "whether there's any hope that the world they have chosen to live in will ever come any closer to Timeheart. They love Ireland, make no mistake; but at the same time, they're of the Powers, and they long for Timeheart, where they were created. But the legends say they must stay in the world they have chosen until the One's Champion comes back with his spear, and they lose the world of their desire." He shook his head. "A while yet, I think. . . ."

"Do you want Kit back?" Nita said.

He passed a hand over his forehead, smoothing his hair back. "Where is he?"

"The Moon."

"That's all right, then. Wait a few minutes before you bring him

134

back here. I can add a limiter to the binding on the Cup that'll make it at least safe for the Sword to be here with it. But the Sword will need its own binding."

Doris poured the tea out. "That's one less problem," she said. "Now if we just knew what to do about the Spear, we'd be fairly ready."

There was silence around the table at that, and some hopeless looks. "You couldn't find anything that would work?" Nita said, as Ronan came in and sat down again.

"My dear," said Doris, "we have the original Stone awake again, and what seems to be the original Sword. The Cup has ensouled very emphatically indeed. We dare not try to conjoin an inferior or weak Spear to them. They would blast it out of existence. The resouled Spear must be at least as strong as they—preferably much stronger. But we have no proper envelope. It's not strictly a change that a physicist would understand, but matter is not quite the robust stuff it was at the beginning of the world, when Creation as an art was young, and the energies of it dwelt new and hot in the nucleus of every atom. As gravity and other forces have declined over many millions of years, so has the basic—'selfness'—of matter. You see how the resouled Treasures make everything around them look insubstantial and unreal. The souls in them are reminding the matter they embody how matter was then. It was much closer to being alive."

"But then the Spear's soul will remind the matter it's in. Won't it?"

"Not if the matter is simply unable to hold the soul long enough in one place for the change to take," Johnny said. "It'd be like trying to hold a burning coal in a Kleenex. The Spear's soul is the fiercest of them all. I had hoped I was wrong about this, but the research I've been doing over the past couple days indicates that no spear on Earth would be strong enough now to contain the soul for long enough to do the trick: whether it had contained it before or not."

"Off the Earth, then," Nita said.

Johnny cocked his head. "It's a thought that occurred to me. But the changes in matter that have happened here have happened everywhere else, too. And we keep coming back to the problem," and he smoothed his hair back again, "that we don't have much time."

Ronan sighed and sat back. "It's a pity we can't just make a new one," he said.

Aunt Annie sighed too. "Even if we had uncontaminated matter

135

from the beginning of time," she said, "we wouldn't have the expertise to do anything with it. I think we're just going to have to keep looking for some other kind of answer." She glanced over at Johnny and Doris. They nodded.

Nita got up. "I'll go get Kit," she said. "Fifteen or twenty minutes be long enough?"

"Fine."

She looked at her aunt. She nodded. "The overlay buffer is still in place. Go ahead."

Nita said the transport spell quickly in her head, considering how much air she would need, doubling it as usual, and arranging the spell intake so that it would take the air from outside the house rather than inside—the memory of the last time she had done such a spell in her own house, without stopping to consider that her father's desk was covered with paperwork, was still much with her. She vanished.

She found Kit sitting on his favorite rock—a pumice boulder on which he had been using a sharp piece of granite to whittle the boulder into the crude likeness of a human face, for the bemusement of future lunar photographic surveys. The Sword was laid across his lap.

She climbed up beside him. "Johnny said he should be ready for you to come back in a little while."

"I don't want to go right back there," Kit said, turning the Sword over in his lap and looking at it. "Someone I want to have a talk with first."

"Biddy," Nita said.

Kit nodded. "Remember what the fox said to you," he said.

"Listen," Nita said. "You remember how you told me that you felt her forge was alive?" He nodded. Nita started to tell him what Doris had said about the relative "liveness" of matter at the beginning of time.

He stopped her. "It's OK, I heard it. I used your ears."

She punched him. "Illegal brain-tapping! You didn't even ask me! What if you had overheard something I was thinking?"

"What, about Ronan?"

She blushed hot and punched him again, much harder, so that in the low gravity he fell sideways off the boulder and bounced a couple of times in the moondust. "Great," he said, as he got up and dusted himself off. "This stuff is all down my shirt. Now I'm going to itch all night."

136

"Serves you right. Eavesdropper!"

"Still," he said, and looked thoughtful. "He's sharp, your buddy Ronan. Why *shouldn't* they make another one?"

"Because they don't know how. Whaddaya mean, 'my buddy?'" She started heading around the rock to punch him again, far gone in embarrassment.

"Hmm," Kit said. "Neets, forget it, I'll lay off."

"Promises, promises."

"Look, let's go see Biddy."

"What are we going to say to her?!"

He shook his head. " 'Come out with your hands up?' I don't know. But if one of Them is here, They need to be giving us a hand. Do you know where we're going?"

"Yeah. I'll pass you the coordinates."

Nita pictured the place in her head—she had seen it often enough when riding past it on the farm's bike—and translated the image quickly into coordinates that could be plugged into a transport spell. "Got it," Kit said. "Just change that bit there. Got it? Go."

They made the jump. Air slid out and away from them, and they were standing not far from the far side of the dual carriageway, near the pub that stood there. It was getting dark.

"Over here," Nita said, and led the way over to the right, where a small group of whitewashed buildings stood near the Kilpedder shop. There was a low iron gate at the entrance to them, covered with ornate and graceful wrought-iron work; and a hanging sign on a nearby wall said B. O DALAIGH, I.F.A.

Carefully and quietly Nita unlatched the gate and swung it inward. There were no lights showing in any of the buildings, though Biddy's truck was parked in front of one of them.

"Maybe she went out," Nita said.

Kit shook his head and went slowly to the truck, and put one hand up against the forge-box at the back. "Feel this," he said.

Nita laid her hand against it, and snatched it back with the shock. Life, for a wizard, is something that can be felt like the warmth from a radiator. This was not just a warmth, but a burning—and totally unlike the kind of low-level awareness that "inanimate" objects normally manifested.

"I can't believe you didn't feel it the first time," Kit said.

"Different specialties, different sensitivities," said Nita. "Besides, I never touched it. But look at that."

She nodded at Fragarach. The dusk was falling all around them, but it had no power over the Sword; Fragarach shone as if it lay out in full sunlight, though the waning Moon was high and the bats were out.

"It knows," Kit said. " 'Uncontaminated matter from the time of Creation,' did they say?" He chuckled. "Let's see if we can find her."

He went off around one of the outbuildings. Nita leaned against the forge, and breathed out.

"Looking for somebody?" Biddy said from the shadows.

Nita jumped, then laughed a little nervously. *Get a grip on yourself,* she thought. *Now what was the wording?* She didn't move; just watched Biddy head over toward her. "Elder sister," Nita said, "in the One's name, honor and greeting."

"Now what do you mean by—" She stopped, as Kit came around the corner, with the Sword in his hand. It had been bright enough. Now, in her immediate presence, it blazed.

Biddy looked at it, and her face altered. Recognition, and affection, and surprise, all appeared in it. "Now I thought that had been put away somewhere safe," she said in her soft drawl.

"It was," Nita said. "But nothing much is going to be safe any more, unless it gets used."

"It knows you," Kit said. "I can feel that. It just about shouts that it knows you." There was an odd exultation in his face; Nita felt inclined to keep her distance for the moment. "And it knows your forge, there. I think maybe you made this." He hefted the Sword, but there was something in the gesture that also looked as if the Sword had moved itself, a small leap of excitement. "Or someone using the metal that's been built into that forge made this. Probably both."

Biddy looked at them thoughtfully, and leaned against the wall, folding her arms.

"Cutlery isn't usually my stock in trade," Biddy said. "Pretty, though."

"Oh, come *on,*" Kit said. And Nita added, "I wish you'd ditch the accent. It's really bad."

"What?" Biddy said.

Nita had to laugh. "I'm sorry. It's probably good enough to fool the people around here, but it wouldn't fool a real American for very long. The morning after I met you, I was wondering why you sounded so weird. Now I know." She laughed again. "You may be one of the Powers that Be, but you're no more perfect than we are. Especially not at sounding like you've lived somewhere you've never been!"

138

Biddy looked faintly shocked. Then she leaned back again, and she too laughed a little, and fell silent afterwards, looking at the Sword.

"Well?" Kit said.

"Well," said Biddy. "May I see it, then?"

Kit went to her and handed her the Sword hilt-first. She took it, and held it up to examine it, laying it for a moment across the flat of her forearm. "Not much changed," she said. "Though it's more tired than I remember."

"You can do something about that," Nita said.

Biddy glanced over at her with a humorous look. "You have a lot of confidence in my abilities," she said.

"You'd better believe we do," Kit said. "We've worked with the Powers before."

"Not all of us are of equal ability," Biddy said. "And spending time in a physical body tends to affect one's ability to do one's job."

"The last Power we worked with took on the Lone One after spending ten years in the shape of a macaw, sitting on a perch and eating sunflower seeds," Kit said dryly, "so I wouldn't sell yourself short, if I were you."

Biddy sighed and looked at the Sword. "How long have you been here?" Nita said.

"Since the beginning," Biddy said. She turned the Sword over again and looked at Fragarach's flat, as if searching for flaws. "I never left. Couldn't bear to."

Nita boosted herself up onto the fence rail. "You were one of the ones who made Ireland, then."

Biddy nodded, turning Fragarach over again. "The first of the blow-ins," she said, and smiled slightly. "Here." She handed Fragarach back to Kit.

"The stories say that the *Tuatha de Danaan* came bringing the Treasures from the Four Cities," Kit said. "Those are just parts of Timeheart, aren't they. And you were one of the ones who made the Treasures in the first place."

"I was the Smith of Falias," said Biddy, "among others. I made Fragarach . . . yes."

"And then the stories tell about Govan, the Smith of the Gods, who came to Lugh the Ildánach," Nita said, "and how they went away together and took the Spear of Victory, Luin, and forged it full of fire and a fierce spirit—"

She looked at Nita and nodded slowly. "That was me as well."

"You could do that again," Kit said.

139

Biddy frowned. "I doubt it," she said. "The worlds aren't what they used to be, and neither is matter."

"Your anvil is," Kit said.

"That can't be used as anything but an anvil," Biddy said. "Its nature is set, from time's beginning almost."

"But if you could get some more of that old 'original' matter—you could do it. You could make another Spear!"

"What do you take me for?!" Biddy said, laughing hopelessly. "You really didn't understand me. When you live in the physical world, you have to do it in a physical body. Those are the rules. And if you're going to spend as long in a mortal form as I have, you give up a lot of your power by necessity. It would burn the body out, otherwise, and the brain; physicality just isn't robust enough to bear our state of being for very long. The memories all ebb away after a while. And why shouldn't they? I did my work well—too well." She laughed, with some bitterness in the sound. "I fell in love with what I made, and couldn't leave it. You're quite right that we're not perfect, especially that way. Once I had finished my part in making this place, I didn't want anything more but to be here in peace, forever. The One released me to do that—just to be here, and be useful in my small way, until I'm required to give my power back at the end of things. I do my forgework, and live in the place I love."

"Then make yourself useful," Kit said, sounding grim. "Otherwise 'this place you love' is going to be nothing but a big pile of cinders, after Balor gets through with it."

Biddy was shaking her head. "This is one use I can't be. I haven't the power to pull matter here from the heart of time, or its beginning either! And wizards or not, not even the Seniors have that kind of power!"

"I know someone who does," Nita said, "at the moment, anyway." Kit glanced at her, uncomprehending for a moment—then got it, and his eyes glittered. "Never mind that now. The memories may ebb—but you can't have forgotten how you made that."

Biddy's eyes lingered on Fragarach. "No," she said. "That I remember very well."

"And the Spear," Kit said.

"I remember some of the details," Biddy said softly. "But I had that other Power to help me, the one they called Lugh the All-Crafted."

"I can't get you someone who knows how to do everything," Nita

140

said, grinning, "but I can sure get you someone who *thinks* she does. Second best, maybe. But take it or leave it."

Biddy stood there, her eyes downcast, irresolute. "Come on," Nita said. "We could require it of you, in the One's name. Once a Power, always a Power, regardless of how much or little of it you have left. Those are the rules, as you say. But—" She broke off.

Nita and Kit stood quiet. Biddy stared at the ground.

She looked up, then. "It's better than doing nothing, I suppose. Tell me what you want of me."

"Come have some tea at my aunt's," Nita said.

Kit groaned.

Some hours later almost all the free chairs in Aunt Annie's kitchen were full of wizards, all talking hard. Most of them there knew Biddy, and there had been some shock at Nita's announcement of who else she was besides the local farrier, but Fragarach's response to Biddy couldn't be explained in any other way. Shock had been quickly put aside in favor of plan-making.

"It was Ronan's idea," Nita said, and Ronan blushed right out to his ears. "We can make another. We can!"

"I'll entertain explanations of how," Johnny said, sitting back and stroking his mustache. "Don't tell me you're thinking of pinching some ur-matter from Timeheart, either, because it won't work. Matter there is structured differently from the way matter was at the beginning of Time in this universe."

"Timeslide, then," Kit said.

Johnny shook his head. "We would need a wizard with enough power to drive that kind of a slide back far enough. You're talking billions of years."

Kit bent over to Nita and said, "Should I?"

"I think you'd better," Nita said, and sighed. It had been so quiet until now, relatively speaking. "It's after dinnertime. See if you can do it without raising the alarm, if you know what I mean."

Kit nodded and went out. "It might help," Aunt Annie said to Johnny, "if we understood a little more about exactly what kind of matter's needed."

"Well, you've got a bard around here somewhere, haven't you?" he said. "Let's hear the authorized version first, and then Biddy can give us what she remembers of the technicalities, so that we can work on the spelling proper."

"Hmm," Aunt Annie said. She went to the door. "Tualha! Kitty kitty kitty! Tuna!"

The kitchen immediately began to fill with meowing cats. "Do you really think this will work, Shaun?" Doris said.

He stretched, then shrugged. "It's our best chance, I think, considering that no envelope presently extant seems to be suitable. It seems as if the Spear's soul burns out its containers the way—well." He looked at Biddy, then away.

The kitty door flapped as Tualha scrambled in through it. She stood there, very small and black, with her small tail pointing straight up in the air, and said, "Mew."

Nita burst out laughing. "Cut us some slack, Tualha. It's the Senior for Europe, and he wants your advice."

"Oh, well, that's different," Tualha said. She looked up at Aunt Annie and said, "First things first. What about that tuna?"

"There was a time," Johnny said, "when bards performed first, and *then* the lord of the hall gave them largesse."

Tualha looked disdainfully at him. "Tuna," she said to Nita's aunt. "And then cream, please."

Annie's aunt raised her eyebrows, and went to get it. It was astounding how fast such a small kitten could eat, especially in contrast to all the other cats, who had to be fed too so that they wouldn't steal Tualha's food. Eventually she was lifted up on the table and given her saucer of cream there, and she lapped it with a thoughtful air, burping occasionally, while the human wizards sat around and nursed their tea.

"Now then," Johnny said.

Tualha sat down and began washing her face. "What do you want to know?" she said.

"Tell us if you would, oh bard, the forging of the Spear Luin."

Tualha began washing behind one ear. "The Spear of Victory itself came from the city Finias; Arias the poet-smith made it there. The song says that Arias took a star and hammered it on the anvil, and so made the blade of the spear. Then the *Tuatha de Danaan* brought it with them through the air and the high air when they came to Ireland. And with them it stayed, and gave light to any place it was in, for the burning that was in it."

Tualha stopped, yawned, and then started in on the other ear. "Then came Balor, and made a tower of glass for himself and his creatures in the sea near Ireland. Balor's likeness was that of a human, but gross and misformed, and one eye squinted away almost to nothing for the hugeness and horribleness of the other. So great was it that it took four Fomori with forks of iron to pull the eyelid up when Balor wanted it so. And when it opened, what its glance fell on scorched and burned and was poisoned, and blasted off the world and out of it."

Glances were exchanged around the table. "It was foretold by other wizards," said Tualha, "that only fire and the spirit of fire would end Balor, and that one would come who had all skills, and was kin to Balor, and would make that end of him. So the *Tuatha* waited, looking for that one to come."

"Another of the Powers," Aunt Annie said, "by the sound of it. And a fairly central one, if Balor is another version of the Lone Power."

Johnny nodded. Tualha had tucked herself down into meat-loaf shape. "Nuada the King did not know who that one might be," she said, "so he gathered to him all the great Powers that were in Ireland in those days: Diancecht the physician, and Badb the lady of battles, and the Morrigan, the Great Queen; he gathered in Govan the Smith, and Luchtar the Builder, and Brigit whose name meant the Fiery Arrow, who was healer and smith and poet all together; and cupbearers and druid-wizards and craftsmen of all kinds. And one day they were feasting when a young man came to the door of their great rath and asked to come in. The doorman asked what skill he had. He said he was a warrior, and a harper, and a storyteller too, and a champion in the fight, and a smith, and a cupbearer and a doctor and a wizard and a poet. And when the Powers heard that, They said, "This must be the All-Skilled, our deliverer. Let him in so that we can test his power." They did that, and the young man could do everything he said he could: and the Ildanach, the all-crafted, is what they nicknamed him. Then they started their plan to drive out Balor and the threat of his Eye, and his creatures the Fomori from Ireland forever."

Tualha looked thoughtfully at the saucer, then at Aunt Annie. Aunt Annie poured her some more cream. "Thirsty work," Tualha said, and had a brief drink. "Then," she said, licking cream off her whiskers, "Lugh went off in private for a long time with Govan the Smith; they took counsel and made a plan, and Lugh had the Spear of Victory brought to him. In secret Lugh and Govan labored for three years, or some say seven, forging the Spear anew. Unquenchable fire they forged into it, and a fierce spirit—" Tualha yawned, and crouched down in meat-loaf shape again. "Then when they were done Lugh returned to the great rath of the *Tuatha de Danaan* with the Spear, just in time to meet a party of the Fomori that had been sent there by Balor to demand a tribute of slaves from the *Tuatha*. He unwrapped the Spear and called on the *Tuatha* to cover their eyes, and the Spear roared with rage, and blasted the Fomori to ash on the instant, all but one that he sent back to Balor to tell what had happened, and bring the message of Lugh's defiance to him." Tualha rolled over on her side, and yawned again, blinking at them. "Then the war starts. Did you want anything else?"

"No, that'll do for now. Thank you."

Something went POW! out in the front yard. All heads turned at that, and there were some concerned expressions; but a moment later they heard the front door slide open, and Kit walked in.

"Noisy, that," Johnny said. "You weren't so loud when you left."

"Not my fault," Kit said, jerking his thumb over his shoulder.

Behind him, Nita's sister Dairine walked into the kitchen: eleven years old, small, skinny and bright-eyed, with a shock of red hair, wearing shorts and sneakers and a Batman T-shirt three sizes too large for her: one of Nita's, actually. Nita started to fume slightly— Dairine had started "borrowing" her clothes lately, and returning them in less than pristine condition—but there were more important things to be concerned about at the moment; she kept her annoyance to herself. Dairine glanced around the kitchen with interest, then said, "Hi, Neets. Hi, Aunt Annie!" And she put down the portable computer she was carrying, and went and gave her aunt a hug.

Johnny and Doris and Biddy and Ronan all watched this with some bemusement. "My sister," Nita said to Johnny. "Dairine."

Johnny blinked. "*This* is the Dairine Callahan who—" He paused, then, and laughed at himself. "It would be, wouldn't it. The youngest ones are always the strongest, after all. They're just getting a lot younger these days. . . ."

Another chair was pulled in from the living room while introductions were made. Nita had to smile as she watched the portable computer unlean itself from against the table leg, flop down flat on the floor, grow short spidery legs, and wander over to the cat food dish where Bronski was still eating. Bronski hissed at the computer, hit it hard with one paw, and when that didn't do any good, went out the cat door in a hurry.

Nita looked over at Kit, and said, "Any problems?"

"Nothing significant," he said. "She'd had her lunch, so we have a few hours."

144

"You brief her?"

"I know what you're trying to do, more or less," Dairine said, reaching out to take a cookie from the fresh packet their aunt had brought out. "Mmm." She chewed for a few seconds, then said, "It's all been updating itself in the precís in my manual for the past few days." She nodded over at the computer, which was still examining the cat food dish with interest.

"The language is interesting," Johnny said, leaning back in his chair. " 'Took a star and hammered it on the anvil—' "

"When I was in Timeheart, I used meteoric iron," Biddy said quietly. "There seemed to be a certain . . . appropriateness to it."

"There's plenty of that around," Kit said. "Not all in museums, either."

"But not ur-matter," Doris said. "You would need meteoric iron from around the time of the birth of the Universe."

Dairine shook her head. "It wouldn't be meteoric," she said. "That early in the physical universe, there weren't any planetary bodies to shatter and turn into meteors, yet; not even in the oldest galaxies." She looked at Nita for confirmation: Nita nodded. "You're going to have to get real starsteel."

The older wizards looked at her. "From the nucleus of a *star*?" Johnny said.

Dairine looked at him with interest. "Plenty of iron inside stars, especially the type A's and F's."

Biddy stared at Dairine. "You're suggesting that someone should put one end of a timeslide into the center of a star light-years away and millions of years back in time, and fasten the other end *here*? And then do what?"

"Forge what comes out at this end," Dairine said. "That's your department, though. You did that—" She glanced over into the next room, where Fragarach lay on a sideboard, with several layers of spell-warding glowing around it to keep its power from combining disastrously with that of the Cup in the back office. "The techniques shouldn't be so different."

"You really think you can do this?" Doris said to Dairine.

"You mean, can I get you what you need?" Dairine said. She sat back in her chair and let her eyes drop closed a little, and then began to speak in the Speech. It was not exactly a spell, but the schematic for one, the outline, with certain key words and phrases left out so that nothing untoward would start to happen just yet. Nita lost the thread of it after about a minute: she had never heard any spell so

145

complex in her life, and several parts of it that she *did* understand, the power control parameters and the description of the matter that would be conducted down the timeslide, along with several Names to be invoked, all rattled her badly. Nita knew that her sister had, in some ways, *become* the Manual since her own Ordeal; and by way of semi-parenthood, Dairine had the power of a whole race of sentient computer wizards to draw on. But Nita had not had those facts brought home to her quite so definitely as they were being brought home now. She shivered; it was a little like being big sister to a nuclear explosion that could pick its own time to go off, and was thinking of doing it soon.

Dairine stopped and opened her eyes again. "That's the procedure," she said. "It won't be easy, but at least it's not too complicated. When do you want to do it?"

Doris was shaking her head. " 'Forged fire into it,' " she said. "That spell would certainly produce *that* result. Shaun?"

Johnny was looking very thoughtful. "If the other end of the slide were to slip out of place in either location or time," he said to Dairine, "it could annihilate the Earth. You realize that, of course."

Dairine shrugged. "At the rate things are going, people might be thankful for something like that shortly. If I were you, I'd take the chance you've got. I can do this now, but whether I'll have the power next week, or next month, is a good guess. If the world still *exists* next week or next month."

There was a silence. "Well, Shaun?" Doris said. "You're the Senior."

He sat and stared into his teacup, and then said, "I guess we haven't any choice. Tomorrow night, then? At Matrix. Assuming the other Planetaries concur."

Doris nodded, and Ronan, and Nita's aunt. "Will the Treasures be all right here tonight, Johnny?" Aunt Annie said.

"I should think so. Let's meet at Matrix around eight-thirty: that'll give us plenty of time to get ready. This ought to be done at about sunset, so that the Spear knows what it's for."

Everyone nodded and pushed their chairs back. Nita looked over at Dairine. "You came a long way for just this," she said.

Dairine stretched and grinned. "Worth it to see the expression on your face when I outlined that spell. What a look! I thought you were gonna—"

"Never mind," Nita said. Becoming a wizard had mostly changed her sister for the better, but it also seemed to have increased some of

Dairine's more annoying traits, like the bragging and teasing. "Listen, runt," she said, "I missed you too. How are Mom and Dad?"

Dairine shrugged. "Mom keeps going on about 'her baby.' Dad looks depressed all the time. They're fine." Then she chuckled. "They'll never try a stunt like *this* on you again."

"Oh?"

"Uh huh. I heard them arguing about it the other day. Went on for about an hour, and finally Mom said, 'If she wants to be a wizard, fine, let her. Better to have a daughter who's a wizard, than not have a daughter.'"

"Aw *right*," Nita said softly. "When can I—" She was about to say *go home,* except that it occurred to her that she didn't want to go home right this minute. *Not until after the business with the Spear was settled, anyway. And besides, I'm on assignment. . . . I'd have to see it through anyway.* "Never mind," she said again. "Did you tell them where you were going?"

"What, and get them all crazed again? No way. Mom hasn't figured out a way to get any promises out of *me* yet, and that's the way it's going to stay. For the time being, anyhow. What time is it at home when it's eight-thirty in the evening here?"

"Three-thirty in the afternoon."

"No sweat," Dairine said. "I don't have to be home for dinner until seven our time. Yes, I know where we're going: it's in the Manual. See you tomorrow. Bye, Kit. Spot, heel!"

The computer scuttled over to her; cats hissed and bristled at it as it went by. Dairine vanished, and not one of the various papers on the table moved.

"Hey, pretty slick," Kit said.

Nita laughed to herself for a second. "Look," she said, "you'd better get back too. Your folks are going to start wondering."

"Let 'em wonder," Kit said. But he started heading for the door. Nita followed and said, "Make sure you get your sleep."

Kit laughed too, a rueful noise. Excitement sometimes made it hard for him to sleep the night before a big wizardry, and Nita was used to teasing him about the circles under his eyes. "I'll try," he said. "Take it easy, huh?"

"Yeah."

Kit vanished too; Johnny and Doris and Ronan headed out past Nita to Johnny's car, saying their goodnights as they went. As Ronan passed her, he said, "That was your sister?"

"Uh huh."

147

"You poor thing," said Ronan.

Nita nodded in complete agreement. "She has her uses, though," she said. "Hang loose."

Ronan chuckled and went out.

Nita went back into the kitchen, where she found her aunt staring moodily at a sink full of teacups. "They breed," she said, "I swear they do."

Nita laughed and reached up to the shelf that held the dishwashing liquid.

148

Caslean na mBronn/Caher Matrices
Castle Matrix

Sleep refused to come easily to her that night. Finally Nita got up about midnight and struggled back into her clothes, thinking that she would go and see whether there was anything worth looking at on TV, even some boring movie on satellite, or the twenty-four hour news channel.

She never made it past the back yard. It was a clear night, where the last few had been misty: and the Milky Way hung there overhead, nothing subtle about it for once, the Galaxy seen edge-on and for once looking it, ridiculously bright. Nita climbed up on the fence between the yard and the riding ring, and just sat there and stared at it for a long time. Only a month or so ago now she had been out that way, among thousands of alien creatures: and she still felt stranger here than she had there. . . .

The crunch of the gravel down the drive got her attention. Nita held very still and listened. Nita waited, suddenly finding herself getting very tense. Who knew what kind of people went sneaking around farms when everyone was in bed—

She knew, though. The tension got worse . . . not to say that it was entirely unpleasant.

By the time the dark shape turned the corner of the house and paused, looking around it, Nita's sight was so night-acclimated that he might as well have been spotlit. And there were other indications, to another wizard anyway. Very quietly she said, *"Dai."*

He said nothing for the moment, just came over to where she sat on the fence. His head was on a level with hers; very faintly, the starlight caught in Ronan's eyes. *"Dai,"* he said. It came out as more of a growl.

She laughed at him, very softly so as not to attract any attention in the house. "You sound angry all the time," she said, "you know that? Doesn't it run you down?"

He turned away from her a moment, leaning against the fence next to her and looking up at the sky. "I couldn't sleep," he said.

Nita grunted softly and looked up herself. "And you walked all the way up here from Bray? I'm glad I didn't bother going in to look at the TV. There must *really* be nothing on."

This time she actually felt him getting angry, sensed it rising off him like steam off a hard-ridden horse. "Look," she whispered as he opened his mouth, "just spare me, okay? *Everything* somebody says to you, you find a reason to get pissed off about it. It's a wonder anyone even talks to you any more. Except you're so—" Words jostled in her head: she shut up. *Cute. Sensitive. Helpless*—

He opened his mouth again, shut it, and then opened it again and started to laugh, almost soundlessly. "Yeah. I guess. I've always been this way. But lately it's been getting worse. Like whatever causes it is getting closer."

And Ronan looked at her sidewise—a sort of wry expression, clearly visible even in this dimness. "Funny. I thought you were pretty different when I met you first—"

"And now you think I'm pretty normal?" Nita said. "Thanks loads."

"No," Ronan said, sounding annoyed. "I think you're more different than anybody around here. Especially the other girls." He sounded less annoyed. "A lot of them talk tough all the time, but if you push them, they give. You, though, you don't talk tough—mostly. When you do, you're scary—" He shrugged. "And as for pushing— you just fall all over whoever does it, like a brick wall."

Nita flushed hot at this, not sure what to make of it. "Well, you're sure different from everyone else *I* know," she said, and then shut her mouth again lest the confusion inside should start finding its way out and make her look like a total dork.

But Ronan just laughed again. "You think loud, too," he said.

The last blush was nothing to this one, but Nita fought it down, starting to get annoyed herself. That broke off, though, when she saw the way he was looking at her. For once, there was no anger about it. Bizarrely, the look made her start to shake a little. Then it occurred to her that there was nothing bizarre about it, for it was not her own physical excitement she was feeling. She knew what *that* felt like—

There was nothing in the Manual about this. *Or is there?* Nita thought. *Have I ever looked? It's not as if the subject has ever come up, working with Kit*—

—and abruptly she knew, or started to know, rather more about it.

Nita sat there in the starlight and swallowed, getting her first taste of what it was like for a native wizard to experience "the Knowledge," the direct input from the wizardly "database" which was the way Irish wizards experienced the information. *Would it keep getting this way for me if I stayed here longer?* she wondered. But that was hardly important just now: there was other information to consider. Of course wizards got physical with each other sometimes, just the same as other human beings did. But they experienced it somewhat differently. It had to do with the Speech, which had physical components as well as verbal and mental ones—and when two people expert in the Speech were attracted, they were likely to overhear one another's bodies as well as their minds—

Nita broke out in a sweat. *Not mine,* she thought, fascinated. She looked at Ronan, and for a long few moments her thoughts chased themselves unintelligibly through her head. Only one finally made itself plain:

Well, heck, I guess you have to start somewhere. And I do like him—otherwise I wouldn't even be thinking *about this—*

Ronan looked away. And Nita said, "You're not going to get any pushing out of me on this one." She was still shaking, but it was her own nervousness this time.

She just sat there and waited.

He leaned back on the fence. His face was quite close to hers: she caught the starlight in his eyes one more time before he bent in to kiss her.

She spent the first two seconds trying to figure out what to do with her nose. After that Nita was simply lost in sensation: the kiss itself, and what underlay it, the rush and pour of thought and emotion that was both of their minds getting tangled together. She was nervous about it at first, but after a moment it seemed completely natural, that odd fresh scent of his mind—green, she thought, of course, and was tempted to laugh; and behind it, another sensation, something faint but familiar, she couldn't place it—

The kiss broke. She blinked at him. Her heart was racing.

The second kiss went on for a lot longer. This time they touched. This time, as the sweetness built in her body, Nita went shouldering through that welcoming greenness in mind, touching it, warm, but curiously hunting that sense of something else. And there in the dark was some of that anger, quite a bit of it actually, fretting, churning against itself; there was something down in the warm dark here, an irritant, a scent or color that she knew, that made Ronan keep lashing out at everything: some kind of energy looking to be properly expressed. Not mere rage, but a righteous anger, turning on itself, without an outlet, impotent at the moment, straining to get out and be put to right purpose. Nita blinked in the middle of the kiss. A flash of scarlet, an impression of something swift and fierce and tempery, and utterly good—

Her eyes flew open with shock as she recognized the mind-sense of what was struggling down inside of Ronan. *"Peach!"* she whispered. But that had been only one of that creature's names. It had many others. Without her being able to prevent it, she felt Ronan's thought follow hers, down to the image of how she had seen Peach last—moulted out of its old body, now superb, immortal, unconquerable, one of the Powers that Be, the one with many names, the One's Champion—

"No," Ronan gasped. "Feck *no!!*"

And he was gone now, running, the sound of his going frantic on the gravel. Fading now. Gone. Nita sat there on the fence, shaking, half in tears, half too amazed to cry.

The night fell silent again around her.

She went back to bed again, but once more it was a long time before she could sleep. . . .

The next evening she and her aunt and Kit got in the car together at about eight. The shadows were just getting long: sunset was not until nine-thirty that night, and it wouldn't be completely dark until maybe eleven.

Castle Matrix was eastward from Greystones and Kilquade, in the mountains beyond Sugarloaf. They drove down many small narrow roads, which got smaller and narrower and bumpier all the way, until finally they came to a driveway with two huge trees at the end of it, each one beginning to be covered with a great mass of red berries.

"Rowan," Nita's her aunt said.

"I know," Nita said. "I have a friend at home who's a rowan tree."

Her aunt chuckled. "It's still so funny to hear things like that come out of one of my relatives. . . ." she said.

"There it is," said Kit. They turned out of the driveway into an open graveled area. Off to one side of it, Castle Matrix rose. The main part of it was a plain square tower, about a hundred and twenty feet tall and fifty feet on a side, of light gray granite. To Nita's intense delight, it actually had battlements on top. There were narrow arrow-slit windows here and there up and down the face of the tower, and a huge iron-bound oaken door at the bottom. Off to one side, the castle had been added to; there was an additional wing about fifty feet high, with diamond-paned windows. A low fieldstone wall ran around the graveled area. She wandered over to peer into it after they got out of the car. Biddy's truck was parked by that wall, and the forge was missing from the back of it.

The oak door swung open for them. There was Johnny in his leisure suit, looking very ordinary except for what he held in one hand. It was a rod that burned with light. Nita recognized a tool she had used once before herself, a rowan wand that had spent time out in moonlight: a potent weapon for a lower-level wizard, though she couldn't imagine what Johnny needed one for. "Come on in," he said.

Nita and Kit went in behind her aunt, looking around in curiosity. About six feet inside the door was a long, heavy wine-colored brocade curtain. "Drafts," Johnny said, pushing it aside; "you wouldn't believe the drafts we get in here in winter."

They passed through it and looked around, and up, and up. This was the castle's main hall, about fifty feet across; it had whitewashed walls, black and white tiled floors, and big handsome polished wooden tables. Immediately to their left was a huge fireplace with a strange sort of grate that seemed to be designed to hold the fire's coals up vertically rather than horizontally; a big iron spit and a crank to turn it stood in front, and there were smaller fireplaces, grills actually, on either side of the main grate. Tall arched windows, about five feet wide, were let into the west and south walls. The wooden tables had been pulled off to the sides of the big room, and in the middle of the floor, where all the tiles were dark, a most elaborate spell diagram was in the process of being laid out in white. Nita sniffed, and from her art classes identified the sweetish smell of water-based acrylic paint.

"Doesn't scuff off in the middle of a spell," Johnny said, picking up a brush. "Anyway. Welcome to Matrix."

"Have you always lived here?" Kit said, looking around in admiration. "Did you inherit it?"

"Oh, no," Johnny said. "I found this place in ruins. A big tree growing through what was left of the roof, right about here—" He pointed to the center of the room, where the spell diagram was. "We had it removed when we started to renovate the place, my wife and I. She's in London at the moment with our son. But the Normans built the place, originally, some time in the eleven hundreds, when they were trying to subdue Ireland." He chuckled and looked down at his work. "They fell in love with it and got 'more Irish than the Irish,' as the saying goes."

"Seems to be a lot of that going around," Kit said.

Johnny nodded. "They built this place on the site of an old holy well . . . it's still here. But there's more than that. Matrix had been a center for a lot of kinds of faith, or power, over the year. The Mother Goddesses were honored here first . . . that's where its first name came from. Matrix means 'womb,' but the older form was probably 'matricis'—the Castle of the Mothers. Then for a while I think the well was sacred to Brigit, the old fire-goddess; and later to Saint Brigid, the Mary of the Gael as they called her. Other mysteries were here later. There was some connection with the Knights Templars; some of them said this was one of the Grail Castles. But all those came later. We have older business tonight. . . ."

"Are you about ready?" Aunt Annie said.

"Just about. Waiting on Biddy and Dairine. Ronan's in the back with Doris, making tea."

"Where else," Kit muttered.

"Give it time, you'll get used to it," Nita said. She wandered over to the diagram that Johnny was working on, noticing the elegance and cleanliness of it. Half the figures in the Speech that she was used to tracing out laboriously and in whole, here were only hinted at; a single graceful stroke "holding the place" for a figure or diagram much more complex. *I guess when you're Senior for half a continent, though, you get enough practice to be able to do that* . . . It was a big five-noded diagram, with a separate circle for each of the Treasures—each written around with the reinforcing and warding spells that each specific Treasure would need—and a fourth empty circle for the starsteel that would become the Spear. That fourth circle was particularly densely written-in, and Nita could understand why. The spell there was for the magnetic bottle that would be needed to confine the starsteel and cool it down until it was safe to work; for in its native condition inside the star it would not be solid metal, or even molten, but iron plasma at something more than 7000 degrees Kelvin. If there was any specific part of the spell diagram Nita would have been interested in double-checking, that was it. But again the shorthand that Johnny was using was a little beyond her. . . .

Nita stopped then, suddenly, and looked down as Johnny finished one character and touched it with the rowan rod. The acrylic flared briefly bright, then died down again.

154

Nita stared at the floor. "Something wrong?" Johnny said.

"There's something down there."

She was aware of Kit looking at her uncomprehendingly from off to one side, where he had been examining a set of old pikes mounted against the wall. "Yes, there is," Johnny said. "I didn't expect you to feel it, but then a lot of wizards older and more experienced than you don't. There's a power in the earth here; not the earth itself, though. The water table runs fairly high here, and this castle's element is water. No surprise, since the place is more or less haunted by the 'female principle.' You saw the little stream that runs down by the forge, out by where you parked? We'll be doing work down there later."

Nita stood there just feeling it—a long, slow swelling, biding its time, caring nothing for the flash and dazzle and busyness of life, but only for slow nourishment, things growing, things prospering, birth, being. She glanced up at Johnny and said, "This is the only place where we could do what we have to, isn't it."

"To keep fire from getting out of hand," he said, "water, always. One way or another, we have plenty of it here."

Doris came in, followed by Ronan with the tea-tray. He put it down on one of the tables and joined Nita and Kit as they looked at the diagram. Johnny finished one last figure, then stood up. "Tidy enough?" he said. "I miss anything?"

Nita shook her head in complete helpless ignorance. Kit said, "Don't look at me," and moved off to pour himself a cup of tea. Doris came to stand by Johnny and look the diagram over.

"All names seem to be in place," she said. Her gaze dwelt particularly on one spot, which Nita had noticed earlier and not known what to make of. While the rest of the spell was written in shorthand, the names of the participants were all written out in full, as was vitally necessary. Your name in the Speech was meant to describe you completely, and to work with a shortened version of your name was to dangerously shortchange yourself of your own potential power. The name written in the spot Nita was examining, though, was not the complex, fussy thing that most human names were. It was simple, just six curves and a stroke. Names that short tended to be like short words in the dictionary—the shorter they were, the more meanings they tended to have—and mortals did not have names like *that* one, all power and age. But then again, one of them spelling tonight was not mortal. *Still—there's something odd about it. The usual 'continuation' curve is cut off awful short—*

155

"Hi, y'all," said Dairine as she swung in through the brocade curtain. "What's shakin'? All set? Oh," she said, stopping at the edge of the diagram and taking a long look at it.

"Does it meet with your approval?" Johnny said.

"Looks fine to me. Yo, Spot!" she called, looking over her shoulder. The laptop computer came scuttling in and sat itself down under a table.

"You picked out a star yet?" Nita said to Dairine, as her sister paused beside her.

Dairine shook her head. "Can't predict the positions that accurately from this end," she said. "We're just going to have to wait until the timeslide's fastened, and then have a look around and pick one that looks good."

"Just make sure you pick a star that's not scheduled to have inhabited planets later," Kit said from the other side of the spell diagram.

Dairine looked at him with mild amusement. "Kit, from that end of time, it's already happened. There never was a star to have planets."

"You hope," Kit said. "If it didn't work, back then, then the star's either still just fine, or it's long since gone nova from its core being tampered with . . . and we're all going to be so much plasma in about fifteen minutes."

Dairine grinned at him. "Adds spice to life, doesn't it? Don't worry, Kit. I'm here."

Kit looked at Nita with an expression that was eloquent of what he thought that was worth. Nita shrugged at him. *She is pretty hot stuff at the moment,* she said privately.

If she screws this up, we all will be, Kit replied. *Oh well . . . we've been in worse spots.*

That was true enough. Nita had never had a Senior spelling with her, let alone the Senior for a whole continent. In the past it would have lent her a lot of peace of mind. At the moment, though, it didn't seem to be helping much.

Pre-spell nerves, Kit said. *Me too.*

It was small consolation. Nita sat down for a moment, watching Johnny go over the last few details of the spell diagram with the rowan wand to activate and check the separate character groups. The curtain to the kitchen wing stirred, and Biddy came in slowly, carrying what looked like a long, wide bar of metal.

She placed the object inside the node of the spell diagram that was meant to contain the iron plasma, and then stood up, massaging her back. It was a bar of metal all right, about six inches thick and six inches wide, and about two feet long. The bar had a long deep groove about three inches by three, right down the length of it, to within about an inch of either end.

"There," she said to Johnny. "That's the casting mold I use for fireplace tools. The best I could come up with."

Dairine wandered over and looked at it. "How much does it hold?" she said. "Molten metal, I mean."

"About twenty pounds."

"I mean in volume."

Biddy looked surprised. "I don't usually think of it in those terms. —About a liter, I'd say."

"Hmm." Dairine looked at the mold, then glanced at the laptop computer. It got up from under the table, came over and looked at the mold itself; then it and Dairine seemed to exchange glances, though how it did that with no eyes was a good question.

"Yeah," she said to it. To Biddy she said, "What's the melting temperature of the mold? I don't want to mess it up."

"It's case-hardened," she said. "About 800 Fahrenheit."

"Okay." Dairine looked thoughtful. "You want some carbon in with the iron?"

"About one and a half percent."

"Gotcha." Dairine looked at the computer for a moment; it made a soft disk-drive thinking noise, which amused Nita, since she could see that its drives were both empty. "Okay," Dairine said to Johnny. "I'm ready when you are."

He took one last long look at the spell diagram as he stepped into the middle of it. "I know that in group spellings people usually divide the work up evenly among them," he said, "but if it's all right with you all, I'd sooner handle everything but the actual timeslide, and leave that part of things to Dairine. The Treasures themselves are going to need watching to make sure that they don't interfere, and I would prefer that each of you in the active diagram concentrate on that. Does that seem appropriate to you?"

Everyone nodded, or muttered agreement.

"All right, let's get to it. Doris, the Cup—"

"Right," she said, and went into the kitchen. A moment later, light swelled behind the brocade curtain, and she elbowed it aside and carried the Ardagh Chalice in. The whole thing blazed, and the knotwork designs running around its bowl and foot were so bright that to Nita's dazzled eyes they looked as if they were moving. Doris

157

carefully bent down to place the Cup in the center of the circle waiting for it. It burned even brighter, and the light-liquid inside it moved gently and threw ripples of brightness on the high ceiling.

"Water knows its own," Johnny said. "Doris, keep an eye on it. If any of these things is likely to get out of hand here, it's the Cup."

"Oh, I'll mind it all right, don't you worry about that."

"We needn't do anything about the Stone," Johnny said, glancing at the empty circle next to that of the Cup: "we couldn't be much more in contact with the earth if we tried, and it's here already. Kit—"

Kit brought in Fragarach and laid it carefully in the circle waiting for it. Its light was burning low, but a breath of wind stirred the door-curtains and the banners hanging from the ceiling as he put it in place.

"Air is ready," Johnny said. "One element only remaining, and that's the one we need. Ready, Dairine?"

She stepped into the circle for Fire, next to the steel mold, and said, "Let's do it."

Johnny put his hands behind his back, bent over a little the way someone might bend over to read a newspaper lying on the ground, and began to speak, reading the spell from the diagram. Things had seemed quiet before—here, far from any town or road, close to sunset, that was hardly surprising—but the silence that shut down around them now, and into which the Speech began to fall, was more than natural. Nita felt the hair standing up all over her, the old familiar excitement and nervousness of the start of a spell combining with the effect of the wizardry itself on the space and matter within its range of influence. Under the silence Nita could hear or sense a constant slow rush and flow of water—or the essence of it—welling up and sinking away again, taking all dangerous influences away with it.

That was something of a problem, of course, for that same flow was likely to perceive the building energies of the wizardry itself as a dangerous influence, and try to carry it away as well. Nita had particularly noticed the careful reinforcement that Johnny had done around the edges of the spell to prevent this. But all the same, the soft rushing sound that she more felt than heard was washing against the boundaries of the wizardry, becoming more insistent as the spell progressed, like waves pushing harder and harder against a coastline as the storm comes up behind them.

The spell was taking. It was always a sure sign when you began to

158

perceive it as a physical thing, rather than just words spoken: reality was being affected by it. Nita put up a tentative hand to the air in front of her and felt smooth cool stone, though the air was clear and empty before her, or seemed that way. The *Lia Fail* was performing its function, holding the boundaries closed against whatever forces might come loose inside them.

The darkness was slowly falling outside, but not in the hall where they stood. Fragarach and the Cup blazed, throwing long shadows back and up onto the walls from everyone who stood there; a clear, warm, pale light from the Sword, a bluer, cooler burning from the Cup. One moment the Cup was brighter, the next the Sword; Nita could hear Johnny's voice straining a little as his mind worked to keep them in balance until the symmetries of the first part of the spell were complete. There was no telling how long it would take. One moment he seemed to have been speaking forever, and the next, for only a few seconds. It was the usual confusion about time when you were in the middle of a spell. The world seemed to hold still while you redescribed it—

His voice stopped. Johnny looked over at Dairine.

She nodded, folded her arms, and began speaking. And if the hair had stood up all over Nita before, now she felt as if every hair had turned into a pin, and was sticking her. Dairine was building the timeslide, the long pipeline through spacetime that would conduct the starsteel where they needed it. It would not, of course, actually exist in space or time, but would circumvent them both; and normal matter disliked such circumventions of the rules, when you set them up, and complained bitterly during the process. Nita looked at Kit and saw him nearly in the same distress, his jaw clenched to help bear it. Ronan looked no better, and neither did any of the grown-ups. But Dairine looked completely unaffected. She paused for a moment, examined the spell diagram, and then said five words, carefully, a second or so between them. She waited again.

Abruptly there was no room. They stood, all of them, on or around a glowing webwork in the middle of nothingness. But a nothingness that was strewn with stars, cluttered with them, crowded with them. *They're too close together!* was Nita's first panicked thought. Not even in the hearts of young galaxies or new globular clusters was there stellar density like this; these stars were so close that some of their coronae were mingling. In other spots, three or four stars were pulling matter out of one another in bizarrely warped accretion disks. New stars were forming all over the place, or trying to, as they stole matter from one another, swirled, kindled as she watched. This was the view from the other end of the timeslide that Dairine had constructed.

She's crazy, Nita thought. *We're barely out of the Big Bang here—the universe can't be more than a few hundred thousand years old!!* But if Dairine heard Nita's thought, she gave no sign of it. One after another of the stars nearby seemed to veer close, then away again, as Dairine considered it, rejected it. For a few seconds the sunspotted globes of stars seemed to pour past them, twisting and skewing. Then one loomed up close, a big white star with a tinge of gold.

Dairine closed her eyes and spoke one more word.

It was as if the world had caught fire. Nita was frozen as much by her own horror as the spell itself. With the outward senses she knew that everything was fine, that the darkness of Matrix and the light of the Treasures was all around her; but her mind saw nothing but annihilation. A ravening light so desperately destructive as to make the thought of physical existence seem ridiculous in the face of it, pressure and heat beyond anything she could imagine—she saw straight into the heart of this, and could not look away. Vaguely she could feel Dairine doing something, speaking again, naming in the Speech the amount and type of matter she wanted, the form, the place of delivery—all as casually as if she was filling out an order form. She came to the end of her specifications, and was about to sign her name—

The rushing sound suddenly became deafening, and the perception of unquenchable fire was suddenly invaded by something; that cooler, bluer light, the feeling of liquid, quelling and subduing. Then, for the first time, she felt something from Dairine: panic, just barely controlled. The Cup had sensed fire, and was trying to put it out—the essence of all quenchings was trying to flow up the timeslide, into the core of a live star. The *least* that could happen was that the timeslide would be deranged, and the whole energy output of that star would backfire down it—

Two more voices were raised then, in the Speech, quite suddenly; Doris's and Aunt Annie's, and their tone was astonishing. Nita almost burst out laughing, despite her terror, as the two of them scolded one of the Elements of the Universe as if it was an unruly child. They sounded as if they intended to send it to bed without supper. Funny it might have been, but if the two of them had anything, they had certainty. The Cup struggled, the blue light washed higher—then abruptly fell away again.

Nita sagged with relief. Dairine had calmed down from her bad moment, and was completing her end of the spell. Through the blinding images still in her mind, Nita could see Dairine look carefully at the metal mold resting on the floor, then crouch down, and poke her finger most carefully at a spot in the air about a foot above it. She lowered the finger carefully to the mold, and said another word.

Fire followed her gesture. It paused in the spot where Dairine's finger had first paused, and Nita smelled ozone as the tiny spark of plasma took shape at this end of the timeslide and destroyed the air molecules in the spot where it had arrived. That one pinpoint of light drowned out even the fire of the Treasures, and threw back shadows from everyone as stark as if they had been standing on the Moon. Then it began to flow downwards in a narrow incandescent pencil-line, cooling rapidly out of the plasma state, into incandescent iron vapor and then a molten solid again, as Dairine let it pass out of the small magnetic-bottle part of the spell and down into the mold.

Slowly the mold filled, the steel of it smoking. All the air began to smell of burnt metal. Nita looked over at Dairine; she was turned into a white-and-black paper cutout by the ferocity of the light hanging a foot away from her nose, but she seemed not to be bothered by it. Nita could see her beginning to shake, though—even Dairine couldn't hold a wizardry like this in place for long. *Come on, Dari,* she thought. *Hang in there—*

The mold kept filling. Nita could feel the Cup trying to get out of hand again, and her aunt and Doris holding it quiet by sheer skill in the Speech and calculated bad temper. Dairine was wobbling where she crouched, and put one hand behind her to steady her, and sat down on the floor, but never once took her eyes off that spot in the air where the plasma was emerging—her end of the timeslide. If it moved, if it got jostled—

Come on, come on—! Nita thought. *How long can it take?! Oh please God, don't let my sister get fried! Or the rest of us,* she added hurriedly, as that possibility suddenly occurred to her. *Come on, Dari, you little monster, you can do it—!*

The light very suddenly went out, with a noise like a large short-circuit happening. Dairine fell over sideways. Everyone blinked; nothing was left but the light of the Treasures, now looking very pale to their light-traumatized eyes. One other light was left in the room, though. The steel mold was full of it; iron, still liquid and burning red, skinning over and going dark, like cooling lava. Just the sight of it unnerved Nita, and filled her with awe and delight. It somehow looked more definite and real than anything else in the area . . . anything else but Fragarach and the Cup.

Nita went over to help Dairine up. Her sister tried to stand, couldn't, sagged against Nita.

"What's this 'little monster' stuff?" she whispered. "It never even got really tough." And she passed out.

"Here," Johnny said from above Nita, and bent down to pick Dairine up. "I'll put her in on the couch. She's going to be out of it for a while. Biddy—"

Biddy was standing there looking at the mold, and shaking all over. Nita glanced at Kit, who had noticed this as well. He shook his head, said nothing.

"I think we're going to have a late night," Johnny said. "You're all welcome to stay—we've got room for you. I think we should all take a break for an hour or so. Then—we've got a Spear to forge."

He looked at Biddy. She was still trembling, as if with cold.

She looks worse than Dairine did, Kit said to Nita privately.

Nita glanced over at him. *If she pulls her bit off that well, we'll be in good shape.*

If, Kit said. *But why am I getting nervous all of a sudden?*

Nita shook her head and went off to see about a drink of something. She agreed with Kit. The problem was, wizards rarely got hunches that didn't have meaning, sooner or later.

She had a feeling it would be sooner.

Lughnasád

Nita went and had a nap immediately. What she had seen had worn her out; and she had been drawn on for general energy assistance during the spell, too, so it was only understandable that she would feel a little wiped afterwards.

When she got up, it was two in the morning. Everything was very still except for a faint clanging sound, soft and repetitive, that wouldn't go away. She had an idea what it might be.

She got up off the ancient bed in the upstairs bedroom Johnny had shown her, and wandered down into the great hall. It was empty now: the spell diagram had been carefully scraped off, and the floor scrubbed. The clanging was closer.

She went gently out the front door of the hall and stood there, in the night, listening. Far off on a hill, a sheep went "baa." There was a faint hint of light about the far northeastern horizon, an indication that the Sun was already thinking about coming up again, and would do so in a couple of hours. *If it's like this now,* Nita thought, *what must it be like around Midsummer? It must hardly even get dark at all. . . .*

The sound was coming from off to her left. She followed a little path around the edge of the castle toward where the drystone wall ran. The sound of water came chuckling softly up the riverbed beneath it, and the clanging continued, louder.

It was quite dark. She made a small wizard-light to help her go. It sprang out of the air by her, a small silver spark, and lit her way down the rough stone steps that went down toward the water.

The clanging paused, then resumed again. Ahead of her was a small, low building with a rough doorway. There was no door in it, just an opening surrounded by stones. She paused there, and looked in.

The castle's forge was larger than it seemed from outside in the dark. Biddy's steel-walled portable forge had been carried in and set

163

up on one side; her anvil stood in the middle of the floor, on a low stone table there. There was a stone trough, like a watering-trough for horses, off to one side, full of cold water that ran in and out from a channel to the river outside. Something else was there as well; the Ardagh Chalice, sitting all by itself on another stone sill to one side, shining. Its light was quiet at the moment, though it flickered ever so slightly in time with Biddy's hammer blows, when the sparks flew up.

Biddy kept hammering—not a simple single stroke, but a clang-tink, clang-tink, doubled with the rebound of the hammered ingot on the anvil; a sound like a heartbeat, but metallic. Biddy's shirtsleeves were rolled up, and her shirt was soaked with sweat, and sweat stood out on her forehead. Johnny was leaning against a wall, watching; Kit was sitting on the edge of the trough, swinging his legs. He raised his eyebrows at Nita as she came in.

"I couldn't sleep," he said. "Even after I went home. So I came back. My folks think I'm still in bed . . . it's not a problem."

"What about Dairine?"

"I saw her home. If she needs to come back tomorrow, she can."

"I don't think we'll be needing her any more at this point," said Johnny. "Also I wouldn't like to put all my eggs in one basket. Some of us might not come back from this intervention, and the newer talents like Dairine may be needed for other defenses elsewhere if we can't pull this off."

Nita came in close enough to see what Biddy was doing, while at the same time staying out of her way so as not to spoil her concentration. The bar of starsteel had been hammered out into a flat now. As she watched, Biddy paused and picked up the hot steel in her tongs, shoving it back into the furnace. She turned up the feed to the propane bottle, and the steel began to glow cherry-red, and brighter. "When are you going to do it?" she said to Johnny.

He sighed and leaned back. "I think we have to make our move tomorrow. May as well be: it's Lughnasád. A good day for it."

"But you can't have the spells ready by then," Biddy said to him. "You can't possibly—"

"They're ready enough," Johnny said. "We can't wait for the poetry of them to be perfect. It's not the old days any more, unfortunately. Brute force and the Treasures are going to have to carry the day . . . or nothing."

Biddy looked with a critical eye at the steel. It was getting crocus-yellow. She pulled it out hurriedly, put it back on the anvil and began beating it with the hammer in such a way that it folded over. Nita looked at the lines running up and down the length of the spearblank and realized that she had already done this many times. This would strengthen the metal and give it a better edge. "When does the 'forging in the fierce spirit' bit start?" Nita said.

Johnny laughed. "Oh, the re-ensoulment? As soon as Biddy's done. We can't wait any longer. Fortunately we don't have to do what the Power that worked with her the first time did, and actually call that spirit out of timelessness. It's here already, somewhere. All it needs is to be slipped into this 'body.'"

"It seems strange, sometimes," Kit said, leaning back and taking a drink out of a Coke he had with him. "The idea of weapons having souls. . . ."

"Oh, it was common in the older days. It was a rare sword that wouldn't tell you its history when you picked it up: and verbally, not just the way one would do it these days, to a wizard sensitive to such things. That may be our problem today . . . that our weapons don't nag us any more, or tell us what they think of what we're doing with them . . . just let themselves be used. But then they take their example from us. And bigger things than just people have lost their spirits, over time; planets, nations. . . ."

Nita looked at him curiously. "Nations have souls?"

"With so much life concentrated in them, how not? You must have seen how certain images, personifications, keep recurring. All our countries have their own 'hauntings,' good and bad. The bad ones get more press, unfortunately." He shifted against the stone of the wall. "But the good ones do keep resurfacing. . . ."

Nita looked at the steel, cooling now on the anvil as Biddy rested for a moment. "How much more do you need to fold it?"

Biddy shook her head. "It's had enough. There are maybe twenty thousand layers in there now, if I've done my figuring right."

"It's not the hardness of the steel itself that's going to make it useful as a weapon," Johnny said, "but you're right; something useful should be beautiful, too. . . . Let me know when you're ready."

"Not too long now," Biddy said. She put the spear-blank in the fire one last time, and turned the gas right up. The length of metal got hotter and hotter, reaching that buttercup-yellow shade again and getting brighter still. She watched the color critically. "About 700 degrees," Biddy said then. "That's all it needs. Kit, you want to move out of the way."

Kit hopped down and went sideways hurriedly as Biddy plucked the steel out of the fire and came past him. It was radiating such heat

165

that Nita could feel it clear across the room by the door. But Biddy seemed not to mind it. To Nita's surprise, Biddy headed, not to the water-trough, but straight for the Chalice.

"Straight in," Johnny said.

Nita opened her mouth to say, *You're nuts, that won't fit in there!* But Biddy, holding the length of metal by one end, eased it straight down into the water-light in the Cup—and in, and in, and in, far past the point where it should have come out the bottom of the Chalice, if the chalice had been any ordinary kind of vessel. She held the metal there. A roar and a bubbling went up, and the light of the Chalice rose and fell; but none of its contents flowed over the edge, and finally the bubbling died away, and the roaring got quiet. Biddy pulled the metal up and out of it. It was dark again, almost a dark blue on its surface.

"So how exactly are we going to do this, Shaun?" Biddy said, as she laid the metal on the anvil again, and reached for a file.

"Well. All the Dark Power's forays so far have been into our own world—twistings of our reality. We're just a beachhead, of course; it's Timeheart that's really being attacked. It's true, we have some limited successes against it here, because we're fighting on our own ground, so to speak. But we can't hope to prosper if we stay merely on the defensive. We'll take it over into the Lone One's reality, into one more central. What happens there will affect what happens here."

"And what will happen here?" Kit said.

Johnny shook his head. "There's going to be a lot more trouble, and it can't be avoided. We'll move as fast as we can, try to finish the battle fast by forcing a fight with Balor immediately. I have a few ideas about how we can do that." He laughed ruefully. "Unfortunately, the only way I can test those ideas is to try them. If they don't work—" He shrugged.

"Then we're no worse off than we were," Nita said, "because the world looks like it's going to pieces at the moment anyway."

Johnny laughed softly. "The directness of the young. But you're right." He looked over at Biddy. "Let's finish this first. We can't do anything until it's done."

She had been filing at the length of metal while they talked. The bar was now looking much more like a spearblade and less like a long flat piece of metal. The steel shone, even in that dim place where the only light was the coals in the forge and the camp-lantern

166

on the shelf, and the Cup standing nearby. It glinted the way Fragarach did—as if it lay in sunshine that the rest of them couldn't see.

Biddy kept working on it, with file and polishing wheel and cloth, and then after about twenty minutes held it up for them to see. "Sloppy but fast," she said. Nita shook her head; she didn't see anything sloppy about it. The flat of the blade gleamed, and the point of it looked deadly, a wicked needle.

"Okay," Johnny said. "Let's get it mounted. Then around dawn, we'll finish the job."

"Dawn will be fine. Then what?"

"Then this afternoon we go to war."

" 'We?' " Nita said.

"They'll be coming in this afternoon," Johnny said. "Wizards on active assignment . . . some just along for the ride, but they live here, and they feel involved. And when everybody's together, we go have us a fight."

He headed off. Biddy was still standing by the anvil, looking at the head of the spear, her expression very still. She looked up, after a little while, to gaze over at Nita.

"Do you know what I've forged here?" she said.

Nita looked at the spearhead, and found that there were two answers to that question. One of them had something to do with Ronan, and the way he had run from her after she had seen the Champion buried in him the other night. That answer was still partially obscure. But as for the other— The edge of the spearhead glinted in the low light, and Nita suddenly saw the way Johnny had written Biddy's name in the circle, and the way it had seemed to cut off short—

"Your death," Nita said: or rather the answer spoke itself.

Biddy folded her arms and leaned back against the stone wall of the forge. "I gave up making," she said after a while. "At least, the kind of making that I used to do once. Can you have any idea—" She shook her head, smiling a little: a hopeless look. "What it's like to ensoul your consciousness in a mountain range while it's still molten, and spend a century watching every crystal form?—and planning the long slides of strata, the way erosion wears at your work, even the scrape of glaciers. To *be* what you make. . . ." Biddy sighed. "And to know what it'll become. You can't do that in one of these bodies. And I said I would do so no more, and that rather than ever do so again, I would give myself back to the One—"

Nita threw a glance at Kit. She had been there: she knew the

167

sound of the kind of promise that means one thing when you make it . . . and then later you find that the meaning has changed, but you are going to be held to the promise nonetheless. *Or you hold to it.* . . .

"And now," Nita said, "you *have* made something again. And you will have to do what you said. Become part of the making, as the Powers do. . . ." But the Powers existed partly outside of time. One living *in* time, in a human body, might not find that body working too well after it came back from such an act of making. Nita shivered.

"I may not," Biddy said. But her voice was still full of doubts.

This tone of mind Nita knew as well. Her heart turned over inside her with pity and discomfort. Any advice would sound hollow to someone in Biddy's position, poised between sacrifice and refusal. But Nita thought of how it must have felt to the wizards who had advised her, at one point or another: and they never shirked reminding her of what she needed to do, though their hearts bled from it. It was the basic courtesy one wizard owed another—not to lie. How much more did a wizard owe that courtesy to one of the Powers?

"You can't very well get out of it at this point," Nita said. "Your name in the Speech is bound into the spelling we did yesterday. The name says who and what you are . . . and for how long." She swallowed. "Change the truth of that now, and the whole spell is ruined. You know that. No Spear . . . no chance of ensouling it. No chance of saving Ireland."

—not to mention the rest of the world, Nita thought. But that would hardly seem germane to Biddy at the moment. "There it is, though," Nita said. "Refuse this making and you'll be part of the destruction of your first one. . . . But you of all people should know what to do to keep this island healing, I would have thought."

Biddy looked at her and said nothing.

Nita was immediately mortified. She had completely screwed it up. "Sorry," she said, "sorry, never mind, forget I said anything—" She went out of the forge hurriedly, feeling totally hopeless and ineffective.

Kit came along after her. He said nothing to her until they were about halfway up to the house. "Sounding a little rattled back there, Neets," Kit said then. "Is there anything—"

"No," she said, and regretted it instantly. "Yes, but you can't do anything. Oh, Kit!—" *So how do I tell him about last night? About what I saw inside Ronan?* And the sight of that cool, sharp metal on the anvil had given her something else to think about. Its image resounded against the image of Ronan in her mind, leaving her with a feeling bizarrely compounded of disaster and triumph. But the resonance was incomplete. *It must be finished,* something, the Knowledge perhaps, said to her. *It has to be fully forged. Otherwise—*

Nita breathed out. "I can't," she said: and she wasn't even sure who she was saying it to, or about what, any more.

Kit punched her lightly in the arm a couple of times and said nothing.

They went back up to the quiet room together. Dawn wasn't that far away.

"It's not like the last time," Kit said, "or the time before."

The room had big overstuffed chairs in it, and a big glass case full of books. "Look at this," Kit said, reaching up for one. " '*How To Build Your Own Staircase . . .*' " He started leafing through it.

"How do you mean, not like the last time?" Nita said, getting up on the bed and leaning back against the big headboard.

"We've always been doing our stuff pretty much by ourselves," he said. "This is different. We don't have a lot of say about what's going on." Kit looked over at her. "Don't know if I like it."

Nita knew what he meant. "Maybe this is more what it's like for grownups," she said. "I guess this is what it'll be like when we're older. If we survive it."

"You think we might not?" said Kit.

"I don't know. We've been in a lot of situations we thought might kill us. Or that looked bad for part of a continent, part of an ocean . . ."

"Sometimes part of a universe."

"I know. But this time it just seems more . . . it seems bigger this time, even though it's smaller. You know what I mean?"

"It means you're away from home," Kit said. "I feel it too, a little."

Nita yawned. "But among other things," Kit added, "it means that if we get killed, it's not our fault."

"Oh, great," said Nita. "You find the strangest ways to be positive. . . ."

"The only thing I don't understand," Kit said, and then stopped. A moment later he said, "I think we're missing somebody."

"Like who?"

"I don't know. But there's something we're missing."

"Well, I hope you figure out who it is pretty quick," Nita said.
"Tomorrow . . ."

"Today," Kit said.

Nita yawned at him again.

"Neets," Kit said. "What happens if we do die?"

"We get yelled at," Nita said, and then burst out laughing at her-self. "I dunno."

"Timeheart?"

"I suppose." She shook her head. "I mean, you know it's going to happen some day . . . but I don't think I've ever thought it would happen today." She thought a moment, then said, "Well, maybe once or twice. —Why? You got a bad feeling?"

"No. That's sort of what worries me. All the times we've been in real big trouble and come through, I've had awful bad feelings. But this time, nothing." He leaned back in the big fat chair and stared at the ceiling. "I keep wondering if that means something. . . ."

Nita looked at him. "Would it be so bad?" she said. "I mean, if you know you're going to die anyway. Might as well go down fighting as die in a bed somewhere, or a car crash or something. It's more useful."

"You sound like Dairine," Kit mumbled.

"Insults," Nita said. "Not very mature of you. I do *not.*"

He fell asleep as she watched him. He had always had a gift for that, except on the night before a wizardry. He was feeling as wiped as she was, though: or else he considered himself off duty at the moment. Nita sighed, and leaned back herself. . . .

When she woke up again, it was very suddenly indeed, and with that feeling of having pins stuck into her all over. She swung herself off the bed. Kit was sitting in the chair with his mouth open; she nudged him with her foot. His eyes flew open, and she said, "Kit—"

He felt it. He spared himself just time for one long stretch, then bounced up and headed out of the room. "They're doing it—"

She followed him around the upper gallery and down a tightly-spiraling staircase in a corner tower of the castle. They came out on the bottom level, peered into the great hall, and saw nothing.

They're out in the forge, Kit said in her head. The predawn stillness was too much for even him to break. *Come on—*

They slipped out the front door: the squeak of it opening seemed as loud as a scream in that great quiet. Nothing spoke, outside, no bird sang; there was only that pale hint of light, high all around in

170

the sky, omnidirectional, bemusing—morning twilight, with thin cloud all over everything, mist clinging low, running along the ground, hanging in wisps and tatters from bushes, hovering over trees.

The top of the dry wall was just visible. Nita and Kit paused by it and looked down to the forge; there was no one there. *Out in the field,* Nita said. *That way—*

They turned and made their way through the dew-wet grass, quietly, toward the shadow that lay beneath a nearby oak tree. Ahead of them they heard voices, speaking in unison in the Speech. There was no light, there was no diagram drawn; just four people standing there at the cardinal points of a circle. Nita could just make out where the circle had been trodden down in the long grass of the pasture: a dark curve where everything else was pale with dew. Struck down into the center of the circle, on a long shaft, was the spear. The shaft was very plain: some light-colored wood— ashwood, maybe. The blade of the spear, almost three feet long, had been socketed into it and bound with more of the starsteel. Very plain, it was; there it stood, pale shaft, paler blade, with wizards around it, setting up the spell. Nita's aunt stood at one quarter of the circle, Doris Smyth at the second, Johnny at the third. The fourth was wrapped in shadow—a thin shape, wearing a long dark cloak. Only above the thrown-back hood did anything show: a faint gleam of silver hair, cropped short. Nita swallowed at the sight of it, kept quiet, watching.

The spell was about half-built, to judge by the feeling of anticipation in the air. More than anticipation—it was a sort of insistent calling. Nita's nerves were jangling at the edges with it, even though she knew perfectly well that it wasn't meant for her. Something very powerful was being called, something that lived in her in some small way, and that fragment or fraction was responding.

The long chorus in the Speech went on, the sound of the wizards' voices twining together, building, insistent, demanding that something, some great power should come here, come bind itself, come be in the world, be physical, real as this world counts reality. . . .

Nita listened to them and heard the wizardry begin to fold in on itself: the knot being tied, the insistence growing that something from outside the world, outside time, should wake up, heed the call, come here *now!* All four voices ended on that tone of command, and the silence fell; and they waited.

Everything waited.

In the East, the sky was going gold, and low clouds were beginning

171

to catch the fire of the sun that had not yet risen. The spear stood there in the cool light, still as a tree. Nita stood there watching it, holding her breath, not knowing what to expect.

Then it moved. Leaned, ever so slightly, eastward; leaned like a branch of a tree being blown that way in a wind. Leaned further. And it was beginning to make a sound as well. *No,* Nita thought then. *Not making it itself.* But the sound was certainly happening around it, a low vibration that sounded like the noise that there ought to be just before an earthquake; a low rumble in the bones and the blood. It wasn't audible by the ears. The mind heard it, though— the fabric of things, the structure of spacetime all around, rumbling, being pushed up from under, or down from above. The feeling of some immense pressure being brought to bear on this spot—

Nita looked at Kit, and with him, put her back up against the tree. The sense of pressure got stronger. And the benevolence—that was the strange part. What was coming definitely meant well . . . maybe a little too well for mortals to bear. It wanted all things healed, everything made well, no matter what pains it cost: *everything* being put right, straightened, filled—Nita held onto the tree as she felt that down-pressing force trying to tamper with her, with the cells of her body, her mind. They resisted, in their dumb way, and so did she, thinking, *Leave me the way I am! Leave me alone! I know you want— I know—*

And that was exactly it. It wasn't a pressure, it was a being; not a thing, but a person; not just a person, but a Power. Coming down, here, now, swift to answer the call, fiercer than even Nita had thought, unstoppable now that it had heard the summons—and with a frightful violent strength, because it wasn't bodied, not chained by entropy and the other forces that worked on matter, not yet.

Get in there, she thought, clinging to the tree as if she might be swept away; *get in there!* The spear trembled, the blade of it shook on its shaft, a faint creaking sound of the wood betraying the strain as the metal binding tried to break, as the power they had called tried to pour itself into this thing of wood and metal. For all the trouble that had gone into making it strong, the spear suddenly seemed to Nita to be very fragile in the face of this awful strength trying to inhabit it. The metal began to glow, the same cherry-red that Nita had seen in the furnace, getting hotter and realer-looking—more solid and concrete and real than anything in this world should look, as that power pressed down into it, making it real, making it alive, waking it up—

172

Expressions were visible now in this light, but the only one Nita could look at, though she could hardly bear to, was Biddy's. Biddy's eyes were fixed desperately on the spear, as if it were some truth she wanted to see denied; an awful look of anticipation, potentially of horror, was on her face. But there was something else there as well. Plain determination—

The metal was golden now, a hot bright gold that didn't bear looking at, and scaling up past it toward white, almost the color of the star it had come from. White now, that blinding color of plasma new-plucked from the core. But not just metal any more. Alive, awake, and aware: *looking* at Nita—

That light fell on her. She hid her eyes and buried her face against the tree. It was useless. The light struck through everything. No escaping it—it would pierce through you, shake you apart—

And then it stopped.

She rubbed her eyes. They were useless for a few moments. After-images danced in them. Nita smelled burning. Wincing, squinting, she glanced around her.

The first light of the sun was coming between two hills to the east. It fell on grass that was scorched in a great circle. She could see the little flakes of ash going up from where leaves of the tree had been burned. And in the middle of the circle, where the four wizards stood, something stood and looked back at them. It was shaped like a spear, but this fooled no one. They knew they were watched, and considered, cheerfully, gravely, by something that would kill any one, or all of them, to do its job—to find the darkness, pierce it, and be its end.

The socket and binding of the Spear had held. Only the wood of the shaft was scorched black, but it was otherwise sound. Above it, the spearhead stood plain and cool and silvery—but there was something moving in the blade. Those lines of layered metal that Biddy had hammered in, black once, now wavered and twisted: needle-thin lines of fire, white and yellow-white, swirling and writhing in the metal. The air above the Spear wrinkled and wavered the way air does above a hot pavement in the summer, and the ozone smell was thick.

"It's awake," Kit said, softly, as if afraid of being overheard. "It worked. . . !" And he looked over at Biddy just in time to see her collapse.

They hurried over to her. Nita looked helplessly at Johnny as he

173

came over, hoisted Biddy up. Her eyes were closed: her breathing was so shallow it was hardly to be seen. He shook his head.

"What's wrong with her?" Nita said.

"I'm not sure. . . . We'll take her inside and find out. Meanwhile—" He glanced over at the Spear, gleaming crimson where the early sun was catching it. "We're ready," he said. "It's Lughnasád. This evening we move."

She nodded, and looked across the field. Dark in his denims, Ronan was standing there. He had no eyes for anything but the Spear. He was wearing an expression like that of someone who finds something that's lost, something he has been wanting for a long time; something without which he's not complete. It was a frightened look, and a frightening one.

What unnerved Nita even more was the way she could feel the Spear looking back at him. It considered Ronan to be just such a lost object, recovered after a long time, that which completes.

She turned away and did her best to keep her thoughts to herself.

174

ag na Machairi Teithra
The Plains of Tethra

All that day, cars came and went at Matrix: people being dropped off, coming to stay, other people heading out to pick up more people from the train station. The house got full. All the wizards that Nita had seen in the Long Hall were there, and many she had never seen before. The gravel parking lot in front got full, and people started parking in among the sheep. Everyone had tea. Nita made it several times (as did everyone else). People went out to town for fast food and brought it back, and a lot of baking and cooking went on back in the kitchen; Doris made soda bread seven or eight times, smiling more and more as the compliments got louder. But Nita had noticed that there was a certain desperate quality to a lot of the conversations . . . the kind of talk meant to keep people from noticing that they themselves were nervous.

The nerves were not just among the less senior wizards, and there were other worries as well. Nita had watched Johnny that morning as he carried the Spear in from the field. He was wincing as he carried it. "Are you all right?" she said to him.

"Yes," he said, and put the Spear down to lean it against the doorpost—hurriedly, Nita thought, and rather gratefully. Johnny rubbed his hands together. "Well, no. It really is hard to hold for even a little while . . . it burns." He laughed. "It can hardly help it—we went to enough trouble to make it do that! But there's someone else it wants."

"We could all take turns carrying it."

"No, I think it's made its choice. He just has to stop fighting it. . . ." Johnny shook his head. "I think he will."

Nita was confused. "Is there something the matter with it, that it hurts to carry it?"

"The matter? Nothing! The matter's with us, I'm afraid. We called the Spirit of Fire, and we got it—the essence of purification, and triumph . . ." He trailed off, then said, "Patience isn't one of its

175

attributes. It sees the dross in us . . . and wants to see it burned away, and us made perfect, *now*. Not possible, of course. It's not easy, meeting one of the cardinal virtues face to face. . . ."

He picked up the Spear again and went off in a hurry.

She could feel it looking at her, though, and she understood now what Johnny had said about some weapons being able to speak. She knew what this one wanted.

She looked over her shoulder and was not even slightly surprised to find Ronan there, looking after Johnny. "Hey, Paddy," she said softly.

"Hey, Miss Yank." But there was none of the good old abrasiveness in his voice now: nothing but soft fear. He was quiet for a moment, and then said, "I hear it calling all the time now. Not just calling me, either. *Him.*"

For a moment Nita wasn't sure what Ronan meant—until the flash of scarlet, of wings or a sword that burned, flickered in her mind's eye. "Oh," she said, and laughed slightly. "Sorry. I usually think of Him as a Her—that's how we saw—"

"*Her??*" Ronan sounded outraged, as if this were one shock too many.

Nita burst out laughing: for the moment, at least, Ronan sounded normal. "Give me a break! As if the Powers care about something like gender. They change names and shapes and sexes and bodies the way we change T-shirts." She rubbed one ear. The One's Champion, in the last shape She commonly wore, had bitten Nita there several times. "Doesn't make Them any less effective on the job."

They wandered off into the field a little way, absently. Nita looked at the scorched place on the ground and veered aside from it.

"He's in there, all right," Ronan said. He sounded like a man admitting he had cancer. "I hear this other voice—not mine— He wants the Spear. It's his, from a long way back. Lugh." He coughed slightly: Nita realized then, blushing with embarrassment for him, that he was trying to control the thickening in the throat, the tears. "Why *me?*" he said softly.

"You're related," Nita said.

He stared at her.

It was true, though: the Knowledge made at least that much plain. "You've got some of His blood," she said, "from a ways back. You remember what the Queen said, about the Powers dipping in from outside of time, and getting into relationships with people here for one reason or another. So He loved somebody when He was here physically, once. Maybe even as Lugh himself. Does it matter? When He finished the other job he was on, the One set Him—or Her, whatever—another one. Busy guy. But as soon as He could, He came hunting—a suitable vessel. Like the Spear did." And Nita smiled at him slightly. "Would you rather a blow-in got the job?"

Ronan smiled, but it was a weak smile. After a moment he said, "You knew Him. What's He like?"

She shook her head, not sure how to describe anything to Ronan that that flicker of scarlet across a dark mind didn't convey in itself. "Tough," she said. "Cranky, sometimes. But kind too. Funny, some-times. Always—very fierce, very—" She fumbled for words for a moment. "Very strong, very certain. Very right—"

Ronan shook his head. "It's not right for *me*," he said. "Why don't I get any say in this?"

"But you do," Nita said.

He didn't hear her. "I don't want certainty!" Ronan said softly. "I don't want answers! I don't even know what the *questions* are yet! Don't I get *any* time to find things out for myself, before Saint bloody Michael the Archangel or whatever else He's been lately moves in upstairs in my head and starts rearranging the furniture?"

Nita shook her head. "You can throw Him out, all right," she said. "You know what it says. 'Power will not live long in the unwilling heart.' Goes for the Powers, too, I think. But first you'd better see what you've got to replace Him with that will be able to use the Spear to cope with Balor, 'cause *I* can't think of anything offhand."

"If I once let Him run me," Ronan said, bitter in this certainty at least, "He's in to stay."

Nita shook her head. She could think of nothing useful to say.

"Miss tough mouth," Ronan said softly. "Ran out of smart lines at last. Had to happen eventually."

"If the advice was any good before it ran out," Nita said, halfway between annoyance and affection, "better make the most of it."

Ronan was quiet for a breath. Then he said, "The other night—"

Nita held very still.

Ronan looked away from her, toward the castle. After a moment he headed off that way.

Nita stood and watched him go. A few moments later, Kit said from behind her, "He's in a nasty bind."

Nita nodded. "It's a real pain," she said softly. "What happens if he's right?"

"Just hope he's saved everybody in the meantime," Kit said.

They went back to being with the many new arrivals. By three o'clock, there were some three hundred wizards there; by eight there were perhaps another two hundred, from all over. "What are all those things they're carrying?" Kit said to her Aunt Annie, during one quiet moment outside.

"Johnny told everybody to come armed," her aunt said. They had, though they made a most peculiar-looking army. There were a lot of rakes and shovels. Some people actually had swords, and there were many wands and rods in evidence, of rowan and other woods; there were staves of oak and willow and beech. One wizard, for reasons Nita couldn't begin to guess, was carrying an eggbeater. Another one, the dark-haired sprightly lady that Nita had seen in the Long Hall, had a Viking axe of great beauty and age, and was stalking around looking most intent to use it on something.

" 'It is a great glory of weapons that is in it,' " said a voice down by Nita's foot, " 'borne by the fair-haired and the beautiful; all mannerly they are as young girls, but with the hearts of boon-comrades and the courage of lions; whoever has been with them and parts from them, he is nine days fretting for their company—' "

"Tualha," Nita said, bending down to pick her up, "you're really getting off on this, aren't you."

"A bard's place is in battle," Tualha said, perching on Nita's shoulder uncertainly, and digging her claws in. "And a cat-bard's doubly so, for we have an example of fortitude and of boldness and of good heart to set for the rest of you."

Kit looked at her with bemusement. "What would *you* do in a battle?" he said.

"What she's doing to me now wouldn't be bad," Nita said, gritting her teeth.

Tualha ignored her. "I would make poems and satires on the enemy," she said, "the way they would curl up and die of shame; and welts would rise up all over them if they did not die straight away, so that they would wish they were dead from that out. And those that *that* did not work on—" She flexed her claws.

"—you'd give *them* cat-scratch fever," Kit said, and laughed. "Remind me to stay on your good side."

Tualha started scrambling into Nita's backpack again. "Anne, what about this one?" someone shouted from the castle. Nita's aunt sighed and said, "I'll see you two later."

178

"Aunt Annie," Nita said, "have you seen Biddy since this morning?"

"Huh? Yes." Her aunt's face looked suddenly pinched.

"She's not any better," Nita said, her heart sinking.

"One of us who's a doctor had a look at her." Aunt Annie shook her head. "The body—well, it's comatose. No surprise. What lived in it has gone elsewhere." She sighed. "It'll wind up in the hospital in Newcastle, I would guess, and hang on a little while before giving up and dying. Bodies tend to do that. . . ."

She shook her head and went off toward the wizard who was calling her.

"Listen," Kit said, "I was supposed to tell you. Johnny wants people to start coming into the big hall," he said, "as many of us as can fit, anyhow."

Not everyone could, though they spent a while trying. Many wizards lined the gallery above, or stood and listened in the outer halls and corridors. Others hung about outside in the parking lot, eavesdropping with their wizardry. Not that the ones closest to the door couldn't hear Johnny anyway. The acoustics in the great hall were very bright, and his sharp voice echoed there as he stood in the center of the floor, his arms folded.

"We're about ready to go," Johnny said, when the assembled wizards got quiet. "I take it you're all as ready as you can be." The crowd shifted slightly. "I can't tell you a great deal about what to expect, except that we're going into what is, for us, the country of myth . . . so expect to see even more of the old stories coming true, the legends that have been invading our world over the past few weeks. They'll be real. Just don't forget," and he smiled now, "that we are the myths to them. In the plains of Tethra, *we* are what they tell stories about, around the fire at night. So don't be afraid to use your wizardry; there aren't any overlays where we're going, or none that matter to what we're doing. At some point we'll be faced by an army. I don't know what it's going to look like. We've seen all kinds of Fomori over here in the last couple of weeks. I don't know how they'll appear on their own ground, but the important thing is not to be fooled by appearances. Anything can look like anything . . . so feel for essence, and act accordingly. Don't forget that the People of the Hills, and the other nonphysicals who live over on that side, are as much oppressed by the Fomori and Balor as we have been in our world . . . maybe more so, and whether they actively come to our assistance or not, they're on our side. Be careful not to mistake them for Fomori and take them out. Don't get carried away in the excitement of things; remember your Oaths. No destruction that's not necessary."

He paused. "One last thing," Johnny said. "Most of us will never have been in an intervention this crucial, or this dangerous. The odds against us are extremely high. Some of us," and his glance swept across the group with great unease, "will not come back. It's a certainty. Please, please, *please*. . . . be careful with your choice. One thing a wizard cannot patch, as you know, is any situation in which his or her own death occurs . . . so any of you with dependents, or responsibilities which you think may supersede this one, *please* think about whether you want to cross over. We'll need guardians on this side too, to keep an eye on the worldgate in case the Fomori try to stage a breakthrough behind the main group. Bravery is valuable, but irresponsibility will doom us. Later, if not now. So *think*."

There was a great silence at this. Nita looked at Kit, and saw him swallow.

"Those of you who need to excuse yourselves, just remain here when we pass through," Johnny said. "Meanwhile, let's open the gate."

He turned to Nita's aunt. "Anne? This was always one of your specialties. You want to do the honors?" He reached over to the table and handed Nita's aunt the Sword Fragarach.

She took it. A breath of wind went through the hall; the hangings whispered and rustled among themselves. Then Aunt Annie laid the sword over her shoulder and headed up the narrow spiral stairway to the top of the castle.

The wizards in the hall began to empty out into the graveled parking lot in front. Nita and Kit went along. Nita was curious to see what would happen. Gatings were an air sorcery; the business of parting the fabric of spacetime was attached to the element of air, with all those other subtle forces that a wizard could feel but not see. She paused out there in the parking lot and craned her neck.

Against the low golden sunset light, her aunt's silhouette appeared at the top of the tower, between two of the battlements. It was incongruous; a slightly portly lady with her hair tied back, in jeans and sneakers and a baggy sweatshirt, lifting up the Sword of Lugh in her two hands. She said, just loud enough to be heard down below, "Let the way be opened."

That was all it took; no complex spelling, not tonight. The barriers between things were worn too thin already. A wind sprang up behind them; light at first, so that the trees merely rustled. Then harder, and leaves began to blow away, and the cypresses down by the water moaned and bent in the wind. Hats blew off; people's clothing tried to jump off them. Nita hugged herself; the wind was cold. Beside her, Kit zipped up his windbreaker, which was flapping around him like a flag. He stared back into the teeth of the wind. "Here it comes," he said.

Nita turned to look over her shoulder. It looked like a rainstorm coming, the way she had seen them slide along the hills here; the darker kind of light, wispy, trailing from sky to earth, sweeping down on them. Behind it, the landscape darkened, silvered, muted, as if someone had turned the brightness control down on a TV. Everything went vague and soft. The effect swept toward them rapidly, swallowing the edges of the horizon, and then passed over, roiling like a thundercloud. The wind dropped off as it passed.

Everything had gone subdued, quieted; that warm light of sunset now a dull, livid sort of light. The only bright thing to be seen was Fragarach, which had its own ideas about light and shining, and scorned to take the local conditions into account.

Aunt Annie lowered her arms, looked around her, and disappeared from the battlements. Nita glanced around and saw that everything in sight was muted down to this pallid, threatening twilight. The sunset was a shadow, fading away. Overhead was only low cloud and mist; no stars, no Moon.

"That's it," Johnny said. "Someone get the Spear. Doris, the Cup—"

"Which way do we go?" said one of the wizards.

"East, toward the sea, and the dawn. Always toward the East. Don't let yourselves get turned around."

Kit looked around. "There are a lot more trees here than there were before. . . ."

"Yeah." The only thing that was about the same was Matrix, which surprised her. She had thought it would take some other shape here, as Sugarloaf had. But it looked like itself; no change. The cars in the parking lot were gone, though, and so was the parking lot itself. There was nothing but longish grass, stretching away to a ride between the trees of the forest and out into a clearing on the far side. It was still a beautiful-looking place, but there was now a grimness about it.

The wizards began moving out. "It was a lot brighter the last time we were here," Nita said to Kit, thinking of Sugarloaf.

He nodded. "They're under attack." *So will we be,* she heard him think, but not say out loud for fear of unnerving her. Nita laughed softly; she could hardly be much more unnerved than she was at the moment.

Off to one side, Nita caught sight of Aunt Annie, carrying Fragarach. Some ways ahead of them, too, they saw Doris Smyth with the Cup, still in its pillowcase. Nita and Kit passed her, and Nita couldn't help looking at the striped pillowcase quizzically. Doris caught the look and smiled. "Can't have it getting scratched," she said. "They'd ask questions when we bring it back."

Nita laughed and turned to say something to Kit, and stopped. Ahead of them she saw Ronan, stalking along in his black jeans and boots and leathers, carrying what looked like a pole wrapped in canvas. Except that she knew perfectly well that it wasn't a pole, since she got the clear feeling that from inside the wrappings, something was looking at her hard. *I think he'll stop fighting it,* Johnny had said.

"Come on," she said to Kit.

They made their way over to Ronan. "You okay?" Nita said.

Ronan looked at her. "What a daft question. Why shouldn't I be okay?"

"The, uh—" Nita almost didn't like to say its name in front of it. "Your friend there. Don't you have trouble carrying it? Johnny was having a real hard time."

"No. Should I? Is the wrapping coming undone?"

"Oh no," Nita said. "Never mind. . . ." But she remembered what Johnny had said about burdens, and cardinal virtues. Either Ronan was just not very sensitive. . . . But no. It couldn't be that. She particularly noticed, though, a slightly glazed look in Ronan's eyes, as if he was seeing something else than the rest of them were seeing; an abstracted expression. Could the Spear make it easier for the person it wanted to carry it, by dulling or numbing their own sense of it?

Or was it something else? . . .

She shook her head, having no way to work out what was going on, and went on with Kit and all the others through the silvery twilight. It seemed to get a little less gloomy as it went on, though Nita suspected this was just because she was getting used to it. Then the darkness seemed to increase suddenly, and a shadow passed over them. Nita's head jerked up. Something big and winged went by, cawing harshly, as the wizards passed through the space between two tongues of forest.

The bird came to rest on one of the tallest of the trees, and looked down at them. The tree shuddered, and all its leaves fell off it on the spot. The crow laughed harshly. It was one of the grey-backed ones called hoodie-crows; Nita had seen her aunt shoot at them, and swear when she missed, since hoodies attacked lambs during the lambing season, killing them by pecking their eyes out and going straight through their skulls. There was muttering among the crowd as they looked at the crow.

Johnny, up near the front of the group, called, "Well, Scaldcrow? Smell a battle, do you?"

"Have I ever failed to?" said the scratchy, cawing voice; and it was a woman's voice as well, and a nasty one, rich with wicked humor over some private joke. "I see it all red; a fierce, tempestuous fight, and great are its signs; destruction of life, the shattering of shields; wetting of sword-edge, strife and slaughter, the rumbling of war-chariots! Go on then, and let there be sweet bloodshed and the clashing of arms, the sating of ravens, the feeding of crows!" And she laughed again.

"Yes, you *would* like that part," Johnny said, not sounding particularly impressed. "The rumbling of chariots, indeed! You've been picking up road-kills by the dual carriageway again, Great Queen."

"Go your ways," Doris said, beside Johnny. "There'll be a battle right enough. But we'll need you at the end, so don't go far."

The crow looked down at them, and the light of the Cup caught in her eyes. She was quiet for a moment, then laughed harshly, and vaulted up out of the tree, flapping off eastward. "I'll tell *him* you said so," she said, laughing still, and vanished into the mist.

Nita looked over at Ronan. "Now who was that?"

"It's just the Morrigan," he said.

Nita blanched. "Just!" said Kit. Apparently he had been researching matters in the Manual as well. But Ronan just shrugged again.

"Oh, she's in a lot of the old stories," he said, "the chief of the battle-goddesses; she loves to stir up troubles and wars." Nita shivered a little: she saw something more than the recitation of myth in Ronan's eyes. That dazzled look was about him again, but it was an expression of memory this time. He knew the Morrigan personally, or something looking through his eyes did . . . "But she can be good, too. She's one of the Powers that can go either way without warning."

"Well, she doesn't look real friendly at the moment," Kit said. "I'd just as soon she stayed out of this."

183

They walked on. Distances seemed oddly telescoped here. The landmarks were the same as they were in the real world, and Nita was seeing already things that had taken them half an hour to reach in the car. She was just pointing Three Rock out to Kit when they heard the first shouts of surprise from the wizards in front; and then the first wave of the Fomori hit them.

They ran out at the wizards, screaming, from the shelter of the trees. Nita and Kit, being well off to one side and their view not blocked, had a chance to look the situation over before it got totally incomprehensible. There were a lot of the same kind of drow that they had seen in Bray; some of them were riding black horselike creatures, but fanged like tigers. There were strange headless humanoid creatures with eyes in their chests, and scaly wormlike beasts that flowed along the ground but were a hundred times the size of any snake. That much Nita could make out before the front line of the Fomori smashed in among the leading wizards, and battle broke out.

The wizards counterattacked; spells were shouted, weapons alive with wizard-light struck. And the fight started to be a very uneven one, so much so that Nita was surprised by it. The drows, at least, had seemed much stronger in her own world. But here they went down fairly quickly under the onslaught of the wizards; many of those not directly attacked turned and ran away wailing into the woods, and some of those who had been resisted simply fell down dead after a simple stunning-spell or in the backlash of a stasis or rebound wizardry.

"It's just a feint," said Kit, shaking his head in disbelief. "That can't be the best they've got."

"I hope you're right," Nita muttered.

"Oh, no," Kit said softly. "Not already."

She looked where he was looking. Off to their left a young woman was lying, loose-limbed and pale, like a broken doll thrown down. There were several drows lying in pieces by her, but it was no consolation, seeing they were spattered with that shade of red so bright even in this dim light that it looked fake. Nita shuddered, for experience had shown her over time that that "fake look" was a sure sign it was the real thing.

"Two more over that way," Kit muttered. "I thought there was supposed to be safety in numbers, Neets."

She shook her head. Two other wizards had gone over to check the

184

young woman: now one of them came back to Johnny, shaking her head.

"They'll have to be left here for now," he said. "We'll see to them later . . . we can't wait. Come on."

There were a few moments of confusion while the wizards got themselves back in order. Then they headed out again.

"It's getting darker," Kit said, looking ahead. "Is that where we're supposed to be going? Downhill there?"

"I think so."

"Great," Kit said. "By the time we get down there, we won't be able to see anything."

That thought had occurred to Nita; it was getting hard enough to see their footing as it was, and since there were no roads here, this was a problem. She had made a small wizard-light to bob along in front of her, like an usher's flashlight in a movie theater, to help her see where to put her feet. Meanwhile, she might not be armed with anything concrete, but she had the spell ready that she had used on the drows in Bray. It hadn't functioned too well there, but here, to judge by the reactions of the drows to the wizardries used against them in the little skirmish just past, it would work just fine. "You got anything ready to hit things with?" Nita said to Kit.

He looked sideways at her and smiled very slightly. "Well," he said. "There's always the beam-me-up spell. If you just leave the locus specification for the far end of the spell blank—or if you specify somewhere, say, out in deep space—"

Nita shuddered. "Yecch."

Kit shrugged. "Better them than me."

The crowd was heading downhill now, on a path paralleling the way the road would have run in the real world, down onto the little twisty ridge of Kilmolin and then further down into Enniskerry village. As they came down there seemed to be some confusion among the front ranks; they were milling around, and the wizards behind were pushing up close behind them.

"Hmf," said the young wizard in the leather jacket, as they came up abreast of him. "Not the best of positions. Look at that." He pointed down the valley. "All strung out like this, if anything should come at us from the sides, it'd break us in two. No, he's doing the right thing, gathering us together. That way if anything happens—"

And then it *did* happen. The Fomori forces came down out of the trees again; they came from both sides in great crowds, hitting the group of wizards in the middle. From where Nita and Kit stood, they could see the crowd being shoved together, in danger of being pinched apart into two groups that couldn't help each other. The fighting broke out in earnest now; flashes of wizard-fire repeating back, a low sound of angry and startled cries beginning to ricochet up the valley. "Here we go," said the young wizard, and he was gone, off down into the press.

Nita looked at Kit and said, "Should we hold off—wait till it gets at us?" And then of course it *was* at them, as another attacking force hit the group up on the hill from both sides, and everything went crazy.

Nita had a great deal of difficulty remembering the fighting later. The one thing she did remember, rather to her horror, was that she enjoyed it a great deal. It helped a lot, knowing you were on the right side; though several times she wondered, as a drow or one of those black tiger-horse-looking things came at her, whether they knew that they were on the wrong side, and whether it affected them much. It didn't seem to. Everything turned into a wild confusion of waving arms and hands, shouting, being jostled and bumped. That was the worst of it, really; you could never tell what was going to bump into you, friend or enemy, and it kept you from reacting as quickly to enemies as you might—or else you accidentally hit a friend. Several times Nita was aware of not-so-accidentally elbowing other wizards, just in case they were something that was about to attack her; better to throw them a little off balance than to take the chance—and then of course you were embarrassed afterwards. She did it to Kit once, knocking him right over, and was mortified.

The other problem was the screaming. At the time it didn't bother her particularly; later on she found herself wondering whether she had been watching much too much television. Everything seemed remote, like something in the crowd scene from a movie. Nita remembered one moment with particular clarity, of seeing a drow come at her, and saying the spell that had not worked in Main Street in Bray, and seeing the spell then work entirely too well as the thing exploded in fragments and splinters of stone that bled hot, and splattered her with ichor that burnt like drops of lava. Her wizard's shield took most of it, but a few drops got through, probably because she was distracted, and burnt right through her clothes to the skin.

She wasn't able to keep track of what Kit was doing; but for those strange few minutes, she didn't really care. She had her hands full. The screaming from all sides got louder, as beasts of the Fomor kind came at wizards to savage them, sometimes missing, sometimes succeeding. That was when it began to come home to Nita that this was *not* a movie. One wizard went by her staggering and white-faced with shock and blood loss, one arm so badly torn that it seemed to be just barely hanging by a string from his shoulder. Another wizard, a young woman in jeans and a sweatshirt, hurried to help, and carried him away. It was not a movie. People were getting killed here. *And what happens then?* Nita thought, in one lull when the fighting seemed to be happening somewhere else, and she had lost sight of Kit. *What happens if you die when you're not in the real world? Where does your soul go? Does it know where to go when you die?* But it seemed unwise to push that issue too far.

After a long while, there came another lull. Nita looked down the hill and saw nothing but human wizards, milling around; there seemed to be no more drows, no more of the horse-things; just quiet. A lot of wizards, maybe ten percent of the whole group, had been hurt, and were sitting or lying down on the ground while others tended to them. She didn't feel so wonderful herself; she sat down to rest on a log under the eaves of the forest, gasping for air.

After a while, Kit found her. His clothes were spattered with burn-holes, apparently from the hot lava-blood that lived in the drows, and he was limping as he came toward her. Nita staggered to her feet at the sight of him; but he shook his head and waved at her. "No, it's okay. I just turned it."

"Well, c'mere, you can't just walk on it like that, it'll get worse. You won't be able to run anywhere if you have to."

He sat down on the log beside her. "Your specialty."

She nodded; she had always had a knack for the fixing and healing spells for either animate or inanimate objects. Spells for the living always required the wizard's own blood, but there was no shortage of that; Nita had bashed herself pretty thoroughly against one drow that had caught hold of her, getting loose. Now the memory made her shiver: but at the time it had seemed simply an annoyance, and had made her angrier. She had blown that drow up while it was still holding her—

Nita shook her head and set to work. She spent five minutes or so working on Kit's leg. It was a strained tendon, and she talked it out of the strain and gave it the equivalent of several days' rest in several minutes. The spell seemed to come harder to her than usual, though, and at the end of it Nita was panting even harder than she had been from the sheer exertion of the battle. "It's not right," she said to Kit when she got her breath back. "It shouldn't take that much energy."

Kit was looking vaguely gloomy. "I think that's the catch," he said. "Wizardry works better here, but it takes more out of us—we can do less of it." He shook his head. "We'd better get this over with fast. In a few hours we won't be worth much."

She was too nervous to sit there much longer. Nita got up and dusted herself off. "Have you seen my aunt?" she said.

"She was down in front with Johnny, last I saw her. That was before the fighting started, though."

"Tualha, you any good at finding people? There's quite a crowd down there."

"In this case it won't be hard. I should look for Fragarach's light, or the Cup's."

It was as good a hint as any. After about twenty minutes' walking they found her, and Tualha had been right; she was with Doris Smyth, and it was the blue-green fire of the Cup that gave their presence away. Doris was working with one of the more seriously wounded people. Two of the larger and more muscular wizards were easing a young woman with a torn leg down into the Cup. She seemed no smaller than she should have been, and the Cup seemed no larger; but nevertheless the woman was lost from the waist down in that cool light, and a few moments later, when the other wizards helped her to her feet again, the leg was whole.

Doris was looking wobbly. "I'll not be doing much more of this," she said to Nita's aunt. "The Cup's able enough for it, but it's just a tool; it can't work by itself without someone to tell it what to do. And nor I nor anyone else will be able to keep doing this again and again—not here. Not today." She looked over at Nita and Kit as if seeing them there for the first time, and her face was very distressed. "Away with you out of here," she said, "you shouldn't be seeing things like this at your age." And she turned her attention away to another hurt wizard who was being brought over.

Nita looked over at Kit; his expression was wry, and a little sad. He motioned Nita over to one side, where her aunt was looking nearly as pale as Doris. "You okay, Aunt Annie?" Nita said, anxious.

Her aunt nodded. "What about you?"

Nita's aunt was wearing an understandably preoccupied expression. She was looking off down the hillside, toward the place where Enniskerry would have been, and past it. "It's awfully dark down there," she said softly.

Nita looked down the slope, past where the valley fell away along either side of the thirteen-bend road. Down where Bray and Shankill should have been, there was a wall of blackness, so opaque as to seem nearly solid. It gave Nita a bad feeling just looking at it.

"Something's on the other side of that," Kit said. "And it's watching us."

Her aunt looked at Nita regretfully. "I'm beginning to wish I'd left you home."

"You couldn't have. I would have found a way to come along, and you know it."

Her aunt suddenly reached out and hugged her. "Don't do anything stupid," she said.

"Listen, I was going to ask you about that—"

"Anne," Johnny said from one side. "Can I have a word?"

Feeling slightly embarrassed, Nita brushed herself off, and was a little amused to see her aunt doing the same thing. "Look," Johnny said, "we can't have another set-to like that. Too many people got killed." It was then that Nita noticed the tears running down his face, incongruous when taken together with that his calm voice. "I think we're going to have to play our aces a little early."

Nita's aunt hefted Fragarach. Or was it the sword itself that lifted eagerly in her hand? Nita had trouble telling. "If we use them too early," her aunt said slowly, "we won't have them for later. You've seen the way wizardry is behaving here."

"That's precisely the problem. First of all, these three Treasures were never much good against Balor the last time. And secondly, if we're all killed or driven off by his creatures before we get to him— or if they delay us past the point where our wizardry, or even that of the Treasures, still works, then all of this will have been for nothing. I want you to use Fragarach on the next lot—because they're out there waiting for us, under cover of those next two patches of woodland. If we get hit again after that, Doris will use the Cup. And I can use the Stone the same way, if there's need." He paused and looked at her. "Something wrong? You look a little pale."

She shook her head. "Shaun," she said, "I just don't know if I can do this."

"Not lack of power, surely."

"Oh, no. It's just—" She held Fragarach up. "Shaun, we speak so lightly of 're-ensouling' these things. The trouble is, it *worked*. There's a soul in this, and an intelligence and a *will*—one much older and stronger than mine, one that considers me mainly a form of transportation. Once I actually start to use it—" She laughed a little. "It's a good question which is going to be the tool and which the

189

user. I don't know how much of me is going to be left afterwards; even now I can feel it pushing, pushing at my mind all the time. I don't know if you get the same sense down your rapport with the Stone—it's Earth, after all, and mostly passive. But if Air, the lightest and most malleable of the Elements, behaves this way—" She shook her head. "And what about Fire, then? I have some experience, some ability to resist. But what's going to come of that poor child? What happens when the Power that comes with the Spear puts forth Its full force—?"

She mentioned no names. Johnny shook his head. "Anne," he said, "we'd better just hope that it does; otherwise we're lost. Meanwhile, can you do your part? If not, I'll look around for someone else. But you do have the rapport."

She looked at him. "I'll manage," she said.

Johnny headed off. "Get yourselves together," he said to the wizards he passed. "We're moving out, and the Fomori are going to come after us again."

Nita's aunt went after him. Nita watched her go, and stood thinking a moment about Ronan. *He doesn't have her experience,* she thought. *But he has the power.*

Not as much, she heard Kit thinking. *Not as much as he might if he were younger . . . What's this going to do to him?*

She glanced over at Kit, unnerved. They tended not to accidentally hear each other thinking any more: but evidently this otherworld had more effects than on merely active wizardry.

And the shout went up from down the slope. Nita saw the mass of dark forms come charging down at the wizards, out of the trees again.

There were a few more moments of confusion, milling around, screams. Then Kit grabbed her arm, and pointed. Down the slope, she saw it, the upraised little line of red light that grew from a spark to a tongue of fire, and from a tongue to a lance of it that arrowed up into the threatening sky. The wind began to rise behind them, moaning softly, then louder, a chorus of voices in the trees, uncertain at first, then threatening themselves, long howls of rage; and the wind rose and rose, bending the trees down before it, whipping leaves and dirt through the air so that it became hard to see. The wizards staggered against the blast of it, but even as she fought to stay upright, Nita had a feeling that the wind was avoiding her, and the threat in it was for someone else—

She and Kit headed downhill, because that was the way the wind

190

was pushing them; but the great mass of wizards were pushing down that way too, their cries mingling with the wind's. The two fronts of Fomori that had struck them from either side were staggering back and away, further down the slope, blown that way, forced down by the raging wind that blew them over and over, that dropped trees on them and tossed logs from the wood after them like matchsticks. The Fomori were almost at the bottom of the hill now, into the little dell where Enniskerry village would have stood. There was no bridge over the Glencree River, in this world; they would have to ford it. The wizards and the relentless wind pushed them down into the dell—

The wind rose to a scream, then; and there were more sounds in it than screams. An odd sound of bells, that Nita recognized; and the sound of hooves, like glass ringing on metal. Nita looked up and saw what few mortals have seen and lived afterward: the *Sluagh Ron*, the Dark Ride of the *Sidhe*. In our time the People of the Hills leave their anger at home when they ride—their day is done, and their angers are a matter of the songs their bards sing to wile away the endless afternoon. But that afternoon was broken, now, and the legendary past had come haunting them as surely as it had come after the mortals. The *Sidhe* rode in anger now, as the People of the Air, in the whirlwind, with a clashing of spears that shone with the pale fire that flickers around the faery hills on haunted nights. Their horses burnt bright and dark as stormclouds with the sun behind them as they came galloping down the air. There was no more chance of telling how many of the riders there were than there was of counting the raindrops in a downpour. But two forms stood out at the head of them: the Queen with her loosened hair flying wild, on a steed like night, and the Fool on one like stormy morning, with their spears in their hands and a wind and a light of madness about them.

At the sight of them, a great shriek of despair and terror went up from the Fomori. The *Sidhe* cried out in answer, a cry of such pure delighted rage that Nita shuddered at the sound of it, and the *Sluagh Ron* hit the great crowd of Fomori from the southward side. The wizards parted left and right to let them through, and the *Sidhe* drove the Fomori straight downward into the Glencree ford, and up against the ridge on the far side. Wailing the Fomori went, and the press of riders and the darkness borne on the wind hid them from sight.

After what seemed a very long while, the wind died down, leaving the riders standing there, and the wizards looking at them, among the dead bodies of Fomor, and the twitching, witless ones, driven mad by the sight of the onslaught. Johnny went from where he had been talking to Nita's aunt, who held a Fragarach much damped-down and diminished-looking, and stood by the tallest of the riders, taking the bridle of her horse. "Madam," he said, "we hadn't looked to see you here."

"We were called by our own element," the Queen said, looking down at Nita's aunt, and Fragarach. "Besides, it has been too long since I went a-foraying; and since our world seems like enough to die here, this is a good time to ride out again. We have not done badly. But I think we may not be able to do much more. All magics are diminishing in the face of our enemy's *draoiceacht*, and I feel the weariness in my bones. Do not you?"

Johnny nodded. "Nevertheless we will press on," he said.

"We will go with you and look on this ending," said the *Amadaun*; and paused. "If an ending is indeed what we are coming to."

"One way or another," Johnny said.

Tir na nOg

Johnny waved the wizards forward, and they started down the winding way that paralleled the river, and led towards Bray.

"Did you hear that?" Kit said.

Nita shook her head; she was very tired. "Hear what?"

"What the Queen said. 'The weariness.' "

She had to laugh at that. "After what we've been through today, you'd be nuts not to be tired."

"Yeah, but that's not it. Don't you feel tireder than you were when we were up at the top of the hill?"

Nita blinked. "You're right."

Kit nodded down at the darkness in front of them. "That," he said. "There's some kind of energy-sapping spell tied up with it. Don't exert yourself if you can avoid it—you may need that energy for later."

She looked at him with very mild annoyance; sometimes Kit's practical streak came close to getting him hit. "What I *really* need right now in terms of energy is a candy bar," she said, "but the only thing I've got left in my pack is a cat. And I can't eat that." She made an amused face. "Too many bones."

Tualha hissed in her ear, not amused. Kit grinned, and produced a candy bar from one pocket. Nita took it, squinted at it in the dimness. "It's got peanuts in it!" she said. "I hate peanuts!"

"Oh, okay," Kit said, grabbed it back, and started to unwrap it.

Nita grabbed it away from him, scowled at him, and began eating. Tualha snickered at her.

They kept walking, along the course of the river: it would have been the route of the thirteen-bend road, in the real world. Trees arched close overhead in the gloom, and the sound of the river down in its stony watercourse was muted. *If something should hit us here, we'd have nowhere to go,* Nita thought, as she took another bite out of the candy bar. And then the screaming began again, very close. *It's not fair!*, she thought, as she saw the drows and pookas come crashing in among them from down the steep slope to their right. At that point she also discovered something else: that a wizard with a mouthful of caramel and peanuts is not much good for saying spells, even the last word of one that's already set up. She pushed backwards out of the way while fighting to swallow, managed it, and shouted the one word she needed just in time to blow away the drow that was heading for Kit on his blind side while he did the same for a pooka.

Something grabbed her from behind by her throat and chest, choking her. Nita fought to turn, for you can't blast what you can't see, but the stony hands held her hard, and she couldn't get her breath; her vision started to go.

Then there was a roaring noise behind her, the pressure released suddenly, and Nita fell sprawling and gasping. She levered herself up, looking around her. "Kit—" she said, "did you—" And she ran out of words. All around them, the path through the forest was awash in blue-green light that rolled and flowed like water; and off to one side, the river was climbing up out of its banks in response, and running up onto the path. Both flows, of light and water together, were rushing with increasing speed eastward, leaving the wizards untouched, but washing the drows and pookas and other monsters away like so much flotsam. Nita struggled to get to her feet again, against the flow. To Kit she said, "Looks like Doris is using the Cup."

Kit nodded. "Come on, we should be breaking out into the open pretty soon. This path comes out in that flat ground by the freeway, doesn't it?"

"The dual carriageway, yeah."

Several more bends of the watercourse brought them out into the open ground. There was a great scattering of drows there, half-buried in the earth as if about a year's worth of mud had buried them there; many others, dealt with by the wizardry of individuals, lay broken or helpless. The last traces of the blue-green light of the Cup's wizardry were sinking into the ground like water, along with the real water, which was running down into the watercourse of the Dargle, which the Glencree stream had just met. Kit and Nita splashed across the ford and up the other side, looking around them.

Nita sagged against Kit as she looked northward along the floodplain of the Dargle, toward Bray. The darkness was getting solider and solider, and she felt about ready to collapse.

You and me both, Kit said. She could feel the fatigue in the

194

thought, and Nita looked around at the other wizards with them and saw that they were suffering too; some of them were having to be helped along by others, and not because of injuries. And far down the flood plain, there was a long line of darkness hugging the ground, coming slowly toward them. It was bigger than all three of the previous forces that had attacked them, all put together.

Oh, no, she thought. *I can't. And neither can a lot of the rest of us. . . .*

"There never was any counting them, even in the old days," Tualha said. "It seems nothing has changed."

There was an awful silence. Many of the wizards looked at each other helplessly, hefted their weapons and watched the Fomori come. Nita looked over at Johnny, who was off to the side of one small crowd, frowning, with his arms folded.

The ground began to shake.

The Stone, Kit said silently, immediately doing the smartest thing: he looked up and around to make sure no tree or rock was likely to fall on him, and then sat down. Nita followed suit. All around them, the earth groaned alarmingly as it was held still where they were, but encouraged to move, and violently, half a mile away. Down by that advancing line of darkness, trees toppled over and huge boulders of Wicklow granite rolled down the hillsides toward the ranks of the Fomori. They broke, screaming and running in all directions. It did them little good. One of the hillsides shrugged itself up and up until it fell over on the Fomori vanguard. Behind them the rest milled about in confusion between the two ridges that paralleled the open ground where it sloped gently away down toward Bray.

The thunder of the quaking ground suddenly became a roar. Nita clutched at the ground as a single awful shock went through it—not one of the rippling waves they had been feeling, but a concussion like two huge rocks being struck together.

Down towards Bray, the horde of dark forms were abruptly missing from the ground. Nothing could be seen but smokes and dust rising upward in the gloom.

"Let's go," Johnny said quietly, and started forward.

No one had much to say as they passed the great smoking chasm that had been a green meadow half a mile long, between two hills. One of the hills was flat now, the other had great cracks in it, and from far down among the rock-tumble in the chasm, as the wizards passed slowly by it, faint cries could be heard. Nita shuddered as she followed Kit; they had to squeeze their way along the side of the meadow, what was left of it. The ground tilted dangerously downward toward the chasm. The riders of the *Sidhe* paced casually along the air above the huge smoking hole, but it occurred to Nita that the wizards might have a slightly harder time of it if they had to leave the area suddenly.

The gloom grew about them, and the tiredness got worse and worse, so that it was almost as much as she could do just to drag herself along. Only the sight of Kit in front of her, doggedly putting foot in front of foot, kept her doing the same. *At least they're letting us alone now,* she thought. *Or maybe there are none of them left.*

We hope, Kit said silently. *Hang in, Neets. Look, Johnny's stopped up at the top of that hill there.*

They went up after him, paused at the hillcrest and looked down over where Bray would have been in the real world. In this otherworld, it was normally a great flowery plain; but the darkness that lay over everything had shut the flowers' eyes. It was a featureless place, flat as heartbreak, right up to where Bray Head should have been; and a wall of black cloud rose there, shutting the sight away.

Nita squinted along the coastline, looking for some sight of the sea. That wall of blackness prevented her, though. *Is it clouds, or some other kind of storm? Why isn't it moving? . . .*

But it was not cloud, as she had thought. There were regular shapes in that darkness, barely visible. It was a line of ships—but ships like none she had ever imagined before, ships with hulls the size of mountains, with sails like thunderheads. They were livid-dark as if full of thunder, and she could see the chains of pallid lightning that held them to the shore. This was the black wizardry that would drag this alternate Ireland out of its place in the sea, up into the regions of eternal darkness and cold, into another ice-age perhaps. What would happen to the real Ireland, and the rest of the world after it, Nita had no idea.

—and under that wall of darkness—

Her mind was dulled with that awful weariness, and at first Nita thought she was looking at a hill, between them and the sea. *Funny about that,* she thought. *That almost looks like a sort of squashed head, there.* But no head could be that ugly. Huge twisted lips and a face that looked as if someone had malformed it on purpose; a sculptor's model of a gargoyle's head all squashed down, the nose pushed out of place, and one eye squinted away to nothing; the other abnormally huge, bulging out, the lid a thin warty skin over it. All this smashed down onto great rounded shoulders, a crouching shape, great flabby arms and thighs and a gross bulging belly—all the size of a hill. Face and body together combined to make an expression of sheer spite, of long-cherished grudges and self-satisfied immobility. The look of it made Nita feel a little sick.

And then she saw it breathe.

And breathe again.

Loathing, that was almost all she could feel. She was afraid, too, but it seemed to take too much energy. *So this is Balor.*

It was not the way she had expected the Lone One to appear. Always she had seen It before as young and dynamic, dangerous, actively evil. Not this crouching, lethargic horror, this lump of inertia, of blindness and old unexamined hates. Before, when confronted by the rogue Power that wizards fight, she had always wanted to fight It too, or else run away in sheer terror. This made her simply want to sneak away somewhere and throw up.

But this was what they had to get rid of; this was what was going to destroy this island, and then the world.

It's really gross, came the thought; Kit, tired too, but not as tired as she was. *They'd better get rid of it quick.*

Nita agreed with him. Off to one side she saw Johnny, looking almost too tired for words, standing there with a Fragarach that looked dulled and tired. But Johnny's back was straight yet. "Lone One," he said, his voice calm and clear, "greeting and defiance, as always. You come as usual in the shape you think we'll recognize least. But this one of our hauntings we know too well, and intend to see the back of. Your creatures are defeated. Two choices are before you now; to leave of your own will, or be driven out by force. Choose now!"

There was no answer; just that low, thick breathing, unhurried, untroubled.

"Ronan," Johnny said quietly. "The Spear."

Ronan moved up, but he looked uneasy. The Spear seemed heavy in his hands, and Johnny looked at him sharply. "What's the matter?" he said.

"It—I don't know. It's not ready."

Johnny looked at Ronan with some concern, and then said, "Well enough. Anne—"

Nita's aunt came up, carrying a Fragarach that looked dulled and tired. She glanced at him, looking slightly confused. Johnny shook his head.

197

"Don't ask me," he said. "I think we've got to play this by ear. Do what you did before."

She held up Fragarach and said the last word of the spell of release. The wind began to blow again, but there was a tentative feel to it this time, almost uncertain. The gross motionless figure did nothing, said nothing. The wind rose, and rose, but there was still that feeling of a hollowness at the heart of it; and when it fell on Balor at last, there was no destroying blast, no removal. It might have been any other wind blowing on a hill, with as much result. It died away at last, with a moan, and left Fragarach dark.

"Doris," Johnny said.

Doris came up holding the Cup. She spoke the word of release, and tilted it downward. That blue-green light rose and flowed out of it again, washing toward Balor. But it lost momentum, and soaked into the muddy ground around the Balor-hill, and was swallowed up; and afterwards the Cup was pallid and cold, just a thing of gold and silver, indistinct in the shadows.

"All right," Johnny said, sounding, for the first time since Nita had met him, annoyed. "Ronan, ready or not, you'd better use that thing."

Ronan looked unnerved, but he lifted the Spear. The fires twisted and writhed in the metal of its head; he leaned back, balanced it, and threw.

The Spear went like an arrow, struck Balor—

—and bounced, and fell like a dead thing.

Silence. The wizards looked at each other.

—and the laughter started. It was very low, hardly distinguishable as laughter at all, at first. It sounded as if the ground should have trembled with it, and with malice, and amusement. *Invulnerable,* Nita thought. *It's not fair. He could be stopped, the last time. Lugh put that spear right through Its eye.* Nothing *should be able to stop it—*

Another sound began, a shadow of the first: rocks grating against rocks, a low tortured rumbling that grew louder and louder. With it, the earth really did start to tremble. People fell over in all directions, tried to find their footing, lost it and fell again. Nita was one of them; when she got up again, she noticed a particular feeling of insecurity, as if something she had been depending on had suddenly vanished.

Johnny was standing up again, having fallen himself. He looked at Nita's aunt in shock, and said, "That was the Stone going. The linkage to it is dead."

Nita's aunt looked at the shadows down by the seashore and said softly, "Then there's nothing to prevent . . . that."

Johnny shook his head. "And what happens here. . . ."

Nita swallowed.

The groaning of the earth subsided; many who had fallen managed to get back to their feet. But there was no relief, for unchanged before them squatted the huge, dark, immobile form with its spiteful, pleased look. A soft protesting noise of distress and anger went up all around.

"It's *enjoying* this," Kit muttered. "We've lost, and It knows it, and It's prolonging it for *fun.*"

"That's as much fun as it's going to have, then," came a sudden small voice: Tualha. She struggled down out of the bag and splatted onto the ground, then climbed up hurriedly onto a nearby stone. She panted a little, and paused; and then her little voice rang out in that sick silence, louder than Nita had ever heard it before.

> "See the great power of Balor lord of the Fomor!
> See the ranks of his unconquerable army!
> See how they parade in their pride before him!
> See how they trample the earth of Eriu!"

Nita stared at first, wondering what Tualha was up to. But the irony and sarcasm in her small voice got thicker and thicker, and she was staring at Balor in wide-eyed amusement, the way Nita had seen her stare at captive bugs.

> "Is it not the way of his coming in power?
> His splendor is very great, he bows down all resistance!
> Never was a better way for the conqueror to come here;
> May all who follow him fare just the same way!
>
> See how the children and beasts flee before him,
> And their elders, just hoary old men and women,
> With their few bits of rusty ironmongery,
> And a crock and a stone, that's all they have with them!
>
> Can it really be so, what we see before us?—
> or is it a trick of the Plains of Tethra,
> where everything seems otherwise than it is,
> and night might be day, if one's will was in it?"

Is it truly what we see, the mighty conqueror,
with his armies ranged and his ships all ready?
Or something much less, just a misconception,
a fakery made of lying and shadows?

No army here, just some shattered stonework,
some poor bruised goblins, all running away?
No ships at all, but just the old darkness,
the kind that used to scare children at bedtime?

And no mighty lord, no mastering horror,
just a bad dream left over from crazier times,
a poor ghost, wailing for what's lost forever?
Some run-down spook complaining about hard times,

and what he can't keep? Can it be that mortals
are too strong for him even here, on his own ground?
—that accountants and farmers, housewives and shopkeepers,
and children and *cats* are even too mighty?

Then all hail the ragged lord of the Fomor,
a power downthrown, a poor weak specter
that ought to take himself off to the West Country
and haunt some castle for American tourists!

Be off somewhere and beg your bread honestly,
and don't come around our doors with your threats,
you shabby has-been! Just slouch yourself off,
crooked old sloth-pile: show some initiative!

Get up and—"

The voice that spoke then made the earth shake again, and a
violent pain went right through Nita at the sound of it, as if she had
been stabbed to the heart with something not only cold, but actively
hateful. *"Let me see this chatterer who makes such a clever noise,"* the
voice said, hugely, slowly, with infinite malice.

Tualha stood her ground. "Get up and do something useful, if you
dare—"

It got up.

The terrified screams of many of the wizards made this seem to

200

take much longer than it did; seconds dragging out to minutes of horror, as the huge shape began to tear itself up out of the ground, bulking up against the darkening sky huger than Bray Head. Indeed the Head looked to be crouching down in terror itself, getting smaller as that form rose up beside it, not just the ugly warped man-shape, but a steed for it as well—black as rotting earth, eyes filled with the decaying light of marshfire, fanged, taloned, breathing corruption. Above it its Rider rose, and Nita heard Its breathing and knew her old enemy again, knew by sight the One That she had been desperately afraid would catch her, that night after the foxhunt went by. Its pack was gathering to It out of the shadows now, ready to hunt the wizards' souls out into everlasting night and tear them to shreds like coursed hares, screaming. In the pack's longing thoughts, dangerously close to becoming real in this otherworld, Nita could hear the shrieks, smell the blood already. But at the moment she could look nowhere but that dark face: see the bitter smile. But there was as yet no glance from Its eye. The Balor-shape still bound It to that shape's rules.

He put the Spear right through Its eye, Nita thought abruptly. *That's it! Unless It opens Its eye first—*

Here it comes, Kit said to Nita. *This had better work!—*

Off to one side, Ronan was holding the Spear. It was immobile no longer; it was shaking in his hands, its point leaning toward the terrible dark shape before them, the fires writhing in its point. "Not yet," Nita said under her breath, "Ronan, not yet—!"

She knew he couldn't hear her; even if he could, it was a good question whether the being he was becoming would recognize Nita as someone it might be useful to listen to. Ronan was wrestling with the spear, holding it back as it pulled and strained in his hands.

A bare slit of light opened in the dark face of the bulk before them, like the first sliver of the sun coming up over a hill. It hit Nita in the eyes and face like thrown acid, searing. She cried out, fell down and crouched in on herself, trying to make herself as small as possible, as the light hit her all over and burned her. All around her she could hear the screams of others going down, and right next to her, on top of her she thought, the sound and feel of Kit crying out hoarsely and rolling over in agony. It was worse than almost anything she could remember, worse than the time the dentist was drilling and the novocaine wore off and he couldn't give her any more; the pain scraped down her nerves and burned in her bones, and no writhing or crying helped at all. The tears ran out and mixed with the mud that her face was grinding into.

But at the same time, something in her refused to have anything to do with all this, and was embarrassed, and angry—the same kind of anger that had awakened in her while she was fighting, and liking it. Shaking her head in that anger, Nita pushed herself up on her hands and knees, even though it felt like she would die doing it, and squinted ahead of them. Through the mud and her tears of pain she could just make out Ronan, still struggling with the Spear. Further ahead, the darkness was broken only by that awful sliver of evil light, getting wider now as the Eye opened. *And if it had opened all the way, all Ireland would have burnt up in that one flash,* she heard Tualha half-singing, half-saying. *But it has to be open enough for him to get a clean shot. He won't get another chance, and if he misses it'll all have been for nothing. Ronan, Ronan,* don't let it go yet!

Tualha yowled and fell off the stone onto Nita. She scooped the kitten up, fumbled for her backpack, couldn't reach it, and stowed Tualha, writhing, inside her shirt, where her clawing made little difference against the storm of pain Nita was already feeling. It could be fought, but not much longer; she could feel the onslaught of the light increasing, its power building. Soon it would be ready— Beside her, Kit stirred and bumped up against her. "Come on," she moaned, grabbed him by one arm and tried to get him up at least on his hands and knees. "Come on. Oh, God, Kit, *Ronan—!*"

She looked over and saw that the Eye was open enough. But Ronan was still holding the Spear, despite its struggles. It was roaring now, a desperate noise, trying to get loose. *What's the matter?* Nita thought. "Ronan!!"

He was nothing but a silhouette against that light, writhing himself, kept on his feet by the Power that had been dwelling in him more and more since they came here. "Ronan, *let it go!*" she cried. "Kit, he has to—he won't—"

Their minds fell together, as they had before. That reassuring presence: frightened, as she was, but also perturbed, looking for an answer. *What's the matter with him?* she heard Kit think. *With me, Neets. RONAN!*

Their minds hit him together, fell into his. Only for a second, for something larger than both of them was fighting for control, and losing. Ronan was holding that Power off, and he had only one thought, all fear and horror: *if I let it go now, if once I throw the Spear,*

I become the Power, become Lugh, become the Champion. Never mortal again—

Make him do it, Kit cried, frantic, to him and the Other who listened. *He's going to get the whole world killed!*

No! It doesn't work that way! Nita was equally frantic. *He has to do it himself! Ronan,* and she gulped,—*go on!*

Silence—

—and then Ronan lifted the Spear. It shouted triumph as Ronan leaned back, and then it leapt out of his hands, roaring like the shock wave of a nuclear explosion, trailing lightnings and a wild wind behind it as it went. That terrible eye opened wide in shock as a fire more terrible than its own hurtled at it. In the instant of the Eye's opening the pain increased a hundred times over. Nita screamed and fell—

—and then came the piercing. Nothing alive on that field failed to feel it, for everything alive had entropy in its bones; all cries went up together as the essence of all burning ate the darkness to its heart, and however briefly, to each of theirs. It was painful, but a terrible relief: terrible because the mortals present knew that, once they returned to the real world, that small personal darkness would be back with them again.

Something else, though, did not find it a relief; something that had almost nothing but entropy about it. The scream of the Lone Power in Its shape as Balor went up, and up, and would have torn the sky if the shy were made of anything solider than air. It took a long time to die away.

The pain was gone, at least. Nita got up to her knees and looked around her, blinded no longer, though her ears were ringing. Kit was just getting up next to her: she helped him up, hugged him. "Are you all right?"

"I'll live," he said, sounding dazed, and hugging back. "Where's Ronan?"

He was standing there not too far away, looking fairly dazed himself. The Spear was back in his hand again, but quiet now, not straining to go anywhere. Ronan was leaning on it, panting, his forehead against the shaft of it; so he did not see the tall shadow rising up over him, towering higher and higher; the immense shape of a woman dressed in black, but with light flickering in the folds of the darkness like a promise, and long dark hair stirring in the wind that had begun to come down from the heights, blowing the blackness of the clouds out over the sea, so that high up the sky began to show again, dark blue, with here and there a star.

Against the growing light, and the clean darkness, that woman raised her arms, and her voice went up into the silence like thunder. "Let the hosts and the royal heights of Ireland hear it," the Morrigan cried, and even Ronan looked up now in terror and wonder, "and all its chief rivers and invers, and every rock and tree; victory over the Fomor, and they never again to be in this land! Peace up to the skies, the skies down to the earth, the earth under the skies; power to every one!"

The wizards and the *Sidhe* shouted approval. And the wind rose, and took the clouds away; and the Morrigan's great shape too bent sideways in that wind and dissipated like a mist, though Nita particularly noticed how her eyes seemed to dwell on Ronan before they vanished completely.

You know, Kit said in Nita's head, *it's funny, but she looks kind of like Biddy. . . .*

She shook her head in bemusement, and she and Kit went over to Ronan. He was looking up at the sky, still leaning on the Spear. But when he looked down at last, and saw them coming, he straightened up slightly and smiled. Nita was very relieved; that abstracted, inhuman look was gone completely.

"It came back," he said to Nita, sounding very bemused. "By itself."

"You put too much English on it," she said, and grinned.

He winced slightly. "Ooh. No puns, please." He looked ahead of him. The great bulk that had first been Balor and then the Hunter was nothing but a hill, now; there was only the vaguest shape about it that suggested that awful bloated bulk. Grass grew on it, and as they looked a rabbit hopped out of cover under a thornbush growing on it, and began to graze.

"I didn't dare let it go," Ronan said.

Nita nodded. "I know. But you're okay—aren't you?"

He looked at her. " *He's* still in there, if that's what you mean."

Kit shook his head. "I think you may be stuck with Him," he said. "But remember which side He's on. I think He'll behave . . . if you do. If you're lucky, you'll never hear from Him again."

"And if I'm not lucky?" Ronan said.

" 'Those who serve the Powers,' " said the small voice from down by their feet, " 'themselves become the Powers.' It's usually the way."

"You," Nita said, picking Tualha up. "I didn't know you knew language like that—that last bit. Don't think I didn't hear."

"I got carried away," Tualha said, her ears going flat.

"Not good technique for a bard," Kit said. Tualha scowled at him, and he laughed and began scratching her behind the ears until finally she gave up and purred.

All around them the light was growing. Nita looked up and around, watching the clouds retreating, and the brightness growing still, though there was no sun now, but a soft violet evening all around them. Everything was beginning to burn with a certainty surpassing anything Nita had seen even in the dúns of the *Sidhe*.

Beside her, one of the wizards, that handsome woman with the dark hair and the Viking axe, said with a chuckle, "Ah . . . the Celtic twilight." But Nita knew a joke when she heard one, and also knew that more excellent clarity drawing itself about them; she had seen it before. All around them, the wizards gathered there began to shine in that light, seeming more perfectly themselves than ever before; the *Sidhe*, already almost too fair to bear, began to acquire a calmer beauty, more settled, older, deeper.

Johnny was standing by the Queen's steed. He looked up at her now, and said, "Well, madam, you asked me a question once. Would your world ever draw closer to Timeheart, and end your exile? And I could only give you the answer that the bards gave us long ago. The Champion must come with His spear, and the world of your desire be lost." He laughed softly. "But then the fulfillment of a prophecy rarely looks like our images of it. Will this do?"

She bowed her head. "This will do, Senior. Do you swiftly take your people home, for shortly this world will perfect itself beyond their ability to bear it . . . at least, just yet. And we . . ." She looked toward the sunset, and said, "We will prepare for the dawn."

Johnny looked at Nita's aunt. "We've got a dawn of our own waiting for us," he said. "Do the honors?"

She lifted Fragarach. It burned like a star in her hands, and the other Treasures blazed in answer as the wind rose in the east and blew into the opening gap in the air before her. The dark outline of Castle Matrix grew in the early morning of their own world, and the song of a single early blackbird drifted through it.

As one the heads of the People of the Hill turned toward that thin, sweet music. But then one by one they looked toward the light slowly growing in their own northeastern sky; sunrise following hard on the heels of sunset, as was normal in this part of the world, in the heart of summer. The splendor of morning in a world growing ever nearer to Timeheart began to swell in the sky, blinding, glorious—

The wizards looked around them with regret and moved through the doorway in the air. Nita and Kit and Tualha, followed by Ronan, were near the rear of the group; they turned, there in the parking lot of Castle Matrix, and looked through the gateway back into Tir na nOg.

"I am sorry," Nita's aunt said softly to Johnny, "to have to leave our dead there. Another world, so far away . . ."

Johnny looked sorrowful as well—but there was a strange edge of thoughtfulness to the look, an expression of mystery, almost of joy. "Yes, but . . . look what's happening to the place. It won't be just another world for long . . . it's being drawn into the very center of things. Can you really be dead if you're in Timeheart?" he said. "Can *anything?* . . ."

Northeastward, over the sea, a line of light, blinding, brighter than a sun, broke over the water. The Spear Luin in Ronan's hands flamed at the touch of that light on its steel. All that country on the other side of the gateway flushed with a light more powerful, seemingly more solid than the solid things it fell on, and burned, transfigured—

The gateway closed.

"So," Johnny said, turning away. "Little by little, we make the Oath come true . . ."

Nita and Kit and Ronan looked at each other. Behind them, the blackbird sang again: and they heard the young wizard in the leather jacket sigh, and say, "Oh, well. What's for breakfast?"

They went to find out.

"Now that things have quieted down somewhat," Johnny was saying to Nita's aunt in her kitchen the day after next, "the Chalice goes back to the Museum, obviously. And the Stone naturally stays where it is. But Fragarach . . ."

"You take it," Aunt Annie said. "The neighbors would talk, if they saw something like that in here. You've got a castle . . . hang it on the wall there someplace."

Johnny chuckled. Nita put the teapot down and moved to look over his shoulder at the newspaper, doing her best to read around Tualha, who was dozing on it. STRANGE OCCURRENCES END?, said the *Wicklow People*, in large, somewhat relieved letters. Things had indeed quieted down a lot, all over the world. "The Spear," Johnny said, "will stay with Ronan, naturally."

"*I* wouldn't try to take it away from him," Kit said from the living room, where he was playing with the teletext functions of the TV set. "It'd probably eat you alive."

"Quite." He chuckled. "And I see that we're losing you two."

"My mom," Nita said, "says they can change my flight home after all." She grinned slightly. "So I go home over the weekend. Not that it hasn't been fun. . . . but every wizard knows her own patch of ground best." And she smiled at Ronan.

He smiled back and said nothing that the others could hear.

"Well, you come back any time," her aunt said, and grabbed her and hugged her one-armed. "She always does the dishes," she said to Johnny. "And without wizardry, even."

"Impressive," Johnny said. "But there was something else I was meaning to tell you—" He sipped his tea. "Oh, that was it. I'd say the odd things aren't quite done happening yet."

"Oh?" Everyone at the table looked at him.

"No. I was out for a walk after things settled down last night, and I saw the strangest thing. A party of cats carrying a little coffin. I stopped to watch them go by, and one of them said to me, 'This is Magrath. Magrath na Chualainn is dead.' And they walked off—"

Tualha's eyes flew open at that. "What?!" she cried. "What? Did you say Magrath?"

"Why, uh, yes—" Johnny said, sounding uncertain, and concerned. "If it's a relative, I'm—"

"Relative, never mind that, what relative! Great Powers about us, if Magrath is dead, then I'm the Queen of the Cats!"

She leaped off the table and tore away into the living room. There was a brief sound of scrabbling, and then from the living room, sounding slightly bemused, Kit said, "Uh, Annie, your cat just went up the chimney. . . ."

There was a moment of silence in the kitchen. "Ahem," Nita's aunt said to her after a breath or two. ". . . Welcome to Ireland. . . ."

"Are you sure you don't want to stay another couple of weeks?" Johnny said.

Nita smiled at him, and went out to the trailer to start packing.

A SMALL GLOSSARY

ban-draoia: She-wizard. In its original usage, "she-Druid."

ban-gall: Gall-woman. Possibly an insult, depending on who says it and how they feel about gallain (q.v.).

"Blow-in": A foreigner who settles in Ireland, and is presumed to be likely to leave suddenly (no matter how long they've been there); not seen as being seriously attached to the place as it really is, but "in love" with some romanticized and inaccurate version of it.

the *Dail* (pr. "Doyle"): The "lower house" of the Irish Parliament (the *Oireachtas* ["oyROCKtas"]), more or less equivalent to the House of Representatives in the US, or the House of Commons in the UK. A member of the *Dail* is called a *Teachta Dail* ("TOCKta DOYLE") or T.D. The upper house of the *Oireachtas* is the *Seanad* ("SHAHnad") or Senate.

Draoiceacht: Wizardry. In its original usage, "druid-craft."

Dún: Used interchangeably in early times for a castle, fortified house, or other strong place. The word persists in many Irish place names, such as Dun Laoghaire.

Faery: One of the inhabitants of the Otherworlds, in this case particularly *Tir na nOg:* or something that has to do with them. Originally derived from the Latin *fatae* or "fates," in this case meaning the Powers that involve Themselves in the destinies of living things. Unfortunately the term has been corrupted by various storytellers, from Shakespeare down to the mushier writers of Victorian children's moralistic tales, so that it now summons up imagery of tiny flying beings who ride butterflies, live in flowers, etc etc ad nauseam. True

Faery is beautiful, but extremely dangerous; the casualty rate of those who interact willingly with it is high, even among wizards.

Gael: A member or descendant of the Gaelic or Goidelic Celts, who settled in Britain and Ireland during and after the Iron and Bronze Ages. The Welsh, Irish, Scots, and some of the Celts of Brittany and parts of Spain are included in this group.

Gall (pl. gallain, pronounced like "gallon"): A non-Gael.

"Guards, the"—The Garda Siochona (GARda shiKOna) or Civil Guards: the Irish equivalent of police. Also found as "Garda" (one policeman) or *ban-Garda* (policewoman): the plural is *Gardaí*, (pr. "garDEE").

Lia Fail (pr. LEEuh FOYLE): the Stone of Destiny, originally supposed to be near the Hill of Tara: now sometimes identified with a different stone near Armagh. Legend had it that the Stone would shout aloud when the rightful High King of Ireland stood on it at his elevation to the throne.

rath (pr. "rawth"): A hill-fort. Sometimes the term includes whatever buildings (halls, towers, etc) are built into or on the rath.

Sidhe (pr. "shee"): the Faery People of Ireland. Sometimes (most inaccurately) confused with elves. Usually considered to be the *Tuatha de Danaan*, the original Children of the Goddess Danu, one of the mother-Goddesses of Ireland; or descendants of those Children. Some legends identify them with "weak-minded" fallen angels, too good to be damned, but too fallible for Heaven. Considered by wizards to be descendants of those of the Powers that Be Who could not bear to leave the place They had, under the instruction of the One, built. They are deathless except by violence, and are expert in some forms of wizardry, especially music, shapechange, illusion, and the manipulation of time; but humans are usually physically stronger, and their wizardries have much more effect on the physical world. Often referred to as "the Good Folk" or "the Good People of the Parish," "the Gentry," "the People of the Hills," (from which is derived their commonest Irish name, *daoine sidhe*), and other euphemistic idioms meant to keep from offending them by invoking their real names, or reminding them of portions of their history they prefer to forget.

Slán (pr. "shlawn"): Hello, or goodbye.

Taoiseach (pr. TEEshock): the Prime Minister of Ireland. Leader of the political party presently in power, who has legislative and political powers somewhat like those of the President of the US or the Prime Minister of the UK. By contrast, the Presidency of Ireland is largely a ceremonial position and is considered to be "above politics."

Tir na nOg (pr. TEER naNOHG): the Land of Youth (or of the Ever-Young), the alternate universe or other-Ireland inhabited by the Sidhe. Time runs at a different rate in this universe, or rather entropy does: experience continues unabated while bodily aging proceeds at a infinitesimal fraction of its usual speed, if at all. Humans who venture there frequently experience untoward side effects on attempting to return to universes with different time/entropy rates. See the legend of the hero Oisín for an example.